IMT

THE MAGIC GLASS

—THE— MAGIC GLASS

Anne Smith

Michael Joseph : London

First published in Great Britain by Michael Joseph Ltd
44 Bedford Square, London WC1
1981

ISBN   0 7181   1986 X

Typeset in Singapore by Colset Ltd.
Printed and bound in Great Britain by
Billing and Sons, Ltd., Guildford.

For Keiko, Freud, and wee Lizzie Brodie

CONTENTS

What do you suppose is the use of a child without any meaning? Even a joke should have some meaning — and a child's more important than a joke, I hope.

(The Red Queen, *Alice Through the Looking-Glass*)

CHAPTER 1

A Star is Born

*A woman when she is in travail hath sorrow, because her hour is come:
but as soon as she is delivered of the child she remembereth no more the
anguish, for joy that a man is born into the world.*

Luke 10

Saturday midnight in Skelf: there is too much darkness in the
streets and wynds; too much isolation in the sound of the sea, just
beyond the main street; no leerie comfort from the gas-lamps — it
is wartime, and the night is absolute. This late, on the cold edge of
winter, the town seems to shrivel into itself, to contract, and to feel
to the few who have to venture out of doors like the last stepping-
stone on the edge of the world. A man hurries along a street as if
impelled by the rising wind that has blown the clouds across the
moon and blanked out the stars.

He is sure of his way, and turns without hesitating at a particular
gate, yet feels for the gatepost as he goes in. He doesn't use the
doorknocker, but raps abruptly with one knuckle on the wood.
Within seconds he hears footsteps in the hallway and, lifting the
flap of the letterbox, he stage-whispers through it, *'It's me —
Wullie!'* The door opens wide to let him in, and stepping forward,
he catches the faint fresh-soap smell: 'Mother?' The door closes
behind him and a lantern-torch is switched on:

'Aye — is't oor Bess?'

'She's started! Will ye come for the bairns?'

'I'll just put my coat on.' The woman's voice is practical.

'Ye're no' in yer bed?'

'No, I was expectin' ye.'

'But — she wasnae due for anither fortnight . . .'

'Nevertheless — I was expectin' ye. Have ye been for the nurse
and doctor yet?'

'No. Bess wanted you first.'

'Well, on ye go noo.'

'I thought I'd see you up the road first . . .'

'Ah'll find ma ain wey, never you fear. Go you an' get the nurse . . .' She puts out the lantern as if to indicate that the conversation is finished. The man understands, and turns and goes, leaving the door open behind him.

Outside, the woman locks her door quietly, then moves off down the path out of the gate as briskly as if she were going to do a day's shopping — her shopping-bag is actually in her hand. 'A rare fresh night!' she whispers to herself, and turns her face into the rising wind with a smile that is a mixture of energy and contentment.

But the mind of the district nurse, as she slants through the streets with a banshee wind at her back, is steeped in the macabre. Even in the placid daylight of a June afternoon, the nurse betrays powers of imagination far beyond the average: strolling along her garden path, which is no bigger than a hall-runner, in an Anna Neagle outfit of flowing chiffon, picture hat, and white cotton gloves, with surgical scissors in one hand and straw scoop-basket in the other, she hums 'We'll gather lilacs in tha spree-eeng again,' and can take a full half hour to gather a posy of short-stemmed, overblown roses. Reality never touches her; she has refined herself with elocution lessons and light opera, and will perform the most efficient enema on the grisliest inhabitant of Skelf with a light touch and an etherial expression, always concluding her act of mercy with an uplifting recitation of Masefield's 'I must go down to the seas again,' unconsciously prompted, perhaps, by his description of wet sheets and flowing seas and winds that follow fast.

Tonight as she hurries to the confinement she paces herself with 'How they brought the good news from Ghent to Aix,' but cannot concentrate on her enunciation, for earlier she has treated herself to an evening at the cinema, the only cinema in Skelf, which by chance was showing Spencer Tracy in *Dr Jekyll and Mr Hyde,* and she expects — but deliciously expects — some depraved sexmaniac with a hairy face and no brow to pounce on her from every next doorway she passes. She shivers in constant anticipation, and is constantly disappointed, for lecherous drunks, of whom there are the usual one or two tottering optimistically through the streets, don't count as far as the nurse is concerned: they are real.

Eventually she reaches her destination. There are no signs on her face, as she waits at the door, of an effort to come down to earth; the nurse has only one expression, and it is a vague one, reminding you of a wax doll's face from another era, with delicately insipid features stuck incongruously above the body of a gangling harlequin. When the door is opened to her she clears her throat purposefully, then recites gaily to the woman who peers out of the darkness at the level of her chest, ' "Is there anybody there?" said the traveller, knocking at the moonlit door!'

'It's *you*, Nurse Sanders,' the woman replies, in a tone of exasperated resignation, and ushers her in, following her along the dark lobby with a rueful shake of the head.

In another part of the town the man stands patiently outside the doctor's door, waiting for him to get dressed so that he can escort him up the road, for the doctor is only a young locum, temporarily taking over. After a while the man gets impatient and begins to pace back and forth, hands deep in his pockets. Finally the door opens and the doctor steps out. The man takes his hands out of his pockets and swivels round, his head bent forward, bullish, heading quickly down the path with a grunt.

'One moment darling!' — a young woman's voice is heard from the house door. The doctor steps back in and the caressing voice comes faintly on the wind: '. . . your muffler and . . .': there is the sound of a cheek being kissed. The man on the path, frozen like a pointer during this scene, gives a snarl which the young doctor, stepping out at last, catches. He blushes to the roots of his hair and is glad of the covering dark as he follows the solid blot of the man's back up the path: they make only one silhouette, for the doctor's slight outline is lost against that of the man. Wounded by the man's contempt, as he falls into step with him the doctor protests, his voice too shrill in competition with the wind, 'Really — you needn't have bothered to wait — I could have found my way alone!'

'No' in *this* stramash ye couldnae!' the man booms back, smiling as if in appreciation of the independent sentiment, but nonetheless casting a sidelong glance at the doctor as he struggles to catch the tails of his muffler and push them inside his overcoat.

'Oh, I've got to know Skelf well in the last couple of weeks!' the doctor asserts, airily, and as the man turns abruptly into a close, turns with him, and walks violently into the fence beside the opening.

'Still . . .' the man gives a grim chuckle, gripping the doctor's arm to steady him, but far too tightly, self-assertive, 'we couldnae risk you gettin' lost, could we noo?' and adds in a threatening mutter, ' — No' wi' a bairn o' mine at stake!'

'No, no,' the doctor yields, quickening his pace till he is slightly ahead of the man. 'Is it your first then?' he shouts back over his shoulder, trying to sound professionally blasé.

'No — it's the third — but it'll be the first *laddie*,' the man replies, with the bold assurance of the addicted gambler challenging his luck.

The doctor smiles to himself in his professional capacity, yet the boy in him is impressed by the man's assurance: 'You sound very sure!' and he laughs to hide the naïveté of his curiosity.

'Oh aye!' the man exclaims, himself in turn puzzled by the note of puzzlement in the doctor's voice, 'it stands tae reason — third time lucky!' and he briskly overtakes the doctor.

So confident is the man's tone that the doctor begins to doubt that there is some area of medicine he has overlooked, but the doubt is only momentary, a slight chink in the armour of medical infallibility, quickly overcome by a comforting swing of his black bag. As he quickens his step again though, he begins to hope with inarticulate spite that it will be a girl.

Unaware of the malice at his side as they fall into step again, the man asks pleasantly, 'Have ye any family yersel', doctor?'

'No — no!' the doctor laughs, 'I was only married last month!' Yet he is immaturely flattered.

'A honeymooner, eh?' the man laughs too, forgiving the doctor his muffler, then has a sudden thought, ' — in that case, I'll better apologise for draggin' ye oot yer bed . . .'

'Eh?' The doctor is innocent, then blushes again to the roots of his hair, and fumbles for a reply, caught between professional dignity and a jolly bedside manner, not knowing which to assume, and confused even more by his religious scruples, which he feels he ought to let the man know about before the conversation degenerates any further. As he fumbles, the man, reminiscing, goes on genially:

'The devil himsel' wouldnae ha'e got *me* oot ma bed on a Saturday nicht when *Ah* was a month mairrit!' The doctor gives up, and pretends he hasn't heard, cupping his ear significantly away from the wind, smiling and shaking his head. 'Ah say: *Ah ken what it is masel'*!' the man bellows at the doctor, smiling back.

The doctor shakes his head in fake exasperation, still pretending he can't hear, and changes the subject with a shrill, 'How nice to have a child born on the Sabbath!'

Despite the wind, an almost tangible silence, like a cocoon, rears itself around them while the man adjusts to this comment. Eventually he answers with what he intends to be polite tolerance:

'No' sae nice when it's the one day o' the week Ah'm no' workin'!'

'What do you do, Mr Ross?'

'Ah'm a miner . . . what aboot you?'

'Eh?' The doctor is stunned by the question.

'No, no — I mean, are ye for the forces after this?'

'No — actually . . .' the doctor hesitates, ' . . . I'm going to a Missionary hospital in Africa . . .' The silence this time is rude, while the man slows his pace to peer at the doctor through the darkness before firing his aggressive question:

'Ye a *Christian* then?'

'Yes,' the doctor answers, shrugging impatiently and walking on.

'Exempt?' the man pursues.

'A Conscientious Objector,' the doctor throws back over his shoulder, casually. The man has heard but asks again, catching up with him:

'A *what*?'

'A CONSCIENTIOUS OBJECTOR!' the doctor bawls, and strides rapidly ahead of the man, as if trying to shake off a terrier nipping at his heels. The man lets him go, and walks more slowly, crestfallen, thinking, then:

'By Christ we're in for a nicht o't. . .' he mutters to himself,

13

suddenly sullen. By the time he looks up again the doctor has disappeared into the darkness. He shrugs as if glad to be rid of him, but then thinks of his son and shrugs again, 'Any port in a storm . . .' and hurries forward. Overtaking the doctor, he is hypocritically pleasant, 'Man, doctor, Ah nearly lost ye there!'

'I *know* the way, I tell you!' the doctor huffs, offended at the patronage in the man's voice, and quickening his step to get away from him.

But the man hangs on: 'The darkness can make a lot o' things different, though, doctor . . .'

'Not if you put your hand in the hand of the Lord and trust to *Him*!' the doctor intones evangelically, hoping to put the man off, but Ross only laughs ruefully:

'Ah'm afraid ye'll no' find mony miners tae agree wi' ye there!' — and laughs again, adding sadistically, ' — maybe we're owre close to the Other Place, eh?' Suddenly pompous, he goes on, '. . . in the *bowels* o' the earth . . .'

But gradually this night in Skelf, with its raw, insistent, and solitary darkness, begins to penetrate even their carefully-wrought defences, and to flay their egos to the bone. They walk faster and faster, pursued by doubts that seem to rise out of the darkness inside themselves like malignant shadows, and in unconscious competition with each other try to assert their manhood, or at least to lay it on the line enough to keep the thoughts at bay. Yet the doctor's mind keeps going back to the shaming recollection of how pleased he was to have this interruption to his by now accustomed hour of post-coital gloom, in which he has lain time and again trying to convince himself that the physical side of love *should* be as short and furtive as he makes it, and that his wife won't miss the orgasm she has never had.

Ross is telling himself for the millionth time that if he hadn't been turned down as unfit for all the services, he would by now have won a medal like his older brother — besides, he comforts himself, this son of his coming tonight will prove that he is a *real* man. He clutches at his contempt for the doctor as a bible-thumping conshie, but the very eagerness with which he finds himself doing so makes him uneasy, and the circle of thought begins all over again.

They are both glad to reach Ross's gate, and arrive at his door neck-and-neck, breathless.

The man ushers the doctor into the firelit living-room with a brusque 'Ye'd better heat yer haunds at the fire before ye go in tae the wife,' and nods to his mother-in-law: 'This is the doctor, Mother,' in the tone of a hard-up housewife producing a meatless dinner. The doctor coughs self-consciously, instinctively raising his hand to his mouth to cover some of his youthful face, but this in itself is a signal to the sharp old woman, who has had her back to them, intent on turning the nappies she's airing on the fireguard. She looks round at him, and the doctor is nonplussed to see a face that is as innocent as it is intelligent; eyes that have learned but not aged. He smiles uncertainly.

'You're *young* for a doctor, are ye no'?' the old woman demands.

He counters with a show of professional impatience: 'Where's the mother-to-be?' — but the woman is still frankly assessing him, and doesn't bother to reply. The doctor claps his hands and rubs them together with false gusto, 'Take me through, will you, and have a kettle ready. Is the Nurse here?'

'Wheesht!' the old woman whispers angrily. 'There's bairns sleepin' through there!' The doctor's hands drop awkwardly to his sides, and there is a pause, during which she manages to make him feel she can read his whole life on his face, the little there has been of it. Seeing his growing self-consciousness she gives a little nod, satisfied that she has control of the situation, and replies matter-of-factly, 'I've twa kettles ready on the stove. The nurse has been here a guid twenty minutes afore ye.'

'Oh — ah . . .' the doctor says, and picks up his bag, turning back towards the door, where Ross has stood all this time.

'This wey, doctor.' The man's expression is enigmatic, his feelings suspended between amusement at the way his mother-in-law has put the doctor down and frustration that he couldn't do it himself.

As the doctor, still trying to adapt to the unexpected presence of this superior authority, numbly follows the man out of the room, the old woman, turning the nappies again, calls out over her shoulder in a loud whisper, 'And see you look after *ma* lassie, young man, or ye'll ha'e *me* tae answer tae!' He tries a patronising smile to himself in the darkness of the corridor, but all he achieves is the expression of a man suddenly made aware of his own bad breath. It is this expression that he turns on the nurse as he enters the bedroom — but the nurse is miles away, humming to herself, a Merry Widow in a Viennese ballroom.

'How's our patient, Nurse Sanders?' he hails her for the second time, conscious of Ross's eyes on him and struggling to repress an unworthy urge to pick the nurse up and shake her till her teeth rattle in her head. He ignores the patient with professional confidence.

The nurse pauses beside the woman's bare belly, reared up like an Alp from the bed, '. . . Oh, Mrs . . . Mrs . . .' — she looks down briefly to remind herself of the patient's identity: 'Mrs Ross? Oh — we've a long way to go yet, haven't we dear?' she replies at last, but as if it was the belly and not the doctor who had spoken to her; and gaily waves a bottle of ether soap to summon the elusive nymph, Memory, then rests it on the belly, which suddenly becomes mobile. As Bess Ross winces she raises the bottle again abstractedly, and continues, gazing vaguely at the doctor, 'But we're shaved and we're ready to be very, *very* brave, aren't we dear?' She turns the same unseeing face to the woman, who protests with an involuntary laugh:

'Maybe *you're* ready to be brave, Nurse, but Ah'm no' sae sure aboot masel'!'

The doctor blinks in bewilderment as the nurse, pooh-poohing, returns to the task of daubing at the woman's genitals with all the delicate concentration of an amateur watercolourist. Then he reminds himself — and with a sense of satisfaction that the process is practically automatic now — that he represents a Power higher than his own inexperienced self, and breaks in with, 'Nonsense!' Looking for the first time straight at his patient, he blasts her with his zealous gaze, modelled on the etching of John Knox he has above his bed, and quotes sternly: 'Remember the words of our Lord — "A woman when she is in travail hath sorrow, because her hour is come: but as soon as she is delivered of the child she remembereth no more the anguish, for joy that a man is come into the world!" '

16

The woman gazes back at him, bewildered for a few moments, then the mists clear and she smiles conspiratorially: 'Oh doctor, d'ye *really* think it'll be a laddie?'

'Oh — ' the doctor falters, 'oh — I — I — don't really know.' Then he falls back on textbook authority: 'Nobody can know for sure. We've no way yet of determining —.'

Bess, anxious to forestall any dampening words of science, interrupts: ' — Only ma man's *awfu'* wantin' a laddie, ye ken!' Ross slips quietly out the door as she continues, 'Ah think, don't you, our luck might turn this time, wi't bein' the third, an' wi' us ha'ein' a different doctor. . .?'

'Well . . .' and the doctor takes refuge in feeling her stomach.

Neither of them has noticed that the old woman has come into the room, until she exclaims from behind, with a snort of impatience and a keen glance of doubt at the doctor: 'It'll be one or the other, ye can count on that! Have ye timed the contractions?' she demands, not failing to notice that the doctor's hand twitched on the woman's stomach as she spoke.

'I'm just coming to that — ,' he answers, too quickly, and the nurse, who has been daubing away all this time and humming 'Goodnight Vienna,' casually reassures in her disembodied voice: 'Oh, we've a long way to go, mother — a long way.'

The doctor sees his chance of escaping the uncomfortable prospect of a night of primitive superstition, frivolous songs from the movies, and a domineering old woman, and says with as much brusque professionalism as he can muster, 'In that case perhaps I may as well go home, and you can send for me later when the pains get bad . . .'

'Nothing o' the kind!' the old woman exclaims indignantly. 'The nurse here — *if she minds* — ' (the last phrase is said with a sergeant-majorish sarcasm that makes even the nurse's eyes open a little wider) ' — will tell you that my dochter comes on very sudden when she *does* start, an' the bairn'll be intae this world *before you've drawn your breeks back on,* young man — never mind runnin' a' the wey back here! Come away through then and have a cup o' tea . . . ye look like ye could dae wi't . . .' and she marches off without waiting for an answer, as the doctor stares at her, in a mild state of shock. He follows her like a sleepwalker, groping in himself for some truly Christian humility to see him through the rest of the night. 'You tae, Nurse!' she throws over her shoulder, and the nurse gives a last gentle swipe with the swab. Standing back to admire her work, she addresses the woman's genitals: 'There! We're all clean and tidy and ready for the little stranger!' Still speaking in that direction, she goes on, 'Be a *good* Mummy till Nurse gets back, and if our pains come, just call!' She has a vague look about her to locate the door, and flutters through to the living-room.

The woman, left alone and exposed on the bed, has the perplexed, reluctant smile of a lost child being amused against its will by a stranger.

The doctor is sitting up straight as a poker, awkward at the table with his cup of tea, while the prospective father makes uncomfortable shuffling noises from his armchair by the hearth. Only the old woman, doing domestic things as naturally as if she were in her own house in the middle of the day, is confidently silent. As she hands the nurse her tea Ross gets up, relief written all over his face, and with 'Oh well, Mother, I'll just awa' through an' see tae Bess!' makes good his escape. The nurse, sipping her tea, goes into a dream, holding the saucer aloft and sticking her pinkie delicately out at a right angle. Awkward in his isolation then, the doctor takes refuge in comforting thoughts of Africa, and fantasises hordes of grateful natives sitting cross-legged at his door, waiting in an awed and patient silence for him to come out like a white god and deliver his Christian wisdom to them.

If the old woman only knew — and the wry half-smile on her face as she sets up the ironing-board hints that she does — it isn't a doctor and a nurse who sit here, pie-faced and gazing into space: it's Albert Schweitzer and Anna Neagle.

The man enters the bedroom and shuts the door behind him with exaggerated, comic caution, holding up his hands and rolling his eyes like a music-hall minstrel. Then, his back to the door, he puts his hands in his pockets and eyes the belly speculatively: 'Ah'll tell ye, Bess — yon's a bonnie pair o'chookies ye ha'e attendin' on ye this time!'

The woman laughs: 'Wheesht! they'll *hear* ye, min!'

'Her? She'll no' hear the Last Trumpet, that ane — she's oot o' this world already!'

They both snigger, and the woman exclaims, 'God help us but ye're richt enough! An' the doctor's a *mish* tae!' They laugh helplessly now, till the woman's face darkens: 'Ah hope this disnae ha'e an effect on ma bairn . . .' Suddenly grim, the man goes over and throws a lump of coal on the fire.

'. . . Aye, they're some pair o' fairies tae ha'e at a birthin' . . .' he mutters, then, straightening up and wiping his hand on the backside of his trousers, he brightens, 'Never mind — yer mither's there tae see tae't that they keep their feet on the ground . . .' He pauses and laughs quietly, coming back now to the bedside and bending over her conspiratorially to whisper, '. . . She's got the doctor faird tae open his mooth already! He's sittin' through at the table like he's shit himsel' an' darenae let bug!'

'Oh, for the Lord's *sake*, dinnae mak' me laugh!' the woman complains, curiously upset by this last remark, 'It's nae laughin' maitter this, ye ken. . .'

'No, no dearie,' the man soothes.

'*And* the Epsom salts ma mither gi'ed me is burlin' through me right this very minute — ' she goes on, moving in fretful self-pity, having seized her chance to slip the news across him.

'*Epsom salts?*' — he is taken aback.

'Aye, Epsom salts — an' Ah dinnae mind tellin' ye — '

'Christ! An' me thinkin' yer mither had the second sicht tae, her waiting' ready wi'r claes on for me comin' . . . Epsom *salts* — that tak's the bluidy ticket!'

'Oh!' Bess, who had started to moan as a diversion, kicks out her feet in real pain. 'Well, ma Mum says it'll be better for the . . . bairn . . . if it's here afore the right cauld weather sets in . . . '

'Are ye OK?' the man asks anxiously, postponing his anger. 'Should Ah bring the nurse?'

'Oh — Ah divnae ken!' Bess breaks out in a sweat. 'Maybe ye'd better, but what wi' the salts, Ah'm no' sure whether tae push or no' . . . '

Ross is embarrassed: 'I'll get the nurse —.' He moves to the door and on an afterthought returns to his wife; leaning over her and gripping her wrist, half-pleading, half-encouraging, he whispers, 'See'n' try tae ha'e a *laddie* this time, darlin'!' As he goes out to call the nurse, she throws a glance of wounded suspicion at his back.

'How strong is the pain?' the doctor enquires, examining the woman while the nurse moves round the bed and takes her hand.

'Well Ah'm no' sure, doctor,' Bess murmurs, more shy than she would have been in normal circumstances. 'Ye see, ma mither gave me salts an' well . . . Ah've been back an' forrit a' day wi them an' — *oh!*' she spares herself from having to explain more by exaggerating the spasm of pain.

'There there noo, dearie . . . ' Ross, gallant in his embarrassment, pats the hand at the other side of the bed from the nurse, and flashes the doctor a threatening look.

'But does it *feel* like a labour pain? It is downbearing?' the doctor pursues, undisturbed by the husband's glower.

'Ah couldnae say . . .' Bess's voice is near a whine, '. . . Ah *think* so . . . '

'Then push down with the next spasm,' the doctor commands.

'Ye'll be a' right, darlin', just grip ma haund,' Ross urges, grimly protective now; all but thumping his chest at the doctor, and giving him an intent aggressive stare as if to imply that this is all the doctor's fault. The doctor catches the stare, and for a fleeting second senses and sympathises with the male vulnerability beneath it; the man's gaze falters and breaks. The woman, alert to the drift of the attention away from herself, whimpers a little to claim it back, and to claim pity in advance, whatever the outcome. The whimper rises to an involuntary '*oh — oh — OH —*' which passes from hope to rue, as, arching her back in response to an urgent spasm, and obediently, but without great faith, pushing down, she abruptly shits the bed . . .

'Oh my *dear,*' the man exclaims in a false-cavalier voice, the first of the rigid tableau to come back to life, and trying to be delicately considerate to his wife's feelings; trying not to laugh; trying to dictate the tone to the doctor and nurse; trying to maintain his and Bess's parental dignity: ' . . . don't you think you're going a bit far now?' He smiles indulgently, with all the Clark Gable sang-froid he can muster.

'*Ah* couldnae help it!' Bess is querulous with resentment and self-pity, as the nurse and doctor rally round and begin to clean her up with expert efficiency, their faces now unreadable professional masks.

'No, no, of course you couldn't!' Ross soothes, desperate and alone in his sense of the humour of it. 'Think nothing of it!' he dismisses, feeling he can afford to be magnanimous with his son on the way, ' — the nurse and the doctor's used to it by now, I dare say . . .'

The doctor's shoulders lift a fastidious, protesting inch, but the gesture is too subtle.

'Get us some newspapers, Father,' the nurse murmurs, preoccupied.

Outside the room Ross stands for a second, his hand on the door-knob, shaking his head and grinning. Composing his face into what he hopes is an expression of stern responsibility, he goes into the living-room and says with sarcastic mildness to his mother-in-law, 'You overdid it a bit wi' the salts, by the looks o'things, Mother.' Ostentatiously weary and martyred, he lifts the cushion of his easy-chair and draws out a sheaf of newspapers.

'Oh aye?' the old woman responds, incurious, abstracted, like a specialist politely pretending to recall a former patient.

'Aye — ' the man draws breath to go on, falters, and goes out again with his newspaper, defeated. Three hours later, Bess goes into intensive labour. As her cries grow to a hysterical crescendo, the old woman shakes her head, 'Eh aye . . . eh dear aye . . . ' more exasperated than worried. Finally, when Bess gives a particularly piercing howl, the old woman rises and goes into the corridor, passing the door of the room where her daughter lies and going on to the bairns' room. Sure enough the oldest, Senga, is sitting bolt-upright in bed, startled and shivering.

'Noo what are *you* daein', sitting' up?' the old woman asks, with tender remonstrance.

'Is that you, Granny? What a *noise*, Granny! Is it the Gerries, Granny? Are they comin' tae get us, Granny? Whaur's ma Mammy?' the wee one's tongue is tripping her, trying to get all her questions out.

The old woman sits on the edge of the bed, cuddles her, and lays

21

her back down: 'No ma darlin', no — wheesht noo, settle doon, *there's* a good lass,' she intones the litany of comfort, patting Senga's shoulder in a steady rhythm.

'But what is it, Granny?' Senga whispers, reassured but bursting with curiosity.

'Mind Ah telt ye about the stork comin' tae yer Mum?'

'Aye!' Senga gasps, instantly thrilled.

'Well, that's him comin' noo . . .'

'But the stork's awfu' noisy, Granny?' she insists, as naïvely as Little Red Riding Hood. 'What's he daein'?'

'He's a big bird, ye ken,' the old woman explains, smiling in the dark, ' — he's tryin' tae get in the windae, that's the noise.'

The bairn isn't totally satisfied by this: 'Why does he no' come doon the lum like Santa then?'

'What!' the old woman exclaims in mock horror, ' — an' get a black bairn?'

'Och aye, right enough,' Senga agrees, more convinced by the tone of her Granny's voice than by her actual words.

'So coorie doon noo,' the old woman admonishes, 'for if the stork hears you up at this time o' nicht, he'll maybe tak' ye back!' Senga dives under the covers and clings to her little sister, who lies at the back of the bed, next to the wall.

'That's her Granny's good lassie,' the old woman croons, rising and tucking her in, and going softly out.

She meets Ross in the corridor: 'They've sent me oot, Mother — she's near her time.' He is pale and scared, but she has no sympathy for him, only disdain: wordless, she leads the way back into the living-room. 'Mother, Mother!' he whispers hoarsely, 'that young doctor'll no' gi'e Bess ony chloroform!'

'*What?*' The old woman is instantly up in arms.

'He says it's against his religion . . . Ah — Ah could ca' the young buggar's heid aff his shooders if it wasnae for Bess an' the bairn!' He takes a few steps, looks around, takes a few steps in the opposite direction, and looks around again, trapped and impotent; suddenly his helpless anger imploded, he sags, slumps into his chair, and gazes a plea at his mother-in-law.

'Now then, there's nae call for your pit language here! I'll see about *this!*' She stalks off to the bedroom.

'Oh Mither, Mither!' Bess calls desperately from the bed.

'Get a grip on yersel', lassie — the howls o' ye would frichten the Free French!' is all the sympathy her mother offers, but the familiar no-nonsense tone quietens her down. 'Doctor?' the old woman continues, almost in the same breath.

'Yes?' the doctor is apprehensive, knowing what's coming.

'A word wi' ye. Why will ye no' gi'e ma lassie chloroform?'

'It's against my principles,' the doctor recites flatly.

'And what "principles" micht *they* be?'

'In Africa the native woman have their children quite naturally, without any kind of anaesthetic, and there are no problems . . . '

'Africa? *Africa?*' the old woman looks at the doctor as if he himself might just have stepped out of the bush at her with a bone through his nose.

'I'm going to be a missionary in Africa,' he answers, in a tone which seems to suggest that this explains everything, but he falters on the last word, and wilts under her moral indignation.

'And ye think this is Africa, do ye?'

'No, but if African women — .'

'What the puir sowels never had they'll never miss, ye mean!' she cuts across his repetition. 'Forbye, this isnae Africa — this is Skelf an' though *you* might no' be able tae tell the difference . . . you bein' *English,*' (this last she says with withering contempt) '*we can.* We're civilised here, an' we dinnae believe in unnecessary sufferin'.' She looks hard at him, tapping her foot.

'But I can't nonetheless . . .' — he comes clean in a burst of bravado — ' . . . for the Bible says — .'

Here Bess roars, 'Aaaw, Mither!' and the old woman's eyes deepen, sharing the pain:

'Ah'm no' goin' intae the Bible wi' ye *noo,* young sir — though Ah doubt if ye'll ken it better nor me — but it's a funny thing that my Minister christened the twa wee lambs through ben withoot a murmur, an' never even speired tae ken if ma lassie had had *chloroform* or no'!'

'Nonetheless — ,' the doctor begins again, ready to fall back on sheer stubbornness.

'Here!' the old woman breaks in, exasperated, eyeing him with blatant disgust: 'Have ye a wife o' yer ain?'

'Yes,' he answers proudly, and falls into the trap.

'Would you be standin' by seein' her sufferin' like that? If that was your *ain* wife lyin' there, would your *principles* haud your haund frae helpin' *her*? Tell me *that!*' she sniffs, folding her arms across her chest in a final Q.E.D. posture.

Involuntarily the doctor's gaze goes to the bed: he pictures his wife there, looking at him with an intensification of the unsatisfied pain with which she'd looked at him on their wedding night, and he nods — he'd do anything to get rid of that image, and the fading shadow of it that has hovered over the guilty month of his marriage: 'All right . . . ' he agrees, as if speaking to himself.

The old woman goes back to the living-room: '*Principles*, indeed! Awa' ye go through — she's gettin' the chloroform noo,' she commands Ross. He hesitates, unwilling. 'On ye go wi' ye! Ye had the pleasure at the makin' o't — it'll dae ye a parcel o'guid tae see the pain ma lassie's ha'ein' tae suffer tae bring it intae the world!' she urges. He goes slowly out, and pauses in the corridor, between the devil and the deep blue sea. 'Men!' she huffs, and then bitterly, introspectively, '. . . *Bess!* A *pair* o' bairns!'

As Ross enters the bedroom, crestfallen, he and the doctor avoid each other's eyes. Bess is drifting away into a chloroformed daze, only her stomach showing signs of activity. The nurse is quietly busy. Suddenly, with a heave and a low moan Bess brings forth the baby's head. 'Here she comes, Nurse!' the doctor calls, and the man instinctively crosses his fingers, touches the wood of the door behind him, and curses the doctor under his breath for that malicious, unlucky 'she'. Bess heaves and groans again; the rest of the baby comes out with a '*Whump!*' and the doctor gives himself away completely with a delighted, 'It's a girl!' He ties off and cuts the chord and holds the baby up by the heels like a butcher with a skinned rabbit, raising his hand to smack her.

'Watch what you're daein' wi' *ma* bairn!' the man growls in retaliation, looking murder at the doctor.

A nervous, gloomy time passes, while the nurse, humming drearily, swaddles the baby, and the doctor struggles with the afterbirth. Eventually Bess comes out of her daze to ask what it is; the doctor joyfully tells her it's a girl, but she's already guessed for herself by the fact that Ross wasn't the first to answer 'Oh, Wull,' she sighs, looking round for him, 'Ah'm sorry . . . ye're no' *too* let-doon are ye?'

'Not at all . . !' the man answers promptly, in fake and dutiful enthusiasm, avoiding her pleading eyes. 'Ah'll awa' ben an' tell your mother.' He all but sidles round the door and escapes.

'Men . . . ' Bess mutters bitterly, after he's gone. The doctor, embarrassed, turns his back and busies himself with cleaning his instruments. The nurse lays the baby on Bess's arm:

'What do you think of my perm dear?' she asks, preening and patting her head, wholly unaware that she doesn't in the least bit resemble Jean Harlow.

'Eh?' Bess can't look at her baby for looking in astonishment at the nurse.

'I had it done on Friday,' the nurse confides, turning all the way round to give Bess the full benefit.

'Eh?' Bess suspects she may still be dreaming under the chloroform, and goes along with it: 'It's fine . . . very nice, Nurse.' Groping for reality, she looks down at the baby, and revives, 'Ach, ye're a fine wee lassie, despite ye're as bald's an egg!' She touches its mottled little face and coos over it, while the doctor hovers awkwardly, his bag in his hands, waiting for her thanks.

He waits in vain, finally gives up and goes to the living-room for his coat. The old woman seems to have succumbed to sleep in Bess's chair by the fire, the shine on the floor and the furniture of the room around her reflecting her efforts to work off the night's anxieties. Ross, on the opposite chair, is smoking and gazing depressed into the fire. 'Oh it's you, doctor,' he says in a flat voice. 'You're away then? Cheerio,' and turns back to the fire before he's finished speaking. The doctor walks down the path at last, his heart set on Africa more than ever.

With the sound of the gate crashing shut behind him, the old woman pretends to wake up, and rises to her feet. 'I'll see the bairn,' she says, moving towards the door, ' — and dinnae you sit there, Wullie Ross, feelin' sorry for yersel': think yersel' lucky Bess and the wee sowel came through it . . . ' Ross grunts, and she adds, losing her temper at the sight of his self-pity, ' — or answer tae *me!*'

Ross gets up wearily and goes to the kitchen to put the kettle on. Gradually the thought that Bess is all right leads to the thought that there will be other chances for a son. He brightens, shrugs, and says aloud in a mock-martyred voice, 'Ah'll just have tae *try again!*'

The nurse and the old woman tidy up the bedroom in silent, practical harmony, then the nurse too, somewhat faded by now, gets ready to leave: her perm tight with the heat and sweat of the night, she looks like a blown dandelion-clock. As the old woman opens the front door for her, she remarks to the nurse, 'My, that's some rain comin' doon Nurse — will ye bide awhile till it's owre?'

'No, thank you, Granny!' the nurse exclaims gaily. 'My hat will save my hair!' Fastening the chinstrap of a hat that would have been more appropriate on a scout in the American army, she steps out, already far away from the scene she has just left, reciting as she walks down the path, ' "Rain, midnight rain, nothing but the wild rain" . . .'

'Eh dear aye — God love ye!' — with a compassionate sigh, and a last rueful shake of the head, the old woman closes the door.

'Look at her Wull — a fine wee lass,' Bess is saying, encouraged to try to win him over by the smile on his face as he brings her a cup of tea. Ross looks over at the bairn with the distant, ruminative assessment of a farmer at a cattle-mart:

'Aye . . . aye . . . she'll dae . . .' he concedes, but instantly, flatteringly, turns his attention to Bess, ' — is there anythin' ye want, darlin'?'

Bess is as ready to fall for this kind of solicitous attention as she was nine months ago, when he'd persuaded her that it was their duty in time of war, since he couldn't join the forces, 'tae try for a laddie'. 'Well . . .' — like the pampered princesses of the fairy tales she seeks a challenging task for him — '. . . have ye a fag while Ah'm thinkin'?'

'Oh dammit no! I've just smoked the last roll-up — it was worryin' aboot you, ye see darlin'.'

'God, an' Ah'm gaspin'! What's the time?'

'About six.'

'The shops'll be shut tae . . . oh Wull, ye micht o' — .'

'Aye, aye — but maybe Mac the milkman'll ha'e a fag tae sell us — he's due by ony minute.'

'Thank the Lord, for ma tongue's fair hingin' oot for ane — that was the hardest birth yet, Wull — .'

'Aye — damn fool o' a missionary . . . Never mind, dearie, ye done well — come through it like a sodger!'

'Come on noo Wull — dae ye *really* like her? *She* cannae help bein' a lassie, ye ken,' Bess cajoles.

'*Sure* I do!' he smiles, chucking the baby's cheek. 'What will ye call her?'

Bess muses, 'We never thocht on a name for a *lassie* . . .' Guilt-stricken, she cuddles the baby closer, ' — *did* we hen? *Ah* ken! Your *Daddy'll* pick your name! Won't ye, Wullie?'

Ross is embarrassed: it's cissy to have to think of girls' names. In this pause, Bess's mouth droops peevishly: 'You're still disappointed, Ah can tell . . .'

'Me? No' me! There's Mac — I hear the horse!' Ross rushes out and along the corridor, while Bess thinks, with a kind of luxurious resentment, that she'll have to go through it all again, to get a son.

'You're up early *this* mornin'!' the milkman exclaims in surprise as Wull looms out of the darkness.

'Aye, well . . . ye ken . . . Bess — .' He doesn't want to admit to the anti-climax of the birth.

'Another lassie?' Mac grasps the situation straight away, and laughs.

'Aye — for ma sins . . .' Ross sighs.

'Whaur's ma cigar then?' Mac teases.

'Cigar? Man, *Ah* came tae ask *you* if ye could sell *us* some fags — Bess is gaspin',' Ross responds, dispiritedly.

Taking pity on Bess, Mac draws out a packet of cigarettes: 'Gi'e her these wi' ma compliments . . . onyway, she'll be bringin' me mair trade afore long.'

'Thanks Mac — I'll see you get a cigar next time, when ma *laddie* comes!' Ross promises with a fervency that makes the milkman give him a quick glance of dubiety. Cheered by his own boast,

Ross expands, and pats the carthorse's flank: 'I see you've a new horse here?'

'Aye, a fine mare. "Stella" we cry her.'

'Helluva fancy name for a cuddy!' Ross snorts.

'No' really. Ye see, she's got a white star on her brow there — go round and have a gander, she'll no' shy.' As Ross goes to look, the milkman adds, ' "Stella" means "star", ye see . . .'

'Oh — Ah see . . . she's a fine bit horse, Ah'll grant ye that!' He strokes the mare's nose, glad of the rough natural smell of the stable after the chloroform and disinfectant smells indoors.

'As guid as gold! She's a star a' right — kens every step o' ma route after four days! By Christ Ah'll tell ye, she's mair brain nor the manager!' Ross laughs with him, remembers his duty with sudden guilt, and, nodding his thanks, sprints back to the house with the cigarettes.

Giving Bess a light he has an inspiration: '*Ah* ken a guid name for the lass!'

'*Do* ye?' Bess cheers up.

'*Stella* — it means "star" . . . eh . . . somebody told me. . . .' He realises what he's just done, but too late — anyway, it'll be days before she finds out. . .

'Stella? It's gey fancy . . . but — aye — Ah like it! Mother!' she shouts, proud and excited.

'Aye?' the old woman puts her head round the door.

'We're cryin' the bairn Stella. What d'ye think o' that? *Wull* picked it — ' She beams at her husband, 'It means "star".'

'Oh aye, that's nice,' the old woman nods sceptically, but as if it were no more than she expected. 'Well, Ah'm awa' hame noo. See'n you rest, Bess. Put that cigarette oot!' she exclaims, on taking a last close look at her daughter. 'Smokin' owre the bairn an' her no' smelt fresh air yet — have ye *nae* sense?' She comes in the door and takes the cigarette from Bess's fingers, and puts it out clumsily in the ashtray on Ross's lap, breaking it in half. While he and Bess look on like guilty, rebellious children, she leans over the baby and says confidentially, as if they weren't there. 'Bless ye ma wee hen!' Then she looks disapprovingly at Ross, who is still smoking: '*Stella*, eh? Well, Ah suppose we maun be glad it wasnae "Pasha" . . . Cheerio!'

CHAPTER 2

The Snow Queen's Palace

The year Stella was seven they went straight from summer into winter: in the middle of September the snow came, and the mornings were frozen over. Waking up early to the white light that made the frost on the windows opaque, Stella could believe she was in the Snow Queen's Palace. She would draw back the curtains and ignore the cold linoleum underfoot while she gazed at the delicate ice patterns, trying to fix them in her mind forever, till her heart was sore at the beauty of them, with a yearning she couldn't understand.

On the fifth morning of snow, she and Sheila had a bit of candle and a match, and they lit the candle and held it to the window-pane, standing hushed and big-eyed till the candleflame warmed its shadow on the glass and the frostflowers melted, sliding into each other before they vanished altogether. But it was just as painful to see them go as it was to see them glisten there.

Coming from the bedroom down to the kitchen on these days was like the descent to a hobgoblins' cave: everywhere was steam and bad temper, on the dark side of the house. Their mother, pregnant again, stayed in bed and left them to it, so it was dog eat dog, fighting — but quietly, not to bring her wrath down on them — for everything every inch of the way: for the cream on the milk, for the heel of the bread, for the strawberries in the jam, for the last crumbs of cheese; for the missing sock-garters, for the socks themselves, for the unbroken shoelaces, and for the place in front of the fire to put them all on.

But Stella always held her own, as independent as any of the heroines in her book, the one book she had, of *Fairy Tales from Grimm and Andersen*. Steadily week by week the school minister had managed to make her believe she was born in sin and outcast of Eden, and she saw the world of these stories as her lost paradise: it was from this world with its miracles and happy endings that she felt banished. She lived in hopes of finding a secret opening that led back there, and wove fantasies about the cupboard below the stairs, low-doored and deep behind the coats in the alcove. Every morning when she jumped up to take her coat off the peg she would give a sudden glance in the direction of that door, hoping to catch it unawares. This morning, again, it was giving nothing away. But she wasn't disappointed, for the frost on the window-panes she took as a reassuring sign that she wasn't wrong about the magic world: she cocked her head to one side, giving a bird's knowing look at the cupboard door, and nodded at it with steadfast purpose: she could bide her time.

It was dismal at school; damp shoes, damp clothes, damp hair where the snowballs had hit her; starting the day with a multiplication sum as long as your arm, and with only the grey teacher to look at, as she cleaned her nose through her hankie, a finger busy in each nostril like a squirrel washing, but examining the results with a monkey's curiosity. 'What a dreariness!' Stella thought, and she kept on thinking that all morning: '*What* a dreariness!'

Just about the only bit of colour in the whole classroom was her pal's head, three rows down, with its hair the colour of old gold like the straw Rumpelstiltskin spun in her story-book. But the rest of Ishbel was more like Rumpelstiltskin himself: undersized and ageless with accumulated grime, sexless at seven, yet all the woman she would ever be, and a patient Griselda at school. She carried with her the atmosphere of the place she came from, and that was what had drawn Stella to her.

Carnegie Mansions was the slum area of Skelf, a deep depression on the other side of the main street from the sea — it was as if the pressure of disapproval from the beach homes of the bourgeoisie on the one side and the brick semis of the aspiring working-class on the other had made this tired, grey little settlement sag and collapse inward with a sigh. The sigh took the form of the steam, smoke and heat from the washhouses and sea-coal fires, and the dip seemed to be haunted by the familiar digestive odour of stockpots constantly simmering their miscellany of exhausted ingredients. You went down a long gentle slope into the central square, and up another slope out of it again, and came away with the impression of poverty so faded it had become something else.

Like the people who lived there, Carnegie Mansions was a relic of times older than when it actually came into being, for it seemed to have been planned along the lines of a tribal village — by some enthusiastic town councillor, perhaps, with a social conscience and atavistic memories of clan life. It was built on a square, with toilets and washhouses running parallel to the cottages and two-storeyed, three-roomed flats, like an intermittent inner line of defence. Cottages and tenements leaned against one another so that the inside of the square was like the courtyard of a medieval castle. All the front doors and gardens faced outward to main streets, but everybody used their living-rooms as bedrooms, and when they sat indoors at all, it was in their back kitchens, so that they could watch what was going on in the square from their low-slung windows without rising from their easy-chairs. None of the front doors had been opened in living memory, for the minister never visited there. When houses changed hands, no front-door keys were passed on: these had all been lost, and the locks rusted over, long ago, so the front doors were ignored as useless archi-tectural embellishment — as irrelevant as cupolas or Corinthian pillars would have been — and the front gardens had merged with the thoroughfare.

Although not many of the individual families were related, the whole community, through years of looking inward on to the square, had the habits and attitudes of a clan. Anyway they were related through failure, for it was from here that the commercial world of Skelf drew its cinema cleaners and casual workers, its sick-nurses and nightwatchmen and squads of seasonal farm-labourers; it was from here that the peace-time soldiers and sailors were recruited, and it was to here that they had come back after the war, to nurse forever after obscure military ailments which forever after excused them from full-time work. Whole families of nine or ten people slept in the three-roomed flats, but home for them was only a roof over your head in rough weather: the real living was done in the square, outside the dark little houses.

And the real living seemed to consist entirely of conversation: roly-poly little women, blown up with their staple diet of starch, squeezed side-by-side like so many Tweedledums and Tweedledees, but bare-armed and in grubby wrap-over aprons, would be sitting on their window-sills talking away ten to the dozen everywhere you looked, a handleless cup of tea in their hands. To Stella these women looked incredibly wise: they were like the gnomes in the fairy-tales — their very casualness was wisdom; the way they sat talking intently, and occasionally looking away into the middle distance, ruminating bitterly or sadly or thoughtfully, shaking their heads at the ways of the world and swilling their teacups round before throwing the dregs on to the packed earth at their feet, then peering into the patterns of the tea-leaves that were left: beyond housework, above cleanliness; undersized and weather-beaten; shunned by the rest of Skelf, speaking an old-fashioned dialect full of strange words — they were magic.

Their men, too. They would squat like miners on their hunkers for patient hours together, their backs to the washhouse walls, engrossed in the racing pages of the newspaper. Stella suspected them of having special powers to see what she couldn't, for they studied it all the time without ever turning a page. It was all a familiar mystery to her, for just about every Saturday morning that summer her father had whispered to her on the fly, handing her a scrap of paper with a half-crown wrapped in it, 'Slip doon tae the Runner at Carnegie Mansions, an' no' a word tae yer Mum!' He made her feel like one of the underground Christians in *Quo Vadis*.

The Runner added potently to the otherwordly atmosphere of the square. He was a thin little man with a suit that was much too big, but which was so moulded to him by the dirt and sweat of years that you could have trimmed off the surplus material like a pie-crust, with no fear of nicking the limbs it encased. Stella had surmised that the impression of spindly knee and shank and arm must have been made by the force of the wind against him as he ran. Yet he didn't look like any kind of runner; he looked more like a clay model wearing away to its wire frame: when she stood next to him to hand over her father's betting-slip, the smell of him was dust and damp clay. And he would take her father's offering without smiling, or looking at her, standing with his eyes fixed on an invisible inner horizon, his hand closing round the paper and falling to his side again like a Sambo bank, as he gave a slight grunt that could have been acknowledgement, but could just as well have been a creak. Then he would turn his head to the side and spit a clot of blood as if it was a receipt or a red seal on the bargain. She half-guessed that the blood came from running like the Marathon man, and she imagined that between taking her dad's money and spitting he had run faster than the eye could see, to the Bookie's and back — so fast that to her he appeared to be standing perfectly still.

As she walked away from him she would glance over her shoulder now and again, hoping to catch the blur of his movement, but the scene would always be just as she left it, the men squatting with their papers in their grey-brown suits the colour of the earth, and their sombre strained faces only a shade lighter, as if they were coming from or returning to the dust.

As far as Stella could see, the folk in Carnegie Mansions toiled not neither did they spin; they did nothing to justify their existence except exist: in this, they were her only human link with the magic world that defied all the laws she'd had drummed into her, so she kept her visits there, and her guesses about the place, superstitiously secret. She thought she had recognised Carnegie Mansions as the place where if any of her friends mysteriously vanished, she would, like Gerda, begin to ask about him; she felt that if she were desperate enough even the starlings there would talk, and give her their secret lore; that any one of these dusky women would, if she herself were only sincere, tell her where the West Wind lived, and that the Runner would in a trice, without a word or a change of expression, transport her there. And when the school minister on one of his lighter, New Testament days, quoted 'In my father's house there are many mansions,' she thought he meant a place like Carnegie Mansions, with Jesus as the Runner for God the Bookie. So she was delighted when Ishbel sought her out for a friend, for that was where Ishbel came from.

When Ishbel whispered to her at the milk-crates, 'Ah'm haein' ma pairty the nicht, just you an' me — are ye comin'?' Stella's heart lurched with excitement. It would be her first private party. She had no friends among the posh ones in her class, who were the only ones who had parties, and she was green with envy when they did. Not long ago, she and Ishbel had been depressed together at the sight of one girl's excited preparations for a party: bringing little toytown invitations to school for her cronies, and them shopping to buy little acceptance cards to give back; everybody talking about what they were going to wear and what present their mothers would buy them to take — it went on for a miserable week, then after the weekend there were two or three more miserable days when the partygoers went into exclusive huddles to relive the event, and Stella got angrily self-conscious in her efforts to ignore them, while Ishbel seemed to sink into some precocious existential despair.

'See that Heather McFarlane?' Stella had burst out in abrupt confession, 'Ah could *strangle* 'er! Her an' her keechy wee pairty!'

Ishbel had responded with a desperate defiance that stunned Stella: 'Wha cares? *Ah'm* gonna ha'e ma *ain* pairty!'

Stella stood and gazed at her as if Ishbel was the light and herself was Paul on the road to Tarsus.

'*And* Ah'm no' askin' her — she neednae think it!' Ishbel glared at Heather McFarlane. 'It'll be just you an' me, Stella. . . .'

Stella nagged her mother to put a ribbon in her hair that afternoon so insistently that her mother rebelled and told her that since she was going to have such a glorious time she wouldn't be needing any tea at home — a typical piece of adult chicanery as far as Stella was concerned, but she was too thrilled about the party to argue the point. She just ran all the way to Carnegie Mansions to avoid her hunger.

Her knees were trembling with nerves as she knocked at Ishbel's door; she was terrified she'd show her ignorance of party manners without her mother there to guide her, and she was in an agony of embarrassment at not having a present with her. She looked round the square; it felt stranger than ever, now that she was on the verge of entering into its mysteries.

34

After a lot of shouting inside the house about who would answer the door, a big surly boy opened it and said, 'What d'ye want?' as if he were protecting his mother from the ticky-man.

It was like a bucket of cold water to Stella: 'Ah'm here for Ishbel's party,' she muttered defensively, shuffling her feet and looking away from him.

'*Pairty?*' he snorted. 'There's nae pairty here!' and looked at her as if she were an importunate, starving dog.

Stella's face went grey and her stomach rumbled; the bottom was falling out of her world, and she all but whispered, humbly, 'Well, is Ishbel in?'

The boy shouted over his shoulder, back into the kitchen, 'Maw! Is oor Ishbel in?' and cries for Ishbel were set up all over the house, while Stella stood, hollowed out by humiliating disappointment. After a minute or so of this the boy said, 'Naw, she's no' in —,' and shut the door, leaving her standing, unconsciously savouring the thick smell of soup that had wafted through the close little house, while she wondered what to do.

She looked around the square, a geometric greyness in the cold and fading light, so harsh and blank that it had to be deceptive: if she only had the power to see, she believed it would turn out to really be a goblins' underworld cave. She blinked and peered, but nothing; she gazed, motionless, till her eyes watered, but nothing; she closed her eyes and rubbed them hard, then opened them. The last of the light had gone, and house-windows here and there glowed like lanterns through the dark, with the cosy inwardness of lamps and fires. But it made her feel so outside, this sudden impression of the secret lives of families drawn together against the night, that she forgot she had a home of her own. In a panic, she strained for the image of her own fireside, but all that came was the image of her mother girning at her because the tea was long since over, and her sisters laughing at her about the party. She was cold, and it would be hot by the fire at home — but hot and tormenting like hell is hot. Stella didn't want to go home.

It started to snow very softly, till the softness of it soothed her, and tempted her: she couldn't connect the cold she felt with the gentle snow falling like feathers, nor with the billowing sky that hung overhead like a plump eiderdown. She would walk in it;

starting from this place of lesser magic, she would look for the Snow Queen's Palace.

So she set off in any direction, and walked and walked, not looking where she was going because she knew instinctively that that was the only way to get there. She only looked up. Eventually the snow stopped and the stars came out, and she began to entirely believe that despite what her dad had told her, it *was* possible to walk off the edge of the world; if you walked far enough you would fall off and endlessly through a starry blackness. But that didn't frighten her, because 'endless' was a fairy-tale word, it belonged to the world she wanted.

Gradually, as she plodded on, a rheumaticky pain up her arm needled her out of her trance. She began to have doubts, that the Snow Queen must be busy somewhere else, or that she only took boys. Looking outward for the first time since Carnegie Mansions, she saw that she was in a waste field with the beach on her right and a hill on her left; nothing ahead but more beach all the way to the next village. She didn't want to go back; she got scared, then got round her fears by slipping back into her vision of the Snow Queen's world, where everything was just cool and clear and you didn't feel the cold. With new heart, and lifting her feet high off the snow like the toy soldier, she marched towards the hill, which she decided was the Ice Mountain she'd have to climb to get to the Snow Queen's Palace.

The first foot she put on the slope of the hill slid back: underneath the snow was rough lumpy ice. It was no more than she expected; the very difficulty of it was convincing. She took her hands out of her coat pockets and began to climb, feeling out each footstep as she put her weight on it. The higher she climbed the more sheer the ice got. Just above the middle she had to begin to climb on her belly, using both hands and feet to scramble for holds, turning first one cheek then the other against the ice. Half-way between the middle and the top she slipped, and slithered in a knobbly way back to the middle. Then she lost her temper and began to burn with determination: 'Bloody Ice Mountain!' she raged, and clenched her teeth and fought her way in a sudden scrambling surge to the top, every little slip backwards making her more recklessly mad.

At the top, the sharp wind off the sea cut through her, and her arm ached. She put her hands in her pockets, but withdrew them in sudden disgust, for the debris inside had gone slithery with the wet ice. And of course, no Palace, just a bleak little country road leading back to Skelf. 'Oh well . . . ' she shrugged, unsurprised, even quite relieved to get back to normal for the time being, for she had a sense that at least her woeful bedraggled condition would spare her the hammering she deserved. In her present state of hunger and cold she would have surrendered all the childhood mysteries — even though it meant believing that what she saw was all there was to see of the adult world (and what she *saw* was a pointless colourless continuum) — she would have surrendered all hope of the Ice Queen and her Palace for a meat-paste sandwich. She puddled away down the slushy cart-road, heading for home, swearing at Ishbel under her breath with every step.

By the time she reached Skelf she had begun to feel as pathetic as the Little Match Girl, in her secret heart. On the surface she just felt that she was being fairly punished as usual for her sins, and she was afraid to let the self-pity through for that was a sin, too, and she didn't want to draw any more punishment down on her. But her knees were like jelly, and she fought the temptation to sink down under the hedge and try for glory the way the Match Girl did. She had a pessimistic suspicion that she was too old and too wicked for that already: what with the cinnamon she smoked on the way home from school when she could afford it, her jealousy over other people's parties, and her swearing, she probably would go straight to Hell.

That thought kept her going as far as her Granny's gate. Exhaustion had stripped her down to her instincts, and for once she didn't reflect the scared awe her mother felt for the stern old woman; her own more subtle sense broke through. She went and rattled urgently at the door. The minute she heard her Granny's footsteps in her lobby her tears started to flow.

'Granny — Ah think Ah'm no' weel, Granny . . .' she sobbed as the door opened.

'Come awa' in an' let's look at ye,' her Granny said, leading the way to the living-room, then, when she saw Stella under the gas mantle she exclaimed, 'Mighty! Ye're like a drooned rat!'

Stella responded to the compassionate tone, and with an almighty snottering sniff, pulled herself together enough to blurt, 'An' Ah'm *awfu'* unhappy Granny . . .!'

'Never! A wee lass like you!' her Granny consoled, half-laughing to cope with the sudden pain Stella's words gave her, coming together with the sight of her standing there puny as a wet dog, with her curls plastered to her head and her handed-down Astrakhan coat sadly diminished, too.

Stella stood numb in the admission of defeat, hurt by the heat of the fire, while the old woman stripped her to the buff, rubbed her with a towel, and wrapped her up in two more dry towels. Then she sat her down in her own chair by the hearth: 'Sit you there and get a heat through ye while your Granny warms up the soup . . .' she ordered. Stella sat.

Her Granny came back eventually with an enamel pudding-basin full of broth, which Stella balanced in her lap to eat. While she took regular sips, like a mechanical toy, the old woman sat opposite and studied her. Slowly the feeling of being watched by a kind, personal eye overwhelmed her, and her heart began to thaw and ache again, and she wept quietly, still taking her soup. When she'd finished she put the bowl on the hearth and looked to her Granny.

'Noo, what have they been daein' tae ye, ma hen?' the old woman asked, protective.

Stella pondered, but she found she couldn't explain; she couldn't even grasp in her most wordless thoughts the sense of what it was. Hopeless tears began to run down her cheeks: 'Ah dinnae ken, Gran . . . but it's no' nothin'.' And she bent towards her Granny with big earnest eyes, hoping against futile hope that she would be able to read it all there for herself.

The old woman responded with the frankly searching look of her own, nodding slowly as if she found what she expected to find, and understood it perfectly. Stella felt the flow of a benign current like a strong beam of invisible light; the sense of a circuit of humanity healed and restored, between them. For a few seconds they were equal and immortal, and her soul opened like a flower. Then there was peace; she lay back in her chair and she and her

Granny gazed into the fire as if this were a lull in a long heart-to-heart conversation, until Stella fell sound asleep.

When she was sure that Stella was in her night's sleep, the old woman got up quietly and filled a hot-water bottle, putting it in the bed that was recessed into the room. She went back by the fire, but got up again twice to move the bottle, so that one whole area of the bed was warmed. Then she picked Stella up and took her across to it, tucking her in and stroking her hair to settle her down as she stirred on contact with the sheets, before going back to her own chair and frowning thoughtfully into the fire.

'Granny — are ye still there Granny?' came the drowsy voice from the bed recess.

'Aye, hen, Ah'm here,' the old woman soothed.

'Granny . . . would *you* gi'e me a party?' (muffled self-indulgent sobs from the pillow).

The old woman rose and went over to the bed, anxious: 'Do ye want a pairty hen?'

'Oh, Ah *awfu'* want a pairty, Granny!'

Patting the bump of Stella's little backside over the blanket in a steady heartbeat rhythm, the old woman indulged her, 'And wha would ye want at your party?'

'Jist only me, Granny . . . ' Stella confided in a whisper, as if it were a deep secret, and went back to sleep. The old woman continued to pat her for two or three minutes, thinking intently, then she rose and gave Stella a gentle shake:

'Listen lass — can ye hear me?'

'Aye,' — Stella was never completely extinguished.

'Just you cuddle in there: Ah'm awa' up tae tell your mother ye'll bide wi' me the nicht.'

'Right Gran,' Stella murmured, from the complacent depths of perfect security.

The old woman got up to go, and Stella, marvelling at the sheer, exquisite luxuriousness of having a sheet over you as well as under you, drifted off to sleep.

When she woke up next morning her Granny was already grilling the toast for her breakfast, and her clothes were all washed and ironed. Even her *knickers* had been ironed! She thought her Granny was like the fairy shoemakers.

'Was ma Mum mad, Gran — ?' she asked hesitantly, but wanting to compensate for the indulgence of having her breakfast made for her by going half-way to meet the certain row.

'Sit doon tae yer porridge,' her Granny answered. And it *was* an answer, for the tone of it told Stella that the matter had passed out of her hands.

'God's *nothin'* compared tae ma Granny!' she thought as she ate her porridge, '*God's* nothin' compared tae ma *Granny*!'

The old woman came back through from the kitchen with a plate of buttered toast, and sat down at the table beside her. 'Nae school for you the day,' she announced, 'till Ah'm sure ye're no' in for the 'flu .'

'Eh?' Stella began to believe she was dreaming the whole thing now, and trembled a little, sudden tears welling up at the prospect of the rude awakening that must inevitably come.

'You'll bide wi' me the day,' her Granny repeated.

'Ah wish Ah could *ay* bide wi' you, Gran,' she said, wistfully.

'And what would your mither dae, withoot ye?' her Granny challenged, with just the shadow of anger, which Stella misunderstood to mean that she was pushing her luck.

'Och,' she tried to make it plain that she had intended it only as a compliment, by turning it all into a wry joke: 'She'd never miss *me* — she's plenty mair at hame!'

'But she'll need a clever lass like you tae help wi' the bairn that's comin',' her Granny argued, smiling now, to draw Stella out.

'What *for* is she ay haein' bairns, Gran?' — Stella was quick to seize the opportunity to solve this puzzle, now that she had her Granny to herself and was talking to her like a person.

The old woman laughed again, 'Weel may ye ask, ma darlin'!' then added, with bitter honesty, '. . . because she's nae mair sense than no' tae!'

Stella smiled with relief: that was what *she* thought too — and confided further, 'Ah mean, she jist seems tae get emptied and filled up again — what for Granny?'

Her Granny choked on her toast, laughing, and pushed her chair back, shaking her head: 'Never you mind why! That's the cross you have to bear, Stella,' she said, almost sternly, remembering Stella's age, but with a secret glance of compassion at the child's head, which was now bent over her empty plate with embarrassed intentness, as if the answer might be somewhere among the droplets of milk there. She rose to take the empty plate through.

Stella yielded up her plate and nodded with an exaggerated grimace, 'Aye, Ah suppose . . .' took a slice of toast, and gazed into space with a matter-of-fact look, in an obvious attempt to seem as old and wise as her Granny. The old woman smiled her approval of this stoicism, and wiped the tears of laughter from her face with the corner of her apron as she went through with Stella's plate.

Basking in that smile, Stella ventured: 'Granny, what you said about the party . . .?' — trying to sound as if she didn't really care much.

The old woman sat down again. 'Your Granny never promises what she willnae dae,' she said emphatically, reaching for the teapot.

'*Really*, Gran? Really an' nae kiddin'!' Stella laid down her toast in astonishment.

'What will ye need for it?' her Granny went on.

'Bridge rolls an' meat paste . . .?' Stella waited to see how this was taken before she would dare go any further.

'Aye,' the woman agreed.

'An' . . . ' she hesitated between delicate self-restraint and the need to make it a real party.

'Aye an' what?' her Granny looked at her with her head on one side and an eyebrow humorously raised. 'Come on, oot wi't!' she urged.

Stella had never seen her Granny like this before. She was emboldened: 'Cocoa — can Ah ha'e cocoa Gran? Naw — cocoa would be too much . . .' she answered herself, shaking her head as if exasperated by her own demands, but casting a hopeful sidelong glance at her Granny.

'Certainly ye can ha'e cocoa,' her Granny dismissed.

Stella began to get self-conscious; she didn't know where to look for embarrassment; for as long as she could remember her mother had been telling her what a hard mother her Gran had been to *her*, but here she was, promising cocoa — and to just Stella: Stella

41

began to suspect that her Gran had a mistakenly high opinion of her importance: 'Are ye sure?' she asked outright, looking straight at the old woman as if to say, 'do you know what you're doing?' But the old woman nodded, 'Aye.'

'Is that no' too guid o' ye Gran?' Stella pursued.

The old woman laughed quietly and answered, 'Allow me tae ken what's too guid o' me and what's no', ma lass!' Then, beginning to be aware herself that this was a side she'd never shown so openly, she added, 'You're the cleverest: your Granny has a special eye for you . . .' and patted Stella's shoulder.

'For *me?*' Stella blurted, incredulous. She'd had no idea.

'Aye for *you* — you're the cleverest,' her Granny repeated.

'Well then, Granny, can Ah ha'e chocolate biscuits tae?' Stella asked quickly.

Stella's Granny had as little idea as Stella herself of what a private party was like, and an onlooker would have thought their version of it more like a wake than anything else. But it was a solemn affair for Stella in any case: justice was being done, and balloons and icecream would have been unthinkably frivolous. So they sat as sober as judges, her Granny silent by the fire, knitting the shawl for the new baby, while Stella ate the bridge rolls and chocolate biscuits as reverently and deliberately as if they had been the Host at Communion, and filled her cup with cocoa from the jug her Granny had put on the table with ceremonious care, sunk in sub-conscious thought the whole time.

The minute she'd finished, leaning her head on one hand with a sigh of content, her Granny rose and cleared the table and washed the dishes. Then they sat at opposite sides of the fire, Stella holding her hands out to it, for occasionally all day she could feel that there were still little shards of ice from the night before going through her bloodstream and giving her a shiver. Eventually she sighed again: 'That was just stu-*pendous*, Gran!'

Her Granny held up her knitting to cast a superficially critical eye over it, then settled down again, equally content. There was very little need for words between them, and they sat in silence together for the better part of an hour. Most of the time Stella watched her Granny's face, to read what she was thinking: it reassured her and gave her peace to see the bright calm eyes go deep with careful thought, assessing the world and coping with it. Her mother was never still and she lived from whim to whim. But then the passing thought of her mother awoke her anxiety. In gratitude to her Granny, she took a deep breath and grasped the nettle: 'Well Ah suppose Ah'll better get hame afore the dark, Gran,' she said, pushing herself up from her chair.

Her Granny set her knitting in her lap, still holding it, and gave Stella a penetrating look. 'How would you like tae stay wi' yer Granny?'

'Eh? *Could* Ah? Forever, ye mean?' Stella leaned forward, on the edge of her chair, not breathing while she waited for the answer.

'Aye,' her Granny said.

'Right noo an' Ah wouldnae need tae go hame?'

'That's it,' her Granny said, easily.

'*Aye,*' Stella said, with all her heart, and sunk back in her chair, so stunned that she felt she was seeing stars.

That night as she lay against the wall in the recessed bed in her knickers and vest, with her Granny's arm around her, cuddled in, she glowed, ' "Safe in the arms o' Jesus" hasnae got a look-in . . . '

Her Granny had no wireless, and in the long evenings after school, she and Stella would sit companionably by the fire, reading. The old woman's taste ran to ingenious murder mysteries, and Stella read and re-read her fairy-tale book, until Christmas came and she got the Woolworth's edition of *Jane Eyre* and *Silas Marner* from her mother. Her Granny got her a dictionary to go with them, and *Everybody's Book of Facts.* With the dictionary she felt she had potentially all the books in the world, and all the words in the world for all the thoughts in the world. Night after night she pored over it, asking her Granny about this and that. One night she looked up, trully puzzled: 'What does it mean, "to read between the lines", Granny?'

The old woman paused in her ironing, 'It means, to read what isnae there.'

'Aw but how can ye read what insae *there?*'

'You'll learn . . . ' was all the answer she got, and she knew not to pursue it, because her Granny always gave the straight answer the first time. But she burned to know, all the same. Here she thought was a clue that maybe the adult world *did* have more to it than met the eye; maybe it *did* have its own mysteries and miracles — maybe that was what the men at Carnegie Mansions were doing when they sat studying the same page of the newspaper all that time — reading between the lines. She was encouraged, and began to read her Granny's newspaper every day to see what might come up from the white lines as if written in invisible ink.

Her Granny noticed her gazing in intense concentration at the paper one evening and asked her, 'What are ye daein', Stella? Have ye sore eyes?'

'No, Gran — Ah'm just tryin' tae read between the lines . . .'

The old woman laughed: 'Well that tak's the ticket! Noo Ah've heard a'thing! Eh aye, wee Stell', Ah dinnae ken aboot you — Ah've a notion you've been here afore! And what do you see?'

'Nothin' yet,' Stella admitted, shaking her head, 'Ah think Ah must be owre young.'

'Aye Ah think sae!' her Granny laughed.

For a treat that night she read Stella *Tam O' Shanter* in bed.

About a week later Stella was lounging on the hearthrug with her dictionary while her Granny sat at the table, still reading her paper after her tea. 'Granny!' she called over, looking up from the book. 'What's "sexual inter-course"?'

Her Granny made no sign of having heard. 'Granny!' Stella tried again, but her Granny was stock-still, with her newspaper in her hand. 'Aha!' Stella thought, ' — at last I've caught her readin' between the lines!' She studied her Granny's back, not wanting to disturb the spell before she could get a good clue to what it all meant, but was finally overcome by curiosity and got up softly, going behind the old woman's chair and looking over her shoulder. Even with Stella breathing down her neck, her Granny still didn't move. Then it dawned on Stella that her Granny was reading the paper *upside-down*. 'So *that's* how ye read between the lines then!' she crowed. When she got no response this time, she became alarmed. Her Granny never played tricks on her. She moved to the side of the chair and looked up into the old woman's face. It was twisted, and her eyes were glazed with confusion, unblinking. Stella knew in that instant, and her whole world came crashing down about her ears. 'Granny! Oh ma Granny! Gran!' she cried, and her heart broke, for with the energetic light of intelligence gone from the old woman's eyes, she could see for the first time the frailty of the shell of flesh that contained it: an old, done woman.

She ran for a neighbour then she ran for the doctor then she ran for her mother and she hated them all for their intrusion on her private world and her Granny's inviolable person. Back in her mother's house, sharing a bed again with Sheila she lay all that night sleepless and rigid as a board with resentment, her teeth clenched and her heart tight as a closed fist. She would gladly have murdered them all to have her Granny back.

The next night her Granny was dead, and Stella lay and sobbed all night, loud and long, till her mother could bear it no longer and came through to the bedside. She looked at her mother's sad broken face and hated her for not being her Granny: 'Ah want *ma Granny!*' she howled, and buried her face, inconsolable, in the pillow.

'Your Granny's gone to Heaven where she'll be happy.' Bess intoned this for the umpteenth time.

'She was happy *here,*' Stella protested savagely.

'God wanted her for his ain.'

'*God's backside!*' Stella roared, and her mother gave her a thick ear. 'Ye can murder me if ye like,' Stella spat, 'Ah couldnae care! Ah only want ma Granny!'

Bess began to whimper, and whined to Stella in a peevish voice, 'She was ma *mither,* ye ken! She was only your *Granny!*'

Stella was utterly dumbfounded. No warmth of consolation went out of her towards her mother at all: her mother wanted to make it into a *competition.* If she'd had the guts, she would have told her mother to go away — that was the next feeling, that her mother was a huge stifling, lumbering weight. And the next feeling was that she was going to have to survive forever after in this world without her Granny; that she owed it to her Granny not to betray their understanding, but to hold it and keep it inside, and survive, and *be strong like her Granny.* 'OK — I'll be quiet noo,' she

45

muttered, turning her face to the wall so that Bess would get up and go away.

'Right then — for a' *your* greetin' willnae bring ma mother *back*, ye ken!' Bess sobbed righteously, rising and moving towards the door.

Stella bit her bottom lip and looked at the wall.

CHAPTER 3

Palm Sunday

'What's Palm Sunday in any case?' Stella asked her sister as they sat side by side on the bus in the rain, on their way to Sunday school. Sheila ignored her, concentrating on learning verses from the open Bible in her lap. Stella never bothered to study hers — by the time the Sunday-school teacher got round to her turn to recite, she'd memorised them from the others' repetition, and anyway, they made no sense at all to her. The first time she'd got verses to learn, she'd said to the teacher, 'But what do they *mean?* Ah cannae understand a word o't!' and the teacher gave her a teacher look, and replied curtly, with less than charity.

'You have to learn them off by heart. I'll explain them next week.'

Of course, she never did explain them — at least, not so Stella could understand.

She knew why she had to go to school, but she never could figure why she had to go to Sunday school: what was Jesus to her after all? Who was he, a total foreigner in a nightgown from a hot country and anyway he was dead, were her weekly thoughts on the subject, which she kept to herself, knowing damn fine they'd only get her into trouble if she spoke them out.

But for the last couple of weeks there had been this tremendous, mysterious build-up to Palm Sunday, with a corresponding build-up of curiosity on Stella's part. She understood that it was an event like Christmas, but like Christmas, she couldn't understand what it was supposed to mean to *her*. Everybody celebrating a birth was peculiar in itself, in a world where it was nakedly obvious that

47

pregnancy was something to be feared, an economic calamity on a big scale. She had sensed the strong relish of righteousness in the hot gossip about pregnancies. She had already heard from Sheila of how her mother had taken hot baths and Beecham's pills and jumped downstairs off the first landing to try to get rid of their youngest sister before she was born, and this she had accepted as a conventional attitude, the conventional behaviour. From what Stella had managed to pick up, the Greatest Miracle was to 'do it' and *not* get pregnant — *not* to do it and get pregnant was sheer stupidity. So the religious side of Christmas, with the maudlin sentimentality it aroused in her mother, had taken a prime place on Stella's list of The Stupendous Hyprocrisies of the Adult World, and she looked forward keenly to understanding it when she grew up — as her mother had assured her she would, along with a whole lot of other weird rituals, like having to go to the toilet to fart when her posh aunties visited, although her father had asserted to her in a moment of confidence (or maybe just of rebellion against her mother) that of course, her aunties farted too: he should know, they were his sisters.

Now, for Godsake, here was something else to add to the list that was growing altogether too fast for Stella's peace of mind. The older she got, the more she felt like she was living in a foreign country, a harsh land where the natives knew everything and told nothing, but if you in your ignorance offended against their unspoken and unfathomable law, you were punished nonetheless. One of her more sentimental aunties, on the birth of her mother's last unwelcome daughter, had persistently recited a poem beginning, 'And into our house a little stranger came,' in a tender voice that had embarrassed everybody. Stella felt the aunt had hit the nail on the head though with the 'little stranger' idea, but she couldn't see what was so marvellous about it, either from the adult point of view, or, more particularly, from the point of view of the little stranger. She knew it in her bones that Palm Sunday must be another bit of pious hypocrisy; she knew it from the way nobody could explain it.

'Aw come on, what's Palm Sunday?' she urged her sister.

Sheila shifted and shrugged, 'God knows — and let me alane will ye, I've tae learn *this* shite for the day!'

Stella subsided; Sheila had social ambitions the furtherance of which required that she be in no way outstanding in public, and it was dangerous to cross her, for she'd lose her temper and start a stand-up fight, and they'd both be thrown off the bus in the rain — it had happened before — and the rain made the dye in their Sunday coats run down their legs, an experience which thrilled Stella personally, for it made her feel like Joseph in his Coat of Many Colours, but which was the last word in humiliation to Sheila.

So when they got off the bus Sheila ran as hard as she could to get into the ante-room of the church hall, before the rain soaked into her coat. Stella dawdled along, hoping for the opposite effect. None of her pals were there; none of her pals had a coat. She wasn't keen, by any means, to join the 'happy band', as the minister called them, of Sunday scholars. She hated them all. She hated their personal smugness, their well-washed well-combed, scarves mittens new coats thick socks shiny shoes complacency, and she writhed impotently under their sneering contempt for her, with her legs blue in cotton ankle-socks, her thin, handed-down coat, piebald with dye, scuffed shoes, no hat no scarf no mitts and a tidemark on her neck under the chin where she flashed the facecloth round it, her hands grey with a week's ingrained dirt, and her seething aggression, her awkward inappropriate cleverness. She saw them now from across the road, cavorting about in the rain in their Skipper's Sardines fishermen's hats, their shiny black wellies, and their snug black Burberrys, and her stomach went cold with social fear. Which she instantly, bitterly, resented: 'Come on God, be decent for once, strike the wee bastards doon where they stand and let me start again with a clean sheet! Come on, God, there's only a handfu' — they wouldnae be much missed!' she hectored between clenched teeth as she crossed the road. But they were still there. 'Aw come *on*, God — ' she waited in the middle of the road for a car to pass, ' — after a' you're cracked up tae be . . . the soul o' kindness — ye've done nowt for *me* so far — just this one wee thing . . .' The car passed and they were still there, running and splashing and pushing, '. . . if, as ma mither says, ye're starving millions tae death in the Sahara every *day*, surely to God ye can get rid o' *them* nae bother, as a special favour tae *me*?' But they were still there.

She tensed her stomach-muscles, raised her shoulders, bowed her head and clenched her teeth, 'Right! *Right!* — an' shit tae you too, God!'

The possibility of atheism hadn't as yet been revealed to her; she went about since her Granny's death burdened by this callous God, to whom, she had gathered, she must be utterly without attraction, for He ignored her like a rich tourist ignores a Bombay beggar. Between her appeals and his silence, nothing changed in the world: it still rained, her legs were still blue with cold, and the wee bastards were still playing jolly pranks in the churchyard. She had an inarticulate suspicion that God was middle-class, and possibly even English — authority, a super-parent, somebody you had to praise and thank all the time for nothing, for being allowed to exist when existence was wretched; somebody who interfered arbitrarily in your comings-in and goings-out — who got the Virgin Mary in trouble, for example — with the complacently bourgeois arrogant assumption of the Ruling Class. But she hadn't heard of revolution either, though if she was helpless, she was far from resigned.

'Ha ha! *You've* got a *green* neck!' One of the boys pointed at her, and they all ran up, laughing in anticipation, to get a look.

'And yours is *black,*' Stella retorted, sick at heart as a baited dog, and irrationally feeling betrayed, for she had fancied the boy who made the comment. He was nearly as clever as herself at school; he had a head like a teddy-bear and an easy-going nature — she had never knowingly done anything to antagonise him. She had even let him feel her up under the desks.

'Sez who?' he challenged, embarrassed by the sudden unwanted atmosphere of confrontation, the sudden pressure of malignant expectation from the crowd gathered round.

'Sez me!' Stella wanted to turn away; to back down and go home.

'Ah widnae let her get awa' wi' *that,* Mike!' one of his tough-guy friends urged, as he stood glaring at Stella with tortured uncertainty.

'I — I could fight ye for that!' he stammered, then brought his words out in a rush, as if somebody had thumped him between the shoulders.

Stella's heart sank to her shoes. As the rain soaked through her coat, making it heavy and clammy and cold as lead, she became conscious of her own too thin, too white body inside, trembling against the material, a feeble little flash of life, guttering like a candle now, and almost as easy to extinguish. She tried to save her face without seeming to back down: 'Och, dinnae be daft!' — she turned on her heel, away from him smiling as casually as she could.

'She's faird, she's faird!' the devil at Mike's shoulder chanted, gloating.

Stella had to turn back: 'Yer Granny's faird!' she defied them both indiscriminately.

'Come on then,' Mike rasped, as if some long-smouldering hatred had finally blazed up, 'fight if ye're no' faird!' and he handed his leather-covered Bible to the friend, who was bouncing up and down with excitement, and squared up, fists forward, like a Victorian boxer.

'Right!' Stella squared up too without hesitation, but as cold as death in the pit of her stomach; weak in the arms with the horror of seeing how she was in his eyes.

He punched out at her face, but she stepped back in time to avoid the blow, and in pulling back his arm he slashed his fist across the metal badge on her lapel — her Sunday badge, a unique one, enamelled, which bore the five Olympic rings and the legend 'Munich, 1939'. His knuckles were ripped open. There was a gasp of sympathy for him from the crowd. Stella was more concerned about her badge: she looked down to her lapel to see if it was damaged. As her head was bent inwards, Mike seized the opportunity, in his blind rage, to deliver an awkward, heavy, dirty punch on the back of her skull. She couldn't lift her head from it, but blacked out for a few seconds, still on her feet, digging her raw cold toes into her shoes to keep herself upright. When she started to looked up, cautiously, again, she could see nothing but a slately dappled greyness: the world was all rainy-day sky, with icy little bubbles of light floating downwards through it. The excited voices round about blended in a rush with the waterspout sound in her ears. She reached feebly out with her fist, but he had got out of its range, and was examining his knuckles, getting madder the longer he looked. She heard his voice through the rush of blood in her ears, 'Ah could *kill* ye for that, ye *damned heathen!*'

Her eyes filled suddenly with tears, but they didn't overflow — 'Thank God,' she thought. He came towards her again, the solid, well-fed stocky figure, still, despite the circumstances, as comforting somehow as a teddy bear to look at. She couldn't get angry, not even after the dirty punch — especially not after that, for it had demeaned him utterly in her eyes: he was ordinary, that was all, like the rest. She was still faint, and the blood that ran from his burst knuckles seemed to burn out at her. It looked like a tiny warm crimson scarf running down to his wrist. He punched her in the gut, but only hard enough to push her clammy coat closer to her body. As he drew back his fist to hit her again she automatically seized the chance and gave him a hard punch on the cheek. He lashed back and hit her on the shoulder; the bell rang to go into Sunday school, and, well-trained, he straightened up, shrugged, and turned to comply with it. The others followed him, exclaiming their outrage at his gashed knuckles, and muttering about Stella.

She walked over to the church wall and leaned against it; she had trouble breathing, the world was spinning with every shade of grey and dirty blue, and she wanted to cry her heart out, but she didn't. She had to pull herself together and go in. Inside, she hung up her coat and felt the better for being rid of it, but dreaded having to put it back on again when she was warmed up from sitting in the hall: it would be even clammier with the wet properly soaked through. Dismally she realised she hadn't change of her threepenny piece for the collection.

She slipped through the swinging doors into the warmth of the hall, looking up at the text along the back wall as automatically as a Catholic crosses himself: 'Suffer the little children . . .' 'Aye, the little children are certainly sufferin', God — ye neednae worry about that,' she thought so bitterly she nearly said it out loud. The first hymn was already starting up, with the pianist, a pie-faced old maid with red hair and thick glasses, joyfully thumping the preliminary notes loud enough to penetrate the general chaos of shuffling feet, hacking coughs, and the several indeterminate restless sounds children can make when they're being bored but good.

This is my story, this is my song,
Praising my Saviour, all the day long . . .

Stella didn't know what 'Saviour' meant, not with a capital 'S' at least; and she saw no point in praising *anybody* all the day long. What's more, she doubted if anybody else in the whole hall would either, despite the fervour with which they were singing. The hymn had nothing to do with her, but she didn't despise it for its mushiness — she couldn't yet rise to that — she envied the children for whom it was written. She envied them their simplicity, and their confidence that it was enough to sit about all day praising somebody they'd never seen, whose only achievement as far as she could make out was to have died — and reluctantly at that, for she hadn't forgotten last Easter's 'take this cup from my lips'. Died for nothing, too, if it was true that he'd died 'that we might be forgiven' — at least in Stella's experience, for *she* wasn't forgiven any of her sins: she got a thick ear for them, or the belt, without fail.

The best she could muster for Jesus was pity: he had been conned, like the bairn in the joke about the Jew, who put his son on the mantelpiece and urged him to jump, saying, 'Come on, who can you trust if you can't trust your own father? I'll catch you!' And the boy jumped, and the father stood by and let him fall, saying, 'That'll show you — never trust nobody, not even your own father.' Jesus jumped. Stella too, though she didn't remember where or when, or maybe she was jumping every day. Her feeling for Jesus was, 'you're one fool and I'm another,' and she didn't respect either him or herself for it: she would have sold her soul to the devil not to feel like that. So the children that could sit and praise him all day were the lucky ones, the ones who were never urged to jump, the ones in whom ignorance was bliss. She knew them from the pre-war picture books, which showed them in vivid colour, succulently fat, fat as pigs, sitting in meadows making daisy-chains, with hampers lying open and despoiled at their sides, and a loving mother in a bonnet pouring tea benignly. *They* were the forgiven ones, she surmised.

As she mouthed the words of the hymn, which was as much as she could bring herself to concede to the collective hypocrisy, signs that she wouldn't be forgiven this time either came to Stella. Sheila turned round and gave her a steady, baleful, 'I've heard about it and I'll see you later' glare. Temporarily safe in the body of the kirk, Stella gave way to pent-up spite and raised her eyebrows in cynical contempt. She and Sheila then glared at each other for a few moments like old European enemies, whose hostility was so ancient that it had become a form of intimacy. Stella was comforted.

When the hymn ended they all sat down and bowed their heads for the Lord's Prayer, which she also found offensive, suspecting that the language was deliberately made stiff and obtuse so that she'd commit herself without knowing exactly what it was she was committing herself to; another string of inhibitions and exhortations, which she already had more than enough of. The minister, having finished the prayer, began his short, simple, and to Stella smug, boring sermon, as usual telling them to be good and grateful to the adults who were kind enough to rear them, and to God in his thoughtful arrangement of this. It was unbearable: the moment the minister cleared his throat, Stella became a deaf adder, it irritated her so much to hear of so many privileged groups of people to whom she should return her humble thanks, when she felt herself to be barely surviving in a moral jungle and a material desert. She had cancelled the unwritten contract with the Sunday school two years ago, at the Christmas party when, thinking there had been some oversight in the distribution of the presents, she had gone anxiously up to Santa, told him her name, and asked for her present. 'I've nothing with *your* name on it — you can't be a regular attender,' he'd said, and that was that. All she got was an orange in her hand going out the door, and that turned out to be sour. Stella would rather be damned than be grateful for what she hadn't got, and knew she wasn't likely to get — but at the same time, she was in constant expectation of a miracle: between her Granny and Hans Andersen her faith had been sustained. Cinderella, Thumbelina, the Ugly Duckling and she had a lot in common, she felt, except, so far, for the happy ending.

She didn't expect the miracle to come from the church, though. She expected it rather in the starry mornings when her father sent her in search of the baker's cart for his rolls, and she was the only one in Skelf between the earth and the sky, and the frost on the pavements twinkled like diamonds. Andersen's and Grimm's

54

worlds were much more real to her than the world of the Bible: their people were frankly bad or greedy or sly; obstacles were real obstacles, like ice and snow and wind and wild beasts and giants; rewards were tangible. So she still had a sneaking faith in the cold Queen of the Ice Palace: a faith that ate her like an invisible disease, while her belief in God was humdrum and perforce.

The minister flowed on with his feudal unsubtleties, and Stella sat complacently deaf, thawing out and drying out, deciding what she would have first when she was granted three wishes, or her father won the pools, and feeling rather inclined to a pony and cart — for all the sunny people in the tales her Granny had told her had a pony and cart — and a lifetime's supply of bubblegum which had just begun to come over from America then and represented the ultimate in desirability: a toy you could eat, play with it while you ate it, and still have it: mentally she blew the biggest bubbles in history. All in all she was sorry when the sermon was over, for she knew she had a test of nerves to face next. There was about to be a scene which would shock her sister far more than any fist-fight.

'Now it's time to give your pennies to Jesus,' the minister made the ritual announcement, as usual with an earnest expression that suggested that Jesus was waiting just behind the door with his hand out, desperate. There seemed to be a hint in it somewhere, too, that forgiveness was purchaseable, if you just got there in time with the cash.

The pie-faced pianist hit the keys with evangelical fervour; the children got up, left-turned, and began to march in a cramped way in a winding snake's path round all the lines of benches, singing with cheerful relief after the sermon:

Dropping dropping dropping dropping
Hear the pennies fall
Everyone for Jesus
He shall have them all . . .

As they passed the minister's wife, who held out a deep red velvet pouch fastened to an open circle of oak, they dropped in their contributions. Those with sixpences or silver threepences dropped them flashily from enough above the bag for the minister and his wife to see; those with just pennies put their hand right into the bag and dropped them hard, hoping they'd sound like half-crowns. Some, it was rumoured, just put in an empty hand and stirred up the loose cash, but Stella had her doubts about that.

As she marched in the snake round the last bench her mind was a battlefield where impulse fought training, with reason on the side of impulse for once. In the last few steps to the bag her knees began to tremble, but then the sense of unfair intimidation that gave her spurred her on: she stopped quailing and began to burn. She burned all the more self-righteously when the girl in front of her, daughter of the illicit bookie, pretended to drop her money on the floor, because it was a whole shilling and she wanted the world to know that. The minister's wife herself stooped and picked the shilling up, and, with a warmly patronising smile, dropped it into the bag.

Stella's turn came. She had been gripping her threepenny so tightly that when she raised her hand to drop it in, it stuck to her palm. She flicked it off, and it fell into the bag with a thick metal jingle. There was a pause, for she didn't then move on as she should have done. The minister's wife shook the bag in a jolly way, as if to rouse her, and Stella said dourly: 'Wait a minute — I need change for my bus home.' Behind her, the last of the snake was impatiently, heavily, marching on the spot. The minister's wife shot her a look of incredulity, and shook the bag again, this time in an authoritative way that said, 'Here it is and here it stays.' Stella steadied the bag with her left hand and dipped into it with her right, searching among the solid copper for the twopence change. 'Really!' the minister's wife exclaimed, looking violated, as if Stella had been searching her intimate garments and not just the bag she held for the money. But Stella persisted, committed now but finding it difficult to grap just two pennies among the money that lay in rolls, without actually peering into the bag in a sacrilegious way.

'What on *earth* are you doing girl?' the minister's wife, red-faced finally hissed, as the pianist began to lose in enthusiasm what she gained in curiosity.

'I need *change*,' Stella repeated. 'It's lashing rain outside. For my *bus*.' She continued to rummage.

'Hurry up then!' The minister's wife held out the bag at arm's length, detaching herself from the whole proceedings. The averted face and snooty look galvanised Stella: she dug fiercely into the bag, grabbed a handful of money, thrust the clenched fist into her pocket, and marched on through to the Sunday school classroom, leaving the minister's wife with a ransacked expression.

'This is Palm Sunday,' the Sunday-school teacher announced, a thin nervous woman who might have been any age between nineteen and thirty-nine, she was so colourless and wrinkle-less. Stella felt that it would be wiser not to ask again what Palm Sunday was. She sat tight, her hand still in her pocket clutching the money. As the verses were monotonously recited, and each successful reciter — *everybody* was always successful here — was rewarded with a stick-on picture to add to their Palm Sunday collages, Stella became more and more conscious, with an incredulous secret pleasure, that she held far more than twopence in her fist. This gave her an intent, abstracted look, which the teacher, ignorant of what had happened at the collection, thoroughly approved. 'It's a real miracle at last!' Stella thought, concentrating all her senses on trying to discern the individuality of each coin in her hand, to count them. Gradually she became obsessed with the need to know if the hiatus in the roll of pennies represented a halfpenny or a shilling — the bookies's shilling — but she had to contain herself. She was afraid that if she took it out to look somebody would tell, and she'd have to give everything back but the twopence. She tried to content herself with simple, miserly gloating.

Finally she controlled herself enough to listen to the verses and learn them. When it came to her turn to recite she rattled them off, and stretched out her left hand for the sticky picture, afraid to let go of her pennies, in case they chinked and gave her away, or fell out of her shallow cardigan pocket. But when the collages were handed out for this last picture to be stuck on them artistically she had to let go, and cautiously, unobtrusively took her hand out of her pocket. The weight of the money stretched her cardigan, but it was safe.

'There will be a prize for the best picture,' the teacher reminded them, as the more artistic of the group studied their pictures intently, making the crucial decision about where to put the last sticky piece. The thought of her ill-gotten gains diverted Stella from the contest. She knew she hadn't a hope of winning, anyway, because her teacher didn't like her, and for weeks back had been giving her tiny stick-on aeroplanes — leftovers from some patriotic wartime project — instead of leaves. Other people had aeroplanes too, but none had been given such a disproportionate amount as Stella. The problem was that the basic picture on to which these decorations were to be tastefully stuck was one of Jesus riding into Jerusalem on a milk-white mule. Messerschmidts and Spitfires and Wellingtons, relatively speaking the size of bluebottles, did nothing to enhance it. For all these weeks, Stella had sensed the teacher's spite, and in revenge she had stuck her little bluebottle planes in the most incongrous places: she had glued one on to the donkey's backside; one between the eyes of a disciple; settled several in a suggestive swarm above Jesus's head, and today she casually put one so that it seemed to be coming out of his nose, like the flies on the African children in the missionary films they showed once a month.

She did wish though, that Palm Sunday and the judgement of the pictures weren't on that particular day. She hardly felt able to cope after the hammering and the collection. 'After this,' she thought, 'Ah'll never be able tae show ma dial again here!' Then the implications of that dawned on her: no more social Sunday torture; no more boredom. 'Thank God!' she added, unconscious of the irony.

'Time's up!' said the teacher briskly. 'Pass your pictures in and let me see who wins!'

'What's the prize, Miss?' one of the keen competitors enquired in anticipation.

'Aha!' said the teacher, archly self-conscious. 'I bought it myself. Wait and see. . . '

The collages were handed to her, Stella's at the bottom because she was at the end of the row. With great and unpretended seriousness the teacher went through them one by one, laying two aside, till she came to Stella's. Stella, her hand back in her pocket, looked at the ceiling in a parody of innocence, and waited for the holocaust.

But it didn't come. The teacher's eyes glazed, and she put Stella's picture underneath the pile of rejects with a grim, determined-not-to-crack smile. There was a disappointed shuffling of feet from the others, who had counted on Stella getting some kind of come-uppance for spoiling the couthy harmony of the occasion. The teacher picked up the two she had laid aside, and said thoughtfully, 'Well, I definitely think Sarah's and Tom's are best.' All the rest except Stella, who didn't dare to, groaned. '. . . But since it's Palm Sunday, I'm going to give you all a prize.' The groans turned to dove-like murmurs of appreciation from everybody but Tom and Sarah, whose turn it was to groan. The teacher reached her seat and brought out a small cardboard carton full of tiny two-ounce bags of sweets. 'You see,' she said with a kindly gleam, 'while you have been working on your verses and your pictures, I have been saving my coupons to give you all a treat.' Stella felt the kindness and was nonplussed. She sat numb, expecting nothing, fondling the money in her pocket while the teacher passed round the sweets; she was sure she wouldn't get any, but her only regret was that she had herself spoiled a good moment. She tried to think 'Tae hell wi' her an' her sweeties!' but couldn't manage it without feeling like a shit, or at least a bull in this super-refined Dolly-mixture china-shop. Then the teacher gave her a bag of sweeties too, and she nearly wept with bafflement and remorse. Never mind if she didn't get a kind look or a kind word to go with them; never mind if the teacher's motives were cowardly, Stella could have none of the comfort of the righteous.

The others were delicately, with exaggerated enjoyment, eating their sweets one at a time, offering their bags politely to the teacher; Stella was too ashamed even to open hers, but nobody commented on it. She stuffed it quickly into the other pocket of her cardigan and sat surly till all the joy was over, the last prayer was said, and they were free to go home. She was first out of the classroom and into the cloakroom. Transferring her money and sweets to her coat pockets she saw that she had indeed picked up the shilling, and it gave her a perverse, self-destructive satisfaction.

She ran as hard as she could up the road — the rain had stopped — to avoid her sister, whom she knew would be after her skin as soon as she heard of the disgrace at the collection-bag. But Sheila was older and faster, and flyer, and had caught up with her within ten minutes, taking a different route.

'What's this Ah hear aboot you fightin' in the kirk an' then holdin' up the march for the collection?' she exploded at the back of Stella's head as she overtook her. Stella's scalp tingled unpleasantly in anticipation of the clout she was sure to get, but Sheila was too shocked for that yet.

'Ah needed change for ma bus back,' she replied, trying to make it sound as reasonable as her logic told her it actually was.

'Ye're walkin',' her sister retorted, flatly dismissive.

'How was Ah tae ken it would stop rainin'? It was pissin' doon when the Sunday school went in!' She tried to turn it into an argument about the weather.

'Maks nae difference if it'd been a bluidy *hurricane,*' Sheila got straight to the point, 'wha ever heard o' onybody takin' change oot the kirk poke? God Almichty — see you? — ye're disgustin'!' Words failed her at last.

'Ah suppose Ah'm tae be soaked tae the skin just because it's no' polite tae ask for change? An' get the 'flu, an' *dee,* for the want o' tuppence?' Stella waxed passionate, feeling she had a case: 'Tuppence that'll go intae the *minister's* pooch, that disnae need it but for greed? Ah'm tae shiver ma wey hame in the sodden rain, an' him tae pass me cosy in's car wi' ma tuppence in's pooch? Fine ye ken the buggar widnae sae much as look who ye was, never mind offer ye a lift!'

'Ach, it doesnae go tae the minister, fine ye ken! It's for the missionaries an' the black bairns starvin' in Africa!'

'So they say!' Stella snorted. She didn't believe it, despite the missionary slideshows: the African children were utterly unreal to her in their starved capacity; her teacher at school had read them the 'Little Black Sambo' books for a treat on Fridays, and told them that the darkies were 'chocolate-coloured', so her image of them was of little animated Fry's Five Boys, running about in the sunshine amongst lush vegetation and tropical fruit. She even had a faint suspicion that if they *were* starving, it must have been the missionaries who thou-shalt-not-ed it away, for by an unconscious association of imperfectly absorbed knowledge, she had come to believe that Christianity itself was to blame for mankind's being bounced out of Paradise. Logic, too, convinced her that the minister couldn't genuinely believe in the starvation of the African bairns, or he himself, and his pink chubby family like marzipan pigs, wouldn't be walking about so obviously well-fed. She believed it to be just one more con in which the entire adult world conspired to keep people like her from living without guilt, or keep them paying, or whatever. One of her posh aunties was a Baptist and kept a box on her mantelpiece, with the same ostentation that better-off people put their phones on their window-ledges — 'for the little starving black babies' she had said with a satisfaction that made it sound as if they were to be fattened up for the kill and she was saving up to buy one. She had outraged Stella when, one day, she had given her a threepenny — the one and only time — and then blackmailed her into putting it into that box. Her father had said he 'didnae ken why oor Mimie's sae worried aboot black bairns, when there's plenty o' white ones hangin' aboot wi' their arses oot their breeks,' and that had clinched it. She knew he was right; she saw it herself every day.

'Onywey,' Sheila broke in to her self-assuring thoughts, 'that was an awfu' thing tae dae; Ah'm fair black-affronted tae show ma face there again!' She didn't argue about the black babies, which was a good sign that showed that underneath she too saw the logic of what Stella had done: it was just the public way she'd done it. But she threatened, 'Wait till you get hame! Ah'm tellin' Mum what you done!'

'Och no, Sheila, dinnae tell on me,' she pleaded, alarmed.

'That Ah will! An' tak' what you get!' Sheila said with vindictive relish. Stella realised then why she hadn't hit her: she intended to be pure as the driven snow so Bess would batter Stella twice as hard later. 'Ah'll gi'e ye threepence . . .' she persuaded.

'Ye havenae — ye've only twopence — ' Sheila sneered.

'Ah have — see!' and Stella brought three pennies out of her pocket, trying not to let the money that was left jingle.

'Ye greedy wee buggar! Ye've stole it frae the bag!' Sheila was amazed, and against her will, before she could control it, a note of respect found its way into her voice.

'Och Ah didnae steal it — Ah had tae hurry up so Ah just

61

grabbed what came tae ma haund,' Stella protested, passionate in her denial, doing her best not to feel guilty about what had after all started out as a piece of fair-dealing. 'Ah only wanted ma twopence change.'

'How much did ye get? Come on, bring it oot!' Sheila commanded, sweeping aside the irrelevant niceties of Stella's conscience. 'Come on!' she ordered again, as Stella pretended to be trying to scrape it all together, but was in fact searching with her cold fingers for the shilling, to keep it back.

Eventually she located it and brought out all the coppers, leaving the shilling behind.

'Christ! How much? Count it!' Sheila looked eagerly at the money.

Stella counted with one practised glance: 'Tenpence,' she announced, her own eyes getting big at the enormity of it, even before she added on the shilling.

'Cough up!' Sheila held out her hand.

'What, the lot?'

'Haund it owre!'

'Ye're kiddin'! No Ah'll no'!'

'Aye ye will, or Ah'll tell on ye, an' Ah'll tell *how much.*'

Stella handed it over as if reluctant, dropping some pence just to see Sheila humble herself to pick them up. In fact she was relieved, for her conscience couldn't have coped with it, and she envied the minister who could take so much more, so easily. She had a contradictory thought that maybe the Christians had appropriated Paradise for their own private benefit. The shilling was something else again, though — she felt she'd a right to that, even if it was a piece of silver — the wages of her sin.

Sheila moved off with a parting, 'Ah'm no' goin' up the road wi' *you,* ya *object* — I dinnae want folk tae ken you're *ma* sister!'

Stella shrugged. She would have preferred the company, for she didn't want to be left alone with her thoughts, but she was used to it, like she was used to feeling like a babyish sap every time Sheila brushed her off. She even despised herself for the constant sentimentality of her sisterly expectations in the teeth of everyday reality. Sheila despised her for it too. But she couldn't figure where the hell it came from, this eternal hope as naïve as if she still believed in Santa Claus — if she could, she'd have torn it up by the roots and lived in peace, for she felt it as an overwhelming weakness, a character deformity. The best she could do was to hide it.

She thought of the shilling she had in one pocket, and the sweeties in the other, and tried hard not to tempt fate by revelling in her lack of conscience about them. What would she do with the shilling? She felt vaguely that she ought to do something significant with it, more significant than just throwing it down in the street and absolving herself from all responsibility for it, like they did in the films: 'That's what I think of your dirty money, Rocco!' No, the reason she'd kept it was because she wanted to have a shot at responsibility.

Yet it was hard and cold and she believed she could actually feel its brightness in her pocket; no matter how tightly she held it, she couldn't feel it getting any warmer, and superstition began to creep up on her. For a few seconds she panicked, reminded of the story of the Ice Queen and the shard of ice that went into the boy's heart through his eye and made him cold and strange and finally go away to the Ice Queen's Palace at the end of the world. Still she thought that wasn't such a bad idea, to be cold, not to feel anything about anybody, and not to feel the cold itself; to be surrounded by a wonderful palace like glass. It was tempting: she pressed the shilling hard into the palm of her hand and began to concentrate, hoping it *would* enter her arm and make its way to her heart. So she walked on, automatically, oblivious of everything and gaining hope from the fact that the shilling still didn't seem to get any warmer.

'Too guid tae speak tae yer freends in yer Sunday coat, Stella?' An uncertain voice, half-humorous, half-aggressive, broke in on her thoughts.

'Eh?' She brought her brain back into co-ordination with her eyes, and saw who it was: 'Oh, it's you Bobby — no, no — Ah was just, ye ken, dreamin'.' From the remoteness of the Ice Queen's Palace she gazed at him, standing in front of her with his little sister, three or four years old, hanging on to his hand. Bobby was one of the poorest boys in her class at school, and one of the smallest, but he could hold his own in a fight. Stella had had an inarticulate secret tenderness for him, neither feminine nor maternal but human, ever since one day when he had lain back on the bench in class opposite hers, and his short trousers, stiff with dirt, had kept their shape like tubes, and she had unintentionally looked up his trouser-leg. His little cock, surprisingly white compared to the ruddy, nut-brownishness of his face and knees, had been lying there like a chubby, boneless, baby's finger, a secret softness, hidden and helpless over his balls, only the side of one of which Stella could see, and which was like some tender seed-pod deprived of its shell. It was the first cock she had ever seen, so she believed it was as individual to him and characteristic of him as his dark forlorn face or short legs. Because he didn't know she could see it, it made him vulnerable, in his lack of the guilty knowledge which would have made any other boy, as soon as he felt the cool air up his trouser-leg, sit up and look aggressive. It endeared him to her.

So now, still recovering from her daze of intense concentration, she greeted him warmly: 'Ma Sunday coat? Oh, ye mean Ah've been tae the kirk! No, Bob, Ah'm tellin' ye, that Sunday school is worse than the bluidy school itsel', even though ye dinnae get the belt. A'body goin' aboot like they couldnae say shite for a shillin' — that's the last they've seen o' me!'

'Ma mither wouldnae let me go . . . I wanted tae because I could join the choir for ma guid singin', but ma Mum says they wouldnae let ye in tae Sunday school withoot a coat, and *she* cannae buy me one.'

'Ye're better aff oot o't! Ye ken, they were criticisin' *ma* coat? *This* coat?' Stella exclaimed, standing back a step to let him see the coat and get the full force of the shock.

'What for? It's a *braw* coat!' Bobby was as puzzled as he was astounded.

'No' guid *enough*!' said Stella. They stood for two or three minutes more, gossiping about it with a repertoire of expressions and gestures of being scandalised that would have done credit to a pair of ancient spinsters, until the little sister tugged Bobby's hand like it was a bell-pull, and moaned:

'Bobby — me *tauld*, Bobby!'

'Aye, in a minute Sadie,' he responded in a kind voice. As the oldest of the family of five who had happened one after the other, he had already acquired maternal patience.

Stella noticed the mite for the first time. She had on a cotton dress, with a thick woollen scarf crossed over at her chest and fastened behind with a nappy-pin, the tails of it trailing over her little backside to brush her calves. She had no socks, and summer sandals that were too big for her. Her nose streamed and she was bluish, but with an overlay of the same gypsy nutbrown colouring as her brother, that set off her black longish hair and big dark eyes. The bare feet in the kipper-box sandals melted Stella, and gave her a sore heart. 'Is this your wee sister?' She squatted down to look at Sadie face to face, smiling.

'Aye, one o' them,' Bobby answered, half-rueful, half-proud.

'My God hen, your nose is tripping you!' Stella exclaimed, as Sadie tried a bleary smile back, like the sun on a damp morning.

'It's the cauld,' Bobby explained expertly, as if he were a zoo-keeper displaying a strange animal.

Stella, with a gesture which to the uninitiated would have looked rough, reached down, and taking Sadie's nose between her thumb and forefinger, tweaked it gently, pulling off the streams of snot at source. Sadie smiled in appreciation as Stella swung the shiny ribbons off her fingers into the road, then wiped her hand on a nearby lamp-post. 'Ye should show her how tae wipe her nose on her sleeve,' she admonished Bobby.

'Right enough,' he agreed, and they both looked towards Sadie with the frankly speculative interest of two specialists agreeing on a course of treatment.

His ready agreement emboldened Stella: 'The wee sowel's frozen: she shouldnae be oot,' she commented.

'Ah've ay tae tak' her oot on a Sunday tae let ma Mum and Dad get a long lie.'

'Oh aye . . . here hen, would ye like some sweeties?' Stella asked. She had been casting about in her mind to do something for Sadie, and now she dug out the Sunday-school bag, and offered it. Sadie's clarty little hand shot out and stopped politely just short of it.

'Just tak' one noo, Sadie,' her brother warned.

'No no hen — tak the hale bag — Ah dinnae want it!' Stella protested, wishing it had been her own bag bought with her own money, because there was a feeling of charity about it coming from the Sunday-school teacher. Sadie hesitated, looking at the bag as if it were too good to be true, almost hypnotised by the sight of it, and Stella put it into her hands, bringing them both together round it in confirmation, and feeling how much colder they were than her own.

'What kind are they?' Bobby asked, tentatively, trying to fathom this miracle.

'Dolly mixtures,' Stella replied, discouraging, any further questions in her embarrassment.

He responded to her tone, and merely said, 'Ye shouldnae gi'e her them a' — she'll just mak' a pig o' hersel',' in a wistful voice.

'No' a helluva big pig on twa ounces o' dolly mixtures!' Stella laughed, but added for his sake, ' — mind gi'e some tae yer big brother noo, Sadie.' Sadie nodded obediently, her mouth solemnly full already, and offered the poke to Bobby, who was too self-conscious to take more than one. She handed it to Stella, but Stella refused, 'No . . . I dinnae like dolly mixtures . . .'

Bobby joked to cover up his childish wish for the sweeties, 'Aye, look at her — her mooth's fu'! Watch ye dinnae choke yersel' oor Sadie! Ye're an awfu' lassie for sweeties, eh?' The wee one grinned at him mischievously, nodding, looking wickedly spoiled.

Stella had put her hands into her pockets, and could feel the shilling again, but it was burning now. She wanted to spend it on them all, but she was puzzled how to make the offer without sounding crazy, like the legendary local madman who'd gone about putting pound notes in folks' letter-boxes at night. She couldn't work it out; she gave in and said, pulling the money out of her pocket: 'Look, somebody gave me a shillin'!'

'*God Almichty!*' Bobby exclaimed, utterly overawed. Stella began to look like Santa Claus to him.

'But . . . but . . .' — inspiration came to her at last: 'if ma Mum kens Ah've got it, she'll want it aff me for the gas, so I'm gonna spend it now.'

Bobby nodded; it was only fair, and anyway he was scared to speak for he saw there was something good coming, and didn't want to break the spell.

'Ah ken!' — inspiration followed inspiration now — 'are ye still cauld Sadie?' Stella bent over the dark little head, close enough to see the lice moving about. Sadie was absorbed in trying to pick her favourites out from the bag of sweeties; a gruff, catarrhal 'Aye' issued from the direction of the bag.

'Would ye like hot juice?' Stella was keyed-up with excitement.

'Scream,' came the gruff little voice.

'Scream'?' Stella repeated, looking at Bobby, who was faintly disgusted with Sadie's rudeness, and reluctant to explain for her. Then Stella got it: '*Ice cream?* Ye're wantin' ice cream on a cauld day like this ye wee besom? Ah'll ice cream ye!' She gave a laugh of maternal indulgence, and turned back to Bobby, 'Would you like hot juice?'

'Hot juice!' he repeated, as if he couldn't believe his ears, then gave a cautious 'Aye. . .'

'We can go tae the caff an' sit doon like real folk, an' have a cup o' hot juice an' a biscuit on a shillin',' Stella announced triumphantly. 'Ah've a twa-ounce coupon: I found it on the grocer's floor.'

'But it's your shillin',' Bobby objected.

'But Ah'm sayin' Ah'll share it,' Stella commanded. She dismissed his absurd finesse and leaned over to Sadie: 'Are ye comin' tae the caff for a biscuit hen? In oot the cauld?'

Sadie didn't know what a café was, but she knew what a biscuit was, 'Aye, bittit!' she exclaimed, and immediately transferred her sweetie bag to her left hand, offering Stella her right.

'Come on, min — the bairn's comin' if you're no'!' Stella laughed at Bobby, setting off along the road to the café without a backwards glance, knowing fine he'd follow.

She marched into the café with Sadie toddling alongside, and went up to the counter. There were no other customers, which was a bad omen, for it meant that the man, notoriously ill-natured, could be as rude to her as he liked. She buried that hesitation as it rose, however, and straightaway demanded: 'How much is it for a cup o' hot juice?'

The man had other things on his mind. He didn't even look up from the football results in his paper, but grunted automatically, 'Sixpence.'

'We'll tak' a cup o' juice an' three tuppenny biscuits — Ah've a coupon,' Stella ordered confidently, knowing that was the only way to be served. 'Sit down, Bob,' she threw over her shoulder, as Bobby, deliberately slow to come in case anything went wrong, came in the door.

Without looking at them at all, the man poured some orange syrup into the glass, filled it with boiling water from the machine, laid it on the counter, and stretching out a hand that knew its way, lifted three chocolate biscuits from the box and placed them alongside it: 'A shillin'.' He sounded bored with the whole business. Stella plonked down her shilling, hung on to her coupon since he hadn't asked for it, and watched him drop her shilling into a cup in his cashbox which held a lot of other shillings, all the same. It made her feel free, that, not being able to tell the bad shilling from the rest. She carried the glass over to the table where Bobby sat still scared and trying to be invisible. Sadie followed like a puppy at her heels, and climbed expertly up into a chair, clutching her bag of dolly mixtures to her chest.

'We'll share this when it cools doon,' Stella said as she laid the hot orange on the table, not feeling the heat of it much, her hand was so cold with holding Sadie's frozen little mitt.

'Are ye sure it's OK tae sit here?' Bobby whispered.

Stella, in all the freedom of a cleared conscience, shouted over to the owner, 'It's a' right tae sit here, eh?'

'Sit whaur ye like,' he mumbled, still absorbed in checking his football pools, and not looking up.

'See?' Stella said, and Bobby relaxed.

'Just think,' he marvelled, 'Ah'll bet that's what thae millionaires dae, sit in a café wi' hot juice every day o' their life! Lucky beezers, eh?'

'Aye, an' cauld juice in the summer,' Stella added, impressed herself at the thought. She doled out the biscuits: 'One to you Bobby, one to wee Sadie,' (Sadie was already reaching for the salt and pepperpots, but Bobby frustrated her by lifting them over to the next table, with a threatening look), 'and one tae me!' In passing out the biscuits she noticed that the impress of the shilling was still clear on the palm of her hand. Her heart missed a beat but she made the best of it with 'Look Bob — I've still got ma shillin'!

Pity Ah couldnae spend it again, eh?' She showed him her palm
and they laughed.

Stella discovered she was ravenously hungry, and she wolfed her
biscuit. Bobby, desperately polite, took three bites to finish his.
They looked at Sadie like a pair of vultures. The steam-heat of the
café had made the child's nose run again, and in the act of putting
her biscuit in her mouth she was also shovelling in snot. It was
unremarkable to Bobby, but Stella noticed it and was touched to
the point of letting herself see that the little red cheeks too, hacked
and rough with cold. 'Gi'e me your poke, hen,' she demanded,
holding her hand out to Sadie. Sadie looked as if she had known
this was too good to last, but well-trained and looking down to hide
her disappointment, passed over the sweetie-bag. Bobby sniffed
and sat back, gazing out the window in embarrassment, but said
nothing. Stella saw all this but didn't bother to explain — action
would be its own explanation.

She tore a strip of the crumpled paper off the bag at the top, and,
leaning forward — with Sadie leaning back as far as she could in
her chair for fear of a slap — used it to wipe the bairn's nose. Then
she handed the bag back to Sadie — who was gaping at her in sheer
amazement — and, dropping the paper on the floor, said 'Noo hen,
ye have tae understand, it's *manners* tae wipe yer snitch!'

Bobby was delighted and couldn't hide his relief, which he
showed by asking without embarrassment, 'Is the juice ready noo,
d'ye think?'

Stella tried it, nodded, and passed it along to him. He drank and
leaned over with it to Sadie, keeping hold of the glass. She drank,
and her cheeks went scarlet, and the snot ran down her top lip
again. 'Och, dae *this*, Sadie!' Bobby exclaimed fastidiously, going
through the motions of wiping his nose on his sleeve. Sadie complied, but only succeeded in smearing a glaze over her forehead.
This was enough to satisfy Bobby and Stella though, and Stella
said, 'She's quite clever, eh?' drinking again, and passing the glass.

They spun out the sitting and sipping for a good half hour, as
complacent as any middle-class family in a school reader. Occasionally Stella would withdraw into herself to gloat at having spent
her shilling in the best and wickedest way possible, sneaking
behind God's back to give the folk he clearly didn't like a treat,

while presumably he was seeing that his pious little Sunday scholars, and the minister and his family, got safe home. Yet she furtively felt the palm of her hand now and again for the mark of the shilling, uneasily suspecting that she might have branded herself for life, like the mark of Cain. Eventually she forgot it altogether.

Nothing was said when she got home, and she had peace for the rest of the day, for Sheila was out at a pal's house. Sunday night was bath-night, a ritual Stella loved. She didn't like the actual getting clean part of it — the fine tooth-comb searching for nits and snagging in her curls; kneeling down in the bath while her mother's hard fingers scraped her scalp rubbing the soft soap in, sitting in the bath then opposite Sheila, with the taps burning one shoulder and chilling the other, and Sheila tickling her between the legs with her toes to make her get out first — but she did like standing bare naked in front of the blazing fire with a fresh towel round her, and putting on a clean vest, even though they were all handed-down and she could get her whole body through one armhole. Most of all she liked the smallness and the heat and the warm light of the living-room, with them all there; it was cosy and intimate and sheltered, as if there was no world outside that could touch them.

She sat in front of the fire in her pyjamas, soaking up the heat, ignoring her father's warning that it would weaken her spine. Her mother brought two oranges and peeled them and leafed them and divvied them up for a treat. As Stella sat enjoying hers slowly, nibbling it like a mouse, Bess bent over her on a sudden maternal whim and, patting her back caressingly, said, 'Aye, you're ma bonny curly-heidit bairn!'

The undeserved tenderness of this riled Sheila, who had to her eternal chagrin poker-straight hair that nothing could curl, and she piped up from across on the settee, 'It wouldnae be her *back* ye'd be pattin' if ye knew what she done the day at the kirk! — it would be her *lugs* — and ye wouldnae be pattin' them, neither!' Stella's stomach turned over, and all that was left of the taste of the orange was the acid rising up her throat.

'What has she done?' Bess's voice was sharp; she was proud of

70

sending them to Sunday school; it was as good as going to church herself, without the effort.

'Only fightin' wi' a laddie ootside, an' haudin' up the hale kirk tae get tuppence change for her bus oot a threepenny!' Sheila exclaimed, heavily sarcastic. Stella noted with some relief that she hadn't told all about the money, but it was a relief mixed nonetheless with disgust, and that old familiar feeling of living in a world where people were like broken mirrors, sending you back always distorted, confusing, crooked images of everything. She merely protested:

'I needed my bus-money because it was rainin', and I was fightin' the laddie because he said I'd a green neck wi' ma Sunday coat.'

'Haudin' up the kirk!' Bess was flabbergasted.

Stella looked across to her father to appeal. He was hiding behind his newspaper, the pages of which were trembling with his silent laughter.

'Aye — at the marchin' marchin' marchin' hear the pennies fall bit,' Sheila got graphic through spite, 'this one here had a'body marchin' on the spot till she howked her change oot the poke!'

Her father's paper rustled like an autumn tree with the wind through it. This antagonised her mother even more: 'Weel may you laugh, ye godless heathen sittin' owre there, Wull Ross! *You* dinnae care aboot your family's guid name!' The rustling stopped. She turned on Stella: 'And you! How could ye ha'e the black effrontery!'

'It was lashin' rain, Mum,' Stella argued.

'In the Lord's Hoose!' Bess went on regardless.

'It's only the kirk hall, no' the kirk,' Sheila interposed, afraid now that her mother would go too far and push Stella to spill all the beans and implicate her.

'A bairn o' mine!'

'It was bucketin' doon, the rain, Mum. . . '

'Have ye *nae* respect?'

'Respect what for?' Stella was getting mad. After all, as far as she knew, Bess herself hadn't been in a church since the last christening, and she honestly couldn't see what was wrong anyway: Jesus took money: she took her change.

'Respect for what? Respect for what! For the *Sabbath* is what!'
Stella didn't answer; she thought she'd better shut up and let the
rest wash over her.

'Are ye an *atheist* or somethin'?' Bess pursued, taking the
opportunity for moral superiority to soothe her own conscience
about never attending church, ' — that ye could dae that tae yer ain
mother in the Lord's hoose?'

'What's an atheist?' Stella asked at once, terrified, for her
mother made it sound like something congenitally psychopathic
and beyond the pale.

'God watches everything ye dae in His hoose,' Bess announced,
dissociating herself from Stella with a vindictive smugness that
had a touch of the bitch.

'Like ma Auntie Nell?' Stella had asked, before she realised how
it was going to sound.

'So ye're criticisin' your relations tae noo!' Bess fumed. 'Wha's
bairn are you? — for ye're nane o' mine!'

This was a remark Stella had heard ever since she went to live
with her Granny; she shrugged if off and tried to changed the
subject without having to climb down: 'What's an atheist?'

'Somebody that doesnae believe in God,' Senga
chimed in from over on the settee, sympathetic to Stella and trying
to help.

'That doesnae believe in *God?*' Stella was stunned. 'What dae ye
mean?'

'Somebody that thinks there's nae sic thing as God,' Sheila
supported, to keep the conversation on a track that was safer for
her.

'Nae such thing as God,' Stella let out a deep breath and subsided,
lost in wonder.

Her mother misinterpreted this as a sign that Stella had been
properly subdued, and relented, saying in a tone that was more
indulgent than her actual words: 'Aye, awa' tae yer bed an' think
that owre! An' think *black burnin' shame* o' yersel' for what you
done this bonny day ma lassie!'

Stella complied quickly, not wanting to provoke more of Bess's
irrelevant wrath, and wanting to be alone with this treasure of an
idea — *no God.* She was so absorbed in it that she forgot to jump on

to her bed as she and Sheila usually did, for fear of werewolves underneath it. She just climbed on like a zombie and lay down, staring big-eyed at the ceiling as if there was a chance she might see through it if God was there. She thought and thought, wordlessly, intensely, then broke out: 'By God, *that* explains a lot!' Then all the things that it didn't explain, the things that made it even more complicated, sprung to her mind against her will. 'Who made me then and why?' — it was beyond her to think that nobody had made her, and for no reason. 'Then whaur's ma Granny?' — that was an alarming thought, that her Granny wasn't up with the angels watching her. But then, she could see her Granny in a better place, in a cosy eternity by the hearth, with the best detective story of all time — better than floating around Heaven singin' in a nightgown praising her Saviour who hadn't saved her but let her die just when Stella was needing her. She canonised her Granny in Fairyland there and then, and turned back, freer, to her rejection of God. 'Ach . . . it would be too guid to be true . . . ' she shook her head in resignation. But then the possibility of its being true, if some adults believe it, that there was no God, made her feel that for the first time a weapon had been put into her hands, and she instantly took up her dialogue with the Great Silence again, taunting: 'So — ye dinnae exist, eh? — or if ye do, *Ah* dinnae have tae believe it: I can ignore ye, just *ignore* ye!' she thought triumphantly, for to her the power of ignoring people was the most dramatic weapon in the adult battery. 'For if *you* can pretend there's nae Stella, then *I can pretend there's nae God!*' — it was a fierce challenge. 'Tae *hell* wi' ye, God!'

She raised her hand in a cut-off gesture, then, a new thought occurring to her, she turned up the palm and looked at it — thank God, the mark of the shilling was gone . . . she snuggled down, and giving a last, puzzled, but sarcastic snarl, 'Palm Sunday . . . Palm bluidy Sunday . . . ' went to sleep almost instantly, lulled by the sound of what she believed was the hum of angels singing in her ears, but was in fact the seashell sound of her own blood.

73

CHAPTER 4

Mighty like a Rose . . .

When she was ten years old Stella passed for twelve and got a paper-round. Paper-boys and girls had a mafia of their own, and if you'd no connections it was hard to break in. The girl whose round she took over was a social outcast with a cleft palate: blonde and underfed, so thin you could X-ray her with a candle, with that look of rapacious sentimentality peculiar to fair women with angled faces, she was disliked for her emotional stickiness in a world of avid realists keen to come to grips with the seamy side of life as soon as they could. What May needed was doting parents to lift her into a sheltered existence, what she had was a boozy pair of fly-by-nights and a tribe of sisters and brothers, all sharper than they were bright: 'hoors and comic singers' as Stella's oldest sister Senga dismissively put it.

Stella, hearing that a moonlight flit out of the district was in the offing very soon for May's family because the ticky-men were threatening to call in the sheriff about bad debts, fell into step with her as she walked home from school one day, and began to try to get on her good side by sounding her out about her teacher. She went through the usual litany of disgust, from the teacher's belting-average to her twin-set and double-chins, but got no response — May just strolled along singing in a honking voice that would have been sweet if she hadn't tried so hard with the words. It really got on Stella's nerves; she dried up and began kicking stones, trying to hit them with her spit as they rolled, like a cowboy hitting a flying dollar.

Eventually she became so absorbed in this that she didn't realise

74

May had stopped honking and was trying to speak to her. 'Eh?' she jerked up as the nasal voice got frantic and close to her ear.

'Ah said, div ye no' think Howard Keele's a hunk?'

'Eh?' For a second they gazed at each other from the depths of different movies, till Stella adjusted and politely agreed.

'Ah mean . . .' May went on, 'he's a *real* man, eh?'

'Oh aye,' Stella agreed again, not giving a damn.

'When Ah grow up Ah'm gonna be a filum star and marry Howard Keele,' May said. 'Ah'm gonna be a *tap-dancer*, Ah've had lessons. Wan' tae see me?'

'Aye.'

May ran and opened the gate of posh house with a flagstoned driveway, and, honking 'Happy feet, I've got those happy feet!' did a pretty athletic Ginger Rogers, tapping and gliding with Stella looking on in sheer disbelief until the housewife rapped on the window and signalled angrily to May to get out. She left matter-of-factly, unhurried because she'd expected it.

'By God you're guid!' Stella commented sincerely. She wasn't impressed by the dancing, but she was deeply impressed by the casual hard neck, and made the one do service for the other. 'You should go in for competitions!'

'Oh, Ah do,' May threw back airily, then added with a frown, 'but I wish I'd tap-shoes. My teacher says they'd mak' a' the difference.'

'Can ye no' buy them wi' yer paper-money?' Stella saw her chance.

'It only pays for ma lessons. I'd have won the competition in the park last summer if I'd had shoes — but I'd tae dance in my bare summer feet, and they got full of splinters frae the stage and I'd tae stop. It was awfu' — everybody laughed when I sat down tae pull them out — I could've *murdered* them! How would they like their feet fu' o' skelves? But ye've tae suffer tae be a star, ma teacher says an' he kens because he was in the *Alhambra* in *Glesca!*' She looked at Stella to see the effect of this.

'Jings!' Stella exclaimed obediently, as much at a loss as if she'd wakened up to find her own whole life to date was only a dream.

'You've tae pay them *cash* you see, or my Mum says she'd get me them.'

'I want a bike,' Stella countered, and sympathy was established between them.

Stella felt like a working man when she got up at half-past five for the first day of her paper-round; master of the silent house, walking through the deserted streets with a sense of purpose, she had a strange sense of peace that she'd never had since her Granny died but different from her Granny's peace, for it was independent and came from some harmony with nothing human but the wind, the stars and the familiar streets — herself and everything in the world she walked on belonging together. Time passing was a mirage. She didn't need God or her Granny, loneliness was just an illusion. She saw the world and herself in it and she rejoiced to be alive in reference to nobody else.

The peace persisted long enough to carry her through the first shock of the paper-shop, which was worse than breakfast at home, with a dozen kids crabbing and grabbing all at once in a room no bigger than a cupboard, while the old newsagent snarled and bullied. She was glad when they came out, and looked forward to more peace, but May started singing almost immediately, a romantic song about a sailor. Stella reckoned the only peace was in a world without people altogether which sent her back to square one in figuring out how the hell to survive. She was curious all the same about what went on in May's head — curious but scared to know it too well: it was so different it made her feel like the contents of her own mind were open to the four wild winds just to begin to think about it.

Her silence was no protection from this, for May sang about the sailor and rattled on about her dancing non-stop, proving the reality of this unreal world of hers, a world in which the chief values were good looks and plenty of fancy clothes. Stella listened, with a growing sense, wordless in her own mind, of being in the presence of monumental triviality. With unconscious motives she groped about in May's conversation for something that would unlock a meaning, but she had the disoriented sensation of a blind man groping in an empty room.

She offered to carry the bag, and nearly kneeled over with the weight of it when May hoisted it on to her shoulder. Then she took another look at May, wondering where she found the strength in that thin body. 'It's helluva heavy!' she grunted.

'Oh that's nothin'! Wait till Thursday when the *Woman* and the *Woman's Own* and the locals all come out at once!' May laughed '— it's *twice* as heavy then!' Stella tried to look debonair about it, but she began to have a sick feeling that she wouldn't be able to manage, and would make a fool of herself. She decided not to think of that.

'. . . an' when Ah'm in Hollywood me an' Howard will ha'e a swimmin' pool an' a party *every night in life* wi' sausage-rolls and jelly . . . and Ah'll get a fur coat an' lipstick and jools . . .' May went on like she'd been wound up, all the way to the first house on the edge of the beach that was to get a paper, and Stella felt trapped by the thoughts she wanted to avoid coming at her from every direction.

They went up the drive. 'Posh houses, eh?' Stella commented with the aggressive resentment she'd been brought up to feel.

'*Ma* hoose in Hollywood'll be better than *that*!' May said, pulling out the paper and thrusting it contemptuously into the letter-box. 'Aw Christ,' Stella thought.

So it went on as they did all the houses along the prom and behind the golf-links, till they came to a great big house with a lawn and a long drive.

'*You* dae this one, Stella,' May said, for the first time speaking in an ordinary voice.

'What for?' Stella was instantly suspicious.

'There's a dug,' came a flat response.

'Ah *hate* dugs — naw me!' Stella refused to take the paper May was handing her.

'Ah'll just have tae tell Mr Williamson you're no' able tae deliver the papers then. . . '

'Oh a' right . . . ' Stella groaned, and took the paper.

'Run across the lawn — it's quicker.'

No sooner had Stella started to sprint across the lawn than a yapping spaniel ran diagonally across it towards her, snapping at her heels. '*Get aff* me!' she howled, holding the paper aloft like the

Olympic torch and dancing away from its muzzle. *'Rich bloody dug
. . .'* she added from between clenched teeth as she ran to the
house-door.

Once she put the paper through the door the dog subsided and
went back to its kennel. All the way back across the lawn Stella
kept a wary eye on it, muttering to herself about kicking its teeth
back into its throat. May was laughing wickedly from behind the
gate. Stella wasn't annoyed at her though; she was too shaken with
fear and anger at the people who owned the dog. 'Rich buggars,'
she snarled, shouldering the bag again, 'What *skunks* letten' oot
their fancy dug on the paper-lassie!' A cold breeze blowing told her
she'd wet her pants and she lost her temper. She opened the gate
and made as if to cross the lawn again, to rouse the dog. When it
leaped forward she shook her fist at it and bellowed, 'Jist you wait!'
and hastily withdrew.

May was tap-dancing in the road humming 'Lovely to look at,
beautiful to see,' but interrupted herself long enough to say,
'Watch what you're saying — that's the manse.'

'I might o' knew it,' Stella said bitterly.

Thursday was as hellish as May predicted. Stella's neck was blis-
tered with the bag-strap after half an hour, and she commented to
May, 'Crivvens, it's no' bairns they need for this job — it's
Shetland ponies!' but May just looked at her briefly to indicate
that the here and now realities didn't exist and shouldn't be mentioned: she was concentrating on fey charm, knocking at the doors
of all the houses and telling an unresponsive public hopefully that
tomorrow was her last day on the round because she was going to
England. Stella tried to get her to knock on the manse door but she
wouldn't. 'Christians is mean onyway,' she said, from long
experience.

One door she knocked on an old man in a dressing-gown
answered. May went through her sales talk and the next thing
Stella saw her disappearing into the house. It was getting
uncomfortably close to school-time, so Stella continued up the
street herself with the paper-bag. May was still nowhere to be seen
when she came back, so she went to the door and knocked. The old
man opened it. 'Where's my pal?' Stella demanded.

'Oh, she's just coming, just coming . . .' he said hastily, turning back into the house. But it was a full three minutes before May appeared, putting her coat on and all flustered gratitude to the man.

'What was ye daein' in there?' Stella asked as the door closed behind them.

'Dancin',' May said without hesitation. Then when they got to the road out of the sight she opened her hand to reveal a ten-shilling note. 'Look what he gave me!'

'A' that just for dancing'!' Stella's eyes bulged in her head.

'Ah'm a guid dancer!' May flung back, stung.

'But Ah mean — only *dancin'!'* Stella insisted.

That evening Stella began to try tap-dancing with her hard shoes on the kitchen linoleum, till her Dad told her to give it up for she sounded like a horse with a bellyache.

'But Dad,' she protested, 'Ah've got tae practise — there's money in dancin'!'

'Aye,' her Dad laughed, and threw her a penny, 'here ye are — awa' an' dance outside for Godsake!'

She sat on the wall outside the house waiting for the chip van to pass so she could buy a sweetie with her penny, and thought of changing her ambition from being a teacher to being a film star, facing it squarely that maybe to be a teacher wasn't the best thing — 'Ah wouldnae mind bein' a *cowboy* . . .' she conceded. She couldn't bear to be a dancer smiling all the time and she'd no notion of being married to Howard Keele, he was much too big.

So she thought she'd practise acting, and did so all weekend, playing to her dad's hens — pretending they were dead settlers in a burnt-out ranch and looking sad at them, saying grimly, 'I'll get them Cherokee if it's the last thing I do Randolph — for you and Mary,' then shouting, 'Dig dirt Tony!' like Lash Larue to his horse and galloping off through the rhubarb. Carried away, she put her two little sisters into the hen-house to pretend they were a wagon-train attacked by Indians — their howls gave it all the desperate edge of authenticity — and defended them with a stick-rifle, till Bess came out and kicked her backside from here to yonder, swearing she'd be all day scrubbing to get the henshit off the bairns' dungarees. Stella galloped off, remarking to herself how sore a day in the saddle could make a man.

On the Monday she had her defences ready for the fancy spaniel. Alone at least, this was the only irritant in the peace to dream in the dark spring mornings and she was determined to get the better of it. Before she decided to be a cowboy, she might have knocked at the minister's door and complained, but now she had to live by the law of the range — shoot first and ask questions later.

Accordingly, she had taken a thick stick with her that day, and when she came to the manse left her bag of papers at the gate, marching in with the paper in one hand and the stick in the other. When the spaniel made its ill-tempered lunge she had a quick look around in case anyone was watching, then stood her ground. As it jumped barking and snapping up at her she smacked it across the muzzle with the rough stick. It howled and turned tail. 'Ah'll show you who's boss on *this* ranch,' she said to its retreating figure, 'you yella-bellied son-of-a-bitch!'

Even when she bought her bike, she kept on the paper-round. In the early summer she became addicted to the sight of the sun rising dark as an orange out of the sea with the mysterious indifference of a silent planet, and would sit in one of the beach shelters for minutes at a time with her feet up, gazing at it and soaking up a sense of eternity.

The flowers in the posh gardens were coming out too. The old man who had given May ten shillings for dancing had a garden full of roses. Stella studied them closely every day when the mornings were light, fascinated by their complexity and by the fact of their growing without anybody's having to do anything. She drew roses all over the covers of her jotters at school, abstractedly, and got the belt for it.

When the summer holidays came and she could take time over her paper-round, the roses were in full bloom. She envied the old man that he could sit and look at them all day, and touch them and tend them, and she stopped wanting to be a cowboy and wanted to be an old man in a rose-garden, watching the sun rise and set. One morning when she was very late he was in his garden cutting roses for the house as she came up the path with his paper. She walked past him and laid the paper down inside his open door, intending to be all anonymous and official, but he said good morning to her, and she turned and blurted from a full heart: 'Man, your roses is fair braw! The brawest I ever seen in ma *life!*' There was a little gleam of consciousness in her that she was being soft and irrelevant to life which was about doing and getting on, and the ghosts of her family if they heard her talking with no motive to the nobbery rose faintly there to mock her, but something that was truly herself and outside time swept this aside: the roses were much more and forever important.

'Aye, they're fine roses,' the old man responded, with a kindly smile.

Stella made no show, and no bones, about looking at them then as she went back down the path. As she was walking up the path of the house next door the old man looked over the hedge, with 'Would you like some to take home?'

'Yes please,' Stella said beaming. She delivered the paper and returned to his garden. He had gone indoors, to emerge with half a dozen different coloured roses wrapped round the stems with a paper bag. He handed them to Stella and she thanked him.

Walking home with the roses she was reassured that they jagged her fingers; it meant that they had an independent life of their own — alive and pricking. She just hoped the old man wouldn't expect her to dance.

She kept the roses in her bedroom but they shed all their petals in a few days and she felt guilty, suspecting herself that she had gazed them to death. Afraid that the old man would ask her about them, she did her round very early for the next week. After that she felt it was all right, and began to hope he might give her more, so left it as late as she could to arrive at his house.

Eventually she found him in the garden again, and greeted him with 'They was braw roses ye gave me mister . . .' He just nodded casually to her and said nothing, but she thought she felt him watching her down the path.

Next day he was in his garden again, and spoke first: 'So you like roses, do you?'

'Oh aye,' Stella nodded, facing him hopefully.

'Would you like more?'

'Yes please.'

'Come back when you've finished your round then, and I'll see what I can do for you.' He smiled, and with his sleek white hair and moustache Stella thought he looked like God.

She would have run through all the rest of her route if it hadn't been Thursday and she was burdened with the *Woman* and the *Woman's Own.* She sped things up as best she could by dropping her bag at every gate and running to the door with the papers, until it struck her she'd have to actually talk to the man when she went back. That stopped her dead in her tracks; her heart fluttered with nerves, and she took her time with the rest of the papers, making up polite replies to what she expected he would say. By the time her bag was empty she felt as prepared as she ever could be.

The man wasn't in the garden when she got back to his house, so she rang his doorbell. He came to the door within seconds, and held it open for her to go in. The interior of the house seemed as black as pitch after the sunshine outside, and she stumbled into and iron umbrella-stand. He put his hand on the small of her back to steady her and she jumped forward again so suddenly with a cold contact on her thin dress she felt she'd left her skin behind. But he put his hand on her again to steady her, and as she moved forward quickly away from it, he let it slide over her backside. Stella fought the strange feeling; she argued to herself that posh folk were more physical than folk like her — she'd seen everybody kissing and petting each other at her posh cousin's wedding like it was nothing.

He ushered her into a sitting-room at the back of the house which smelt like moth-balls and mould, cold and damp and dead. She'd expected posh folk's house to be like the houses in the movies, bright and clean and full of brand new things, but the dull leather chairs were worn in patches, and loomed up in front of her like stuffed animals; and all the furniture was dark and the light was stagnant. She looked for something to cheer her up as the old man went over to sit down, and suddenly caught sight of a dead stag's orange-brown head over the fireplace with its mouth open and a black tongue showing. It stunned her: what on *earth* would anybody want a dead beast's head sticking out of their wall for? That went a stage worse even than seeing them alive in the zoo —

and she had loathed the zoo with its foul smell of tigershit and all the animals prowling in cages looking useless. 'The puir auld buggar's bananas,' she thought with a pang of compassion, and smiled at him understandingly.

He had sat down on an armchair by the empty fireplace which gaped like a black toothless yawn. There was a tiny table by the arm of his chair, with a vase of roses on it, but in the shadowy room the colour had all bled out of them, and they looked like the ghosts of roses — papery too, like the roses the tinkers sold round the doors in winter. The old man patted his knee: 'Come and sit her m'dear . . .'

'Eh?' Stella felt this was a bit too familiar.

'Come and sit on my knee.'

'Ah dinnae ken about this . . .' Stella thought to herself, warily, as she complied. The tweed of his trousers scratched the back of her legs, and he smelt mouldy like the room. He laid his hand on her thigh and bounced her up and down, and the flesh crept on her bones. 'Ha ha!' she managed, then tactfully, 'I'm a bit auld for this carry-on . . .' trying to rise.

He held on to her with his cold horny old hands, and she struggled to get away. He laughed, 'Come on now, I'll be just like your grandad!'

'I haven't *got* a grandad,' Stella protested, still struggling.

'Don't you think this is what your grandad would do if you had one? Don't you *like* sitting on my knee?' he said, patting her thigh in that grisly way.

Stella was embarrassed. 'I'm no' accustomed tae it,' she apologised.

'Sit back and relax and we'll talk about the roses,' he said in a persuasive voice, pulling her to his chest and continuing to pat her thigh.

She complied, thinking the quicker she humoured him the quicker she'd get away, but she felt like a booby, a big Mammy doll, sitting there her size.

'You're just like a rose yourself,' he murmured, stroking her leg. '. . . skin like a petal. . .'

'Oh gad *sake!*' Stella thought, rigid with horror and embarrassment.

'Are you going to give me a kiss?' he whispered in her ear, and she would have shot up like a rocketting pheasant if he hadn't been holding on to her.

'Naw,' she said flatly, thinking she'd had enough of this. 'What nonsense!'

'Nice nonsense, give me a kiss,' the old man whispered again, trying to turn her head round.

'Ah never kiss *nobody,*' Stella retorted, emphatically, swivelling her head back with a determined effort.

'Oh well . . .' the old man quietened down. 'Do you like these roses?' — he took of his hand off her leg long enough to wave it at the table, but put it back again right away.

Stella saw then that they were white wax roses. 'They're no' *real,*' she protested.

'They're winter roses,' the old man laughed, ' — like me. I'm a winter rose and you're a little summer rosebud.'

Stella couldn't stop herself from sniggering at the mushiness of this: she could see Sheila and Senga's faces if she'd told them she was a little summer rosebud — like when she went to the Evangelist's tent on the beach last summer, and had come home singing 'Jesus wants me for a sunbeam' — Sheila had said, 'The Devil wants ye for a *stoker,* mair like!' But she squirmed on the old man's knee nonetheless, uneasy to get away and feeling down in her stomach as if she'd swallowed his tweed suit and was choking on it, suffocating.

He took her behaviour for coltish coyness and joined in, laughing longer than Stella, but stopping abruptly after a little while and saying 'I'll give you the roses if you'll take off your knickers . . .'

'What *for?*' Stella was astounded at the irrelevance of his proposition. If a boy at school had said it she'd have understood straight away, and probably done it, but she was slow to connect the boy with the old man. She felt him tense under her, though, and he was silent but for his harsh breathing, and for a few seconds they both were stock still, the old man waiting for her answer and Stella waiting to find it was all a bad dream. Except she never had dreams like this. She sought for a way out, and finally had an inspiration just as the old man's hand began to crawl up her leg again. 'Ah'll dance for ye!' she exclaimed, jumping off his knee so suddenly he hadn't time to grab her, and going into an imitation of May's routine, waving her arms, shuffling her feet about, heading for the door and singing in a cracked voice, 'There's no Business like Show-business, There's no Business I know. Yesterday they told you, you would not go far, tonight you open and — ' broke off, her hand on the doorknob, to interject — 'like May did, ye ken, and you gave *her* ten bob!'

'May?'

'My pal wi' the papers . . .'

'She didn't *dance,*' the old man laughed, rising ' — no, no!' he gave a fake laugh, coming towards Stella, then whispered hoarsely, *'She took her knickers off and let me touch her little rosebud. . .'*

Stella broke then and yelled, 'Ya durty auld pig!' and dodged out of the door, along the corridor, picking up her paperbag as she made for the front door. She was running down the path when the old man's voice rang out behind her:

'Here, here my dear — a moment!'

She went out of the gate and shut it before she turned round. He was coming down the path holding the wax roses. She gave him a sharp look but waited. At the gate he handed the roses to her, bent down and whispered, 'I'll give you these if you won't tell your mother and father about this morning.' Stella took them silently, contemptuous: she wouldn't have told anybody anyway — how *could* she explain that to her Mum or worse still her Dad? Offering a bribe to a bairn she felt he was a coward, and she despised him, but also she felt a sneaking fellow-feeling for his weakness just as a weakness.

But when she got a bit along the road and the sun warmed her again, her repressed spirit rose, and she shouted at the top of her lungs, 'YOU — DIRTY — AULD — BUGGAR!' and ran with trembling knees as fast as she could. When she stopped she saw the heads had fallen off all the wax flowers, and she cast the stems into the road in disgust. She found that she was still trembling though, and she hated the world till it made her wild. Half-way home an impulse seized her: she walked into a well-kept garden, and began to pick some roses, snapping and pulling them off with bare-handed boldness. A woman came out and began to shout at her what was she doing.

'Ah'm pickin' roses for Ah like them,' Stella said, impudently as she'd ever dared to in her life.

'These are *my* roses!' the woman bawled.

'Forget it!' Stella waved her away and just brazenly walked out with the roses, ignoring the outraged spluttering of the woman behind her.

She walked at first in the direction of home, but more and more numbly, till she was walking as in a trance, gripping the roses masochistically till they jagged into her fingers. Instead of going home she changed direction and went back toward the beach. When she came to the centre of a little stone footbridge over a burn that ran down to the sea she stopped, gazed almost unconscious into the water for awhile, then abruptly thrust her hand with the roses over the parapet and opened it, letting them drop into the water. Then she ran to the other side to see them come through, and watched till they'd either drifted out of sight or had snagged among the rocks and weeds. That satisfied her. With a deep breath, she turned to go home, thinking, 'I *will* be a cowboy . . .'

CHAPTER 5

Performing Monkey

The Salvation Army Hall, a utilitarian cube of concrete, stood at one corner of the square formed by Carnegie Mansions. Because it was in the slums, only the slum bairns attended it. Even at ten years old Stella couldn't accept that what she saw in the Mansions was all there was to see, but her hopes of uncovering the magic were nearly gone, she felt that somewhere along the line she'd missed her chance. As she walked down the hill to the Salvation Army with Senga in the early autumn evening though, she needed all the bitterness she could muster to fight the glamour that was falling over her.

They joined the straggling little queue that was waiting outside the hall for the doors to open. Stella knew the names and faces of everybody there, but no more than that now, for since Ishbel had let her down she hadn't spoken to her ever again, and had no connection with the Mansions bairns. She and her kind mingled with Ishbel and her kind as naturally as shoals of different types of little fishes, silently and without aggression. Except, Senga's best pal came from the Mansions, and Senga had joined the Salvation army with her. That was why Stella was there, she had latched on to Senga out of curiosity, and the easy-going Senga didn't object.

As far as Stella was concerned, Senga, being three years older than herself, was practically an adult. Stella had noticed Senga's pubic hair one bathnight, and this had given her instant promotion to another stratum of society, much as a sergeant is neither an officer nor a private. There was very little communication between them then, but they had a friendly atmosphere always.

87

They didn't talk much on the way down the road. When Senga's pal Rachel joined them at the Hall Stella just stood anonymous, a little sister, not interested in their conversation but looking at the other bairns or studying the billboard on the wall again and again with a wry mixture of hope and embarrassment. For it said 'JOY HOUR. Every Tuesday at 5.30. Everybody welcome.' Joy was a word you never heard in Skelf, it was an English word and a Bible word, and it couldn't have been more incongruous than it was here in the Mansions, to Stella's mind, looking at these bairns who moved through life with their heads down, as wary of jungle lore as little animals, or prematurely resigned to their fate.

When the doors opened they all charged forward, elbows out and desperate as automatically as Pavlov's dogs, from sheer habit. Stella was among the first to get in, but once inside the hall she stood transfixed, absorbing it all while the rest of the bairns surged past her. The place was as nothing inside as it had been on the outside, except that outside it had been daylight. She was bewildered, and turned to Senga who had paused beside her to do her sisterly duty: 'It's awfu' *dreich*, is it no?'

Senga shrugged, 'What did ye expect? The Hollywood Bowl?' and went on with the rest.

There were guttering gas-mantles, plain dark-varnished pews, and tiny barred windows high up on the north and south walls. The contrast between the bleak autumn light outside which made everything starkly geometric, and the soft fluid smudgy darkness in here was overwhelming. Down at the bottom of the hall the bairns who had hung about disconnected and laconic outside had suddenly found their tongues, and the buzz of their excitement seemed to be making the gas-lamps flicker. Still in their faded summer prints they looked like a patch of blown flowers swaying in a breeze, mysterious beings, a congress of elves in a dark grotto, with the silver crescent of the edge of a pair of cymbals gleaming on the bandstand above them like a new moon. Stella was tantalised with that on-the-edge-of-discovery feeling like she got when she looked at the illustration in her nursery-rhyme book for 'Boys and girls come out to play, The moon is shining as bright as day.' She walked forward uncertainly to join in, half-afraid that once she got there she would play forever without knowing it and never get back to the real world again; elbowed her way through to Senga and stood beside her, surreptitiously holding on to her dress in case they got separated.

'Hullo hullo *hullo!*' a hearty voice suddenly boomed out over their heads, which made Stella jump, suspecting for a flashing second that it was God interrupting her thoughts from nowhere. 'Have you started to enjoy yourselves already? Without me?' The bairns all tittered nervously, looking at each other, and Stella tittered too with relief that she wasn't the only one startled. Senga nudged her and nodded upwards: 'That's Captain Cross,' she whispered, and added with a good-natured laugh ' — an' dinnae hang ontae me like that — ye damn near ripped ma frock aff there!' Stella looked away casually as if the last remark hadn't been addressed to her, and saw the Captain standing smiling on the bandstand, a ruddy, full-blooded man in a uniform.

Two more people came in and joined him on the stand while the bairns clamoured to talk to them, a young man and a woman in uniform. The young man's hat was on his head at a little more than a jaunty angle, his face was pale, his mouth not quite shut, and he dragged one leg, club-footed. He looked simple-minded.

'Yon's Sammy Dalgleish,' Senga whispered, nodding and smiling at him '. . . he's no' as daft as he looks mind! — And that's Major McIntyre, the woman.'

'Thank God,' Stella whispered back, 'it's no' as bad as the Brownies, wi' their Snowy Owls and Tawny Owls . . .' although privately she thought the woman's Miss Muffet bonnet was nearly on a par.

Next thing she knew they were all scrambling into a line and marching on the spot. She'd to run after Senga, to whisper in a panic, 'Ah've nae collection money!'

'Nor does onybody else!' Senga shrugged. Stella fell into line behind her, listening cynically to the shuffling of sheet-music from the bandstand, not doubting it to be the same Sunday school every-spinster on the same gutless piano. But there was a toot and a tinkle, and suddenly the hall seemed to be bursting at the seams with the blare of an aggressive trumpet and a tambourine well and truly thumped.

As a body all the bairns, including Stella, straightened their backs, held up their heads like warhorses scenting gunpowder, and began to march in a hard-heeled military way to the strains of 'Onward Christian Soldiers', all singing as loud as they could. Stella felt like she'd lost a sixpence and found a pound; with the first forward step she became a war hero with the rest, marching like the real thing, not knowing the words but bawling to the tune. Their line wound round all the pews like the Sunday school, but there was no collection, no minister to pass, and it had all the gusto of a hot gospel meeting in Harlem. They went round the hall twice and a bit more, and only stopped when the trumpeter ran out of puff. She looked then and saw it was Sammy Dalgleish.

Immediately after Captain Cross shouted, 'What night is this?' and all the bairns roared back, 'It's Refugee Night!', then some ran into a back room and began to pull out a huge cardboard box. Stella pulled Senga's dress and asked her what was Refugee Night, and Senga told her, 'It's the night we knit squares for the refugees.'

'Knittin'?' Stella drew back horror-stricken. 'Knittin', for Godsake! Ah cannae knit ye ken!'

'Ye'll bloody well try,' Senga commanded. 'It's for the refugees, for a guid cause.'

'Well, wha's the Refugees when they're at hame?' Stella demanded in return, setting her lips tight and tapping her foot impatiently, hand on hips.

'It's folk wi' nae hame frae the war, livin' in tents in Germany an' that,' Senga explained, her eyes big with pity, shaking her head.

'Eh? It's the first Ah've heard o' them!' Stella eyed her with narrow suspicion.

'Ye've heard o' them noo well,' Senga said authoritatively. 'Run owre tae the box and bring three knittin's.'

Stella went obediently and fished out three clumps of knitting of different colours, with pins of different sizes stuck through them. The box smelt so powerfully of sweat and wool it made her cough when she rummaged in it 'God, what a niff aff that box!' she gasped, wriggling her backside to worm her way on to the seat, between Senga and two little fat women from the Mansions, who seemed to have sprung up from nowhere. Senga kicked her ankle and glared at her, as she took two bits of knitting for Rachel and herself, then smiling apologetically over her head at the two women, said in an offhand way, 'It's ma wee sister Stella — she's got the manners o' a pig!'

Both the women laughed and Stella laughed with them, confidential as a sweetie-wife. Then she found that, jammed between Senga and the roly-poly woman, she couldn't move her arms to knit, and had to draw them forward like wine-corks to free them. She rested her elbows on her thighs, leaning forward like a working man, the knitting dangling in her hands, and looked round about her at the rest of the bairns. A group of laddies on a pew opposite were knitting in unison, laboriously, like a chain-gang, while Sammy Dalgleish paced them in *'In . . . over . . . through —* through? — and . . . Off! *In . . .'*

'Knit!' Senga kicked her again.

'Ah can barely breathe here never mind knit!' Stella protested. The fat woman next her instantly moved along and said, 'Here hen, sit back now.' Stella sat back and began to pretend she could knit, stabbing away at the wool with the needles which felt like pokers in her hands. Senga glanced down, sighed, looked to see if anybody was watching Stella's fiasco, and began to make her excuses for her to the women, 'She's real clever at school, this one, for a' how she's handless at the knittin'. . .' Stella shrugged and knitted a hole.

'Never mind hen — ' here a third little woman, tiny and thin and worn, who'd been hidden by the two chubby little buddhas between her and Stella, stuck her head out like a squirrel round a tree and interrupted with a flash of real passion, to which Stella instantly responded ' — naebody's ever made a fortune knittin' yet, tae *ma* knowledge.'

'Aye,' the woman next to her came to life, but without stopping her knitting, ' — look at Cis here . . .' she nodded at her mate, ' — she can knit the bonniest Fair Isle ye ever clapped eyes on, and hasnae twa ha'pennies to rub thegither!'

'Ma *Granny* was a rare knitter,' Stella responded, 'but she said I'd tae stick in at the book-learnin' and leave the knittin' tae the mugs.'

All the three women laughed, while Senga kicked Stella's ankle yet again and groaned, 'Sheila's right — ye cannae take you onywhere!'

Stella ignored this, eager to get into conversation with this interesting trio, and got her own back on Senga anyway by asking the woman next to her, 'What's *really* a refugee and how would this' — she held up her knitting — 'help them?'

'No' at a', by the looks o' *that!*' the woman laughed.

'Dinnae torment the bairn, Nellie,' Cis said, laughing too. 'A refugee's somebody whose house was bombed and had naeplace tae stay — puir sowels — ' she shook her head as if she knew what it was like, ' — and these poor wee knitted squares will make blankets for their beds in the cauld.'

Stella gazed at her and nodded solemnly all the time she spoke, and when she'd finished, said, 'Well, Ah'll dae ma best, but the fact is Ah cannae knit . . .' ruefully, holding the knitting up again to cover up her confusion, for the idea of people with no houses was as hard to grasp as the idea of no God: a person had a house like a tortoise had a shell, she'd never doubted it. Yet there was a bleak picture in her mind, from the cover of one of her newspapers, of people standing grey-faced behind fences in heavy coats, and she knew it was true. She studied the holey little grey square in her hands and burned with shame. 'I've got threepence,' she confessed, 'I could give them *that* . . .' scraping off one of her sandals with the other.

'What are you taking your shoes off for now?' Senga looked at her in amazement.

'For ma *threepenny's* in the *toe,*' Stella explained, exasperated.

Nellie patted her knee, ' No no hen, you hang on to your threepenny.' Stella looked round in surprise; all the three women — but they looked like two and a half women — were nodding at her, solemnly impressed.

She turned her attention back to her knitting with a new feeling that she might be somebody who mattered after all.

After a while Captain Cross appeared, 'Now then, it's time for the hymn and go home, but first I want to tell you about the painting competition!' Heads perked up all round, but Stella lifted her shoulders and pursed her lips, thinking here she was missing something again. She didn't listen, but knitted holes all through the rustling of paper and excitement round her, as grimly determined not to be swayed as Madame Defarge. Senga nudged her eventually and she looked up to see Sammy Dalgleish standing in front of her holding out a piece of paper, 'You have to go in for the competition, won't you?'

'But I've only been here once,' Stella demurred — though she took the paper eagerly.

'That doesnae matter — have a go and bring it back next week!' he smiled. Nelly said to him with a knowing wink, 'She's bound tae win it, Sammy — she's a gey clever lassie, her sister says!'

The tiny serious woman, whose name Stella learned was Mrs McCosh, piped up in her anxious voice, 'Aye hen, go on and win it — show them what you can do!'

Stella was red with embarrassment, for her painting was as bad as her knitting, but she was ashamed to admit it. She looked to Senga for help, but Senga had risen and said, 'You go up the road yoursel', Stella — I'm going back to Rachel's for my supper.'

So Stella stood up too, painting-picture in one hand and knitting in the other, and felt burdened by the cares of the world.

Cis and Nell took this for reluctance to go home alone, and Cis said to Sammy, 'You be a good boy Sammy, and see the lassie hame.' They wouldn't listen to Stella's refusal, and walked out of the hall with her and Sammy encouraging her to do her best with the painting all the way, till she began to tell herself that if she forced herself to be patient and keep within the lines she could actually probably do it. But she was nervously self-conscious all the same, and had to put the whole thing out of her mind to be able to converse with Sammy on the way home.

'Did ye enjoy it then?' Sammy asked as they started off up the road.

'Aye,' Stella said.

'Do you like the Army?'

'Aye — it's much better than the kirk!' she blurted in her enthusiasm, though with a vague sense of disloyalty to her family's world.

'Maybe you'd like to join up?'

93

'Would I get a tambourine and a uniform?' Stella asked, after pretending to think about it for a few seconds.

'Aye, if ye join, when ye're bigger,' he responded, serious: the questions of uniform and the trumpet had been crucial ones for him too.

'How big have I tae be?'

'Oh . . . maybe about twelve or so . . .' He was vague because he didn't know: nobody except him in Skelf kept attending after puberty.

'But — would I get a hat like *yours?*'

'Oh, ye'll get a hat nae bother.'

'But like *yours?*' The women's bonnets reminded Stella of Mary Quite Contrary, whom she'd had to spend long cack-handed afternoons colouring in for a school Christmas calendar. She couldn't stand the thought of them. She wanted a real army hat.

'Mines is a man's hat — you'd get a bunnet, like the women.'

'Ah dinnae want a *bunnet,*' Stella was emphatic, 'Ah want a *real* hat like yours! Would they gi'e me it if I asked, d'ye think?'

'Oh they might — they're awfu' nice folk,' he said, reassuringly.

'Aye I like them,' Stella agreed, immensely cheered and warming more to them by the second.

'Just helpin' folk tae be decent and guid an' believe in the Lord,' he parrotted happily. 'Nae side tae them,' he added, nodding significantly at Stella, who picked up his whole history in the gesture.

But then she had a pang of conscience looking at this simple man and remembering her own defiance of God. Maybe though there would be another, better version of God, one you could believe in, here. She shut up and listened with an open mind as Sammy went on, praising the Army and all its works to the skies — but praising them for practical things she could appreciate: black babies were never mentioned. When he finally ran out of examples she added: 'And they're lettin' *me* go in for the competition, even though I've only been once!' — as if that capped the lot.

'Oh, everybody's welcome!' he said casually.

Such generosity amazed Stella: 'Really?' she said.

'Aye!'

'It's just *great,* the Salvation Army!' she enthused, giving a skip in the air. He laughed, well-pleased, and went on to tell her about how to live the Good Life.

By the time they reached her gate he had persuaded her to sign the Salvation Army pledge, and she was feeling uneasily idealistic. Her father was working in the garden and looked up as they approached: 'Aye, my lady! It's high time you were hame!'

'See's a pencil Dad, for a minute,' she pleaded, 'Ah'm just goin' tae sign the Pledge.'

'What?' he looked up from his weeding again at her and Sammy, and half-smiled, half-shook his head, but stood up and fished a pencil out of his pocket, handed it to her, then went back to work, hiding his face.

Sammy brought the slip of paper out of his breast-pocket and handed it solemnly to Stella.

'Ah'll just read it afore Ah sign,' she mumbled, embarrassed at his evidence of distrust, but wanting more to impress her father, who had been ranting on for the last week about reading things before you sign them, ever since he'd been swicked, as he believed, over the H.P. for his Saturday suit. It was a promise, the pledge, not to smoke or drink or swear, to keep the Commandments — and reading this she was relieved that it wasn't more specific, for she didn't know the Commandments anyway — to honour her father and her mother . . . she got as far as that and signed, reassured at least that money wasn't going to come into it, and hurrying to make it appear that she could read as quickly as an adult.

Yet as she signed, leaning on the gatepost, with the pocky grain of the cement making her signature in the soft black pencil look thick and tremulously illiterate, she despised herself a little: the knowledge flashed through her like sudden electric that she wouldn't keep any of it, for she wanted, wickedly, to try everything. She hesitated therefore before she handed it back, and Sammy, taking her hesitation for conscientious sincerity, went home content, thinking the Lord had rewarded him on the spot for his kindness in escorting her home, his faith reinforced.

Stella lingered at the gate, unconsciously rubbing the gatepost where she'd signed, disturbed, feeling like a hypocrite, sensing for the first time the irrational compromises that lie behind the paradoxes of adult life. Her father looked up at her, laughing, 'Signin' the Pledge, eh? I suppose you'll be a good lassie frae noo on?' She blushed and ran indoors, hating him for his cynicism. She brooded for the rest of the week. She had enjoyed the Army better than anything, but she couldn't paint. Yet, such was the encouragement she'd received from Cis and Nell, she believed she could only try, or never go back: it never crossed her mind she could just not enter. She wanted to keep going to the Joy Hour, so she had to try.

This thought tormented her, and made her moody and aggressive, so that she was in more fights, and had more beltings, at school, than in the past three months put together. Finally on the Sunday afternoon she brought out her paints, determined to do or die. When she opened her paint-box it made her savage: her mother had let the bairns play with it, and each square of paint was the same mud-colour as the next. She had a tantrum about this, till her father, intent on the Sunday paper, gave her a thick ear.

She went to the bathroom to sob and wash her paints, more desperate the closer she got to having to sit down and fill in the picture. As each bright colour appeared beneath the tap, she admired it, and felt more helplessly humiliated by her inability to use it properly. Putting off the evil hour, she washed the paints so thoroughly that she washed off the little of the red that was left; it was the last straw, for how could you paint a picture without red? She felt suicidal in her child's way: she wished there was no Stella Ross, that she could just disappear off the face of Skelf. The intensity of the misery made her dumb, and she sat for ages on the edge of the bath, loosely holding her paint-box and scowling in pure hate at her red-eyed image in the mirror.

Eventually somebody tried the door-handle, then thumped on the door. It was Sheila: 'Let me in will ye? Ah'm burstin'!' Numbly, Stella rose and unfastened the latch, then went back to sit on the edge of the bath while Sheila pulled down her knickers and started to pee. 'What's up wi' you?' she demanded, irritated by the gloomy, unseeing presence. Stella sobbed out her problem.

'Is that a'? *I* could paint it for ye!' — but it was a remark, not an offer.

'Would ye?' Stella clutched at straws.

'Aye — but I'd want somethin' for it . . .' Sheila opened up the dealing.

'What would ye want? — but it wouldnae be right . . .' Stella concluded mournfully.

'Wha's tae ken?' Sheila asked brightly.

'Everybody would ken it was too guid for ma age . . .'

'What's the diff.?' — you're no' gonna win, as sure as guns are iron: thae things is ay fixed — '

'No' in the *Salvation Army!*' her sister's cynicism shocked Stella.

'Aw Christ — dae ye no' think every bairn — *every single bairn* — in the competition 'll be gettin' somebody else tae dae't for them?'

Stella's eyes widened, and she brightened up, '*Would* they?'

'Och aye!'

'Ah dinnae want to win — ' Stella hastened to explain, 'Ah just dinnae want tae mak' an arse o' masel' in front o' — '

'So ye say, so ye say,' Sheila broke in, bored as always by Stella's deeper motives, ' — what'll ye gi'e me for it?' She rose briskly, pulled up her knickers, and led the way upstairs. They haggled until a reluctant Stella with a sad heart finally agreed to hand over her Hocus Pocus Magic Ball, to get the money to buy which she had scoured Skelf for a week — even knocking at doors and asking for returnable lemonade-bottles and jelly-jars. Sheila, afraid of being asked to give it back, made a perfect job of the painting, all in blue and yellow and green, not smudging over a single line. It captivated Stella. She temporarily lost all guilt in the feeling that she had been instrumental in the creation of such a beautiful thing.

But the guilt flooded back intensified when she saw the high hopes on the faces of the other bairns as they handed their paintings over at the next Joy Hour. She forced it away from her conscience by reminding herself of what Sheila had said, and marching harder than ever, and avoiding the wee women who were there knitting again, smiling at her every time she passed them during the games they played that evening.

When no more games were suggested and they all sat around exhausted, Captain Cross walked out of the side room on to the bandstand with some paintings in his hand. There was a strained desperate silence in which several bairns went into contortions to see whose paintings he held. Stella could hear her own heart thumping in her ears, and she sweated in the palms of her hands, so much that she had to keep wiping them on her dress. Her head was bowed and she gazed hard at the floor in an attempt to hypnotise herself numb. She wished to be deaf, but through all the scuffling and shuffling she thought she could actually hear Captain Cross breathing and the paintings rustle in his hand.

'. . . in reverse order. Third . . .' not Stella. 'Second . . .' not her, thank God. 'First — Stella Ross!' For a few seconds she kept her head down, trying to pretend she wasn't Stella Ross, then Senga nudged her and she rose on weak legs, went forward, held out her hand, took the prize, and returned to her seat, with Sammy playing a fanfare behind her that felt like the Last Trumpet. She sat tense and white, the money clutched in a clammy hand, wanting to cry and spew out the shame of it.

'What is it?' Senga was asking her. Without looking at it herself, she opened her hand and thrust it out.

'A tanner!' Senga announced. 'You're a lucky lassie!'

Stella sat dumb and oppressed, feeling so heavy with shame that she felt she wouldn't be able to get up when it was time to go home. She clung to Senga all the way out, hiding behind her to avoid the wee women.

Walking up the road Senga said, 'Come on then, oot wi' it! What's up? Is a tanner no' enough for ye after all your carry-on on Sunday?'

Stella mumbled, 'Sheila did the paintin' for me. . .'

Senga laughed, 'By God *you're* a fly ane!'

'Ah wish Ah was *dead!*' Stella burst out, tears springing up with the words.

'Why?' Senga stopped and looked at her.

'Because I hate *me,* that's why!'

When she got home still sobbing Bess came forward to cuddle her, but Stella pulled away with 'Dinnae notice me! Just dinnae *notice* me! Ah'm seek o' bein' *noticed!*'

Next day she still felt like she wanted to jump out of her self and leave it behind like a picked-off scab; her body irritated her; when she started to think anything she smothered the thought the instant she became aware of it; she tripped and fell two or three times in the playground and looked on her bleeding knees with a distant, cool interest, doing nothing to staunch the flow but letting it trickle and harden uncomfortably in her socks. Walking home in the rain she trudged straight through every puddle. She lived like that for nearly a month, feeling there would be a streak like black lightning down through the inside of her if she were split open, and the only relief was the passing of time, the gradual acceptance of self-hatred.

She didn't go back to the Salvation Army in that time, but when Senga asked her to go with her to a fashion show there, saying Mrs McCosh was disappointed she hadn't come back, she was tempted and gave in. When they arrived Senga took her over to sit beside Nelly and Cis and Mrs McCosh.

'Why didn't you come back?' Mrs McCosh asked, and before she could stop herself Stella blurted out,

'Because I cheated and got Sheila to do my paintin', an' I was . . . a — *ashamed* o' masel' for it.' She looked at the three women, blushing, sick in her stomach.

'Why didn't ye dae it yoursel', a clever quine like you?' Cis asked, surprised.

'Ah cannae paint either,' Stella confessed, her lip quivering and her nose twitching with tears held in.

Senga came to her rescue: 'Aye, as ma mither says, for a clever lassie she's awfu' thick!'

They all laughed and Stella laughed too, turning her head away though and weeping through it a bit, suddenly struck to the heart with longing for her Granny.

'She's a guid lass though,' Mrs McCosh commented, ' — no' mony would admit their fau'ts like that.'

Stella felt a precious little flicker of hope; her soul was like a candle not properly snuffed, just needing a breath to make it flame up again. She took her seat between Senga and Nelly, waiting for the fashion show, looking but seeing nothing for all the emotions vying with one another, and trying to quell her heart's swelling longing for her Granny who could have put it all right just by looking at her.

There was a clash on the cymbals and the fashion show began, but it was nothing like the fashion show she'd gone to with Bess at the local co-op drapery. There, it was all new clothes and the women walking up and down looking like dolls with pink faces and glazed eyes. Here it was all the dafties of Skelf in old clothes, and as they walked up and down the bandstand people shouted bids like 'A tanner for the troosers!' or 'Ninepence for that frock if it's a forty bust!' Stella leaned forward wide-eyed with her mouth open when Daft Geordie, the local half-wit, came slobbering and giggling on to the stage in a pair of combinations with a back panel, gazed into the audience and waved 'Hullo Mum! D'ye ken it's me?' Everybody roared with laughter, and he held out the sides of the legs of the combinations like Nelly Egg the hare-lipped woman had done with her frock before him. They stretched as wide as a clown's jodhpurs.

Stella's mum had hammered her before for laughing at Daft Geordie, and she'd had a strapping from the headmaster at school for leading him on to buy brown bananas with tap-washers at the fruit shop, so she was amazed that all the adults were laughing so openly now, and was still scared to laugh herself. Geordie, though, was so carried away with the spotlight that Captain Cross had to come out to lead him off the stage, or he'd have capered there all night. Stella looked round to catch Cis's eye. Cis winked to her, 'Puir sowels, they've tae ha'e their moment o' glory tae. . .' and turned back and yelled, 'Threepence for Geordie's drawers!' adding in an aside to Nelly, ' — they'll dae fine for ma John wi' a bit aff the legs. . .'

'Moment o' glory' buzzed through Stella's mind as she sat thrilled to bits on the edge of her seat watching the show. While Sammy made his way between the pews with the drawers for Cis, Tam the Mongol came galloping on to the stage on an imaginary horse, dot-carry-one because he'd one leg longer than the other, and did a round before stopping to face the audience, donning a silk top hat that was perched so precariously on his big head that he'd to hold on to it like Carmen Miranda. Stella was still scared to laugh, feeling the ghost of the back of Bess's hand hovering over her head, but she rocked up and down on her seat with the thrill of it, admiring Geordie and Tam and Nelly Egg for their unselfconscious panache — they were much better than May, with her artificial, fixed smile and her standard, sub-Ginger Rogers moves — they were themselves and bold and *original*, and she hadn't been so gripped and taken out of herself in all her *life*.

A laddie in the body of the hall stood up and bawled, 'A tanner for yer topper, Tam!'

Tam faltered, peering out into the hall, and caught sight of the bidder, 'You wan' ma hat Hughie?' Then his mood changed abruptly as it dawned on him that this meant giving it up, 'Naw!' he bellowed nasally. 'Ye cannae! It's *Tam's* hat!'

'Come on Tam — a tanner for yer topper!' Hughie cajoled, holding up a sixpence.

'Naw. *Naebody* gettin' *Tam's* hat!' Tam the Mongol shouted back, taking it off and clutching it to his chest, glaring down at Hughie with bug-eyed aggression.

'HAUND OWRE THE HAT!' a stentorian voice boomed down the hall, clearing a path of silence through the general laughter. Everybody recognised Tam's mother without having to look round, and immediately fell quiet, tense with laughter held fearfully in.

Tam had dropped the hat like a hot potato at the sound of his mother's voice. He picked it up now and held it out towards where Hughie sat, gesturing impatiently for Hughie to come and get it, moving from one foot to another in his anxiety to be rid of it, while a big dark stain of frightened pee spread over the front of his hodden grey trousers, and a pool appeared on the stage at his feet.

Hughie must have seen it and taken pity on him, for he shouted up to Tam, with a wave of dismissal.

'Naw never mind, man, keep yer hat!'

Tam shook his head and kept thrusting the hat towards him. Hughie came forward then and handed him the sixpence, taking the hat with a shrug that denied all responsibility.

Tam stood staring at the audience, nodding his head for approval in the direction of his mother's voice till Sammy came and led him limping and bewildered off the stage, with a glance at the pool on it. Seconds later, blushing and smiling, Major McIntyre emerged with a mop. The audience stirred restlessly, as embarrassed at a lady doing the dirty work as if they'd peed the stage themselves, until a wag at the back shouted, 'A bob for the mop!' like an ordinary bid, and Major McIntyre burst out laughing so they could all laugh. Stella looked for Tam's mother, and spied her, a big brosey woman with a chin like Desperate Dan and a face like a putten stot lowering, with folded arms, and she thought, thank God she didn't have *her* for a mother.

By the time the show was over she had laughed herself hollow, the black shame burned out of her. She treated Senga to a bag of chips off the paper-money going up the road home; in return, Senga asked her not to tell their mother about the fashion show: 'She wouldnae see the funny side o't, ye ken — she'd just be gi'en us a row for consortin' wi' the likes o' *them* . . .'

Stella understood, and was sobered, 'Aye — why though? What's wrang wi' them but they've got nae money?'

Senga thought it over for a while and kicked a tin can, 'Ah suppose because they divnae try tae get on in the world like us or somethin' . . .'

'But they're guid folk,' Stella objected. 'Cis and Nelly and wee Mrs McCosh — they're fell an' awfu' guid-natured — '

'Aye but wee Mrs McCosh's man hammers the tar oot her every Friday in drink, and Cis's man's yin o'yon that never works nor wants and Nelly's in tick up tae the lugs.' Senga explained. 'And their bairns are like mulattoes wi' dirt, and they've got nits.' She brought it all out automatically, as if she'd been reciting it in her head for a long time, but still hadn't grasped what it meant.

'Aye,' Stella spared her, knowing that neither of them understood it. She changed the subject, 'Wasn't Daft Geordie a *scream* in thae drawers!'

'God aye,' Senga laughed, ' — an' Tam the Mongol's mither: she'd a voice like a drill-sergeant!'

'Puir buggar peein' the stage in's moment o' glory though . . .' Stella added, with a guilty laugh.

Senga laughed too then wickedly, laughing even harder so she could hardly get the words out, added, 'But mind you, Ah — Ah thocht when *you* won the paintin' competition you'd *shat* yoursel', the knock-kneed wey you walked up for it!'

'*What?*' Stella exclaimed, laughing archly like the cavalier, 'in ma moment o' glory? — No' me!'

CHAPTER 6

Blood Brothers

The only thing she and Roberta had in common was tits: in every other respect they were ill-matched. Stella was dark and thin and mercurial, Roberta was the slow strapping fair peasant her surname suggests: Roberta McLusty. Stella was invariably the top of the class; Roberta was irredeemably of the Fourth Row Down, out of six rows. Stella was in the middle rank — that is, she was one of a family of four and her clothes were neatly darned but not always with matching wool. Roberta, from the Children's Home and with holes everywhere, was so far down as to be out of sight. They had nicknamed her 'Bubbles' because of the two bright green tube-like snotters that glinted perpetually under her nostrils and occasionally, for no apparent reason, inflated themselves, but never burst. Stella at least, when she had a cold, always had a token square of old sheet, fraying on every edge where her mother had torn it off. No matter that it was so thin as to be virtually useless by the time she reached school: the main thing was she had something that passed for a hanky: the proprieties had been observed. Roberta, anyway, was no more conscious of her snotters than she was of her arms.

All she had to alleviate this depressed condition was one of those rubberised, waisted jackets that were in vogue in the early fifties, called, with a cruel irony that deceived only parents, 'windcheaters'. She had a red one, and Stella had a blue one, and they suffered together for fashion like Spartan boys in the cold east wind that blew off the sea and into their cuffs, filling their jackets out like sails and bringing the rubber backing down to almost zero temperature. They were only ten, but they were both tall and they both had tits, and that was enough to draw them together.

Until Roberta came Stella had fought a lonely battle against convention in the school gym every week, stubbornly refusing to undress for 'drill', keeping on her tackety shoes and zipping her windcheater puritanically up to her neck. This was partly because Bess wouldn't buy her a bra, but even with a bra to hold her steady during the initial warm-up 'jumping on the spot' exercise, she wouldn't have taken off her windcheater, because the boys were so fascinated with her tits that they made her feel like a freak. She kept the hard shoes on to distract the teacher's attention from the real issue. A dried-up old maid with a sandy perm and no lips, who ate her lunch in the classroom cupboard, the teacher hadn't the sense to ignore Stella, but every week insisted on a power-struggle. All Stella did at these times was to look at the floor and give a sullenly emphatic 'no' every time the teacher paused to draw breath: as far as Stella was concerned, it had nothing at all to do with the teacher — but the teacher wasn't to know that, and took it personally. So every week Stella had to endure this embarrassment, till she began to feel victimised by puberty: if she hid her tits she was a social freak; if she showed them she was a physical one. She wished she could unscrew them like light-bulbs.

The first time Roberta entered the gym everybody but Stella was unlacing and unbuttoning. Stella stood monolithic in the centre of the floor, waiting, the Immovable Object, trying to look contemptous but feeling like a toad on a stone when the lake had suddenly gone dry: in her clothes, more naked than anybody. She had undone the cuffs of her windcheater as a gesture in the right direction, hoping it would be noted in her favour. Roberta sauntered over to her with all the panache of one who has come from another, tougher school, and asked:

'What for are ye no' takin' aff yer claes?'

'A'body gowks at ma tits,' Stella replied, bitter and insulted by this attention.

'Nor will I then,' Roberta announced, determined, 'for I ha'e tits tae.' They stood shoulder to shoulder, waiting to face the flat-chested teacher.

On the way up the road from school Roberta presented her credentials: 'Ah've got a *mither,* ye ken,' she opened, dissociating herself from the unwanted children at the Home, and went on, earnest, 'and my Mum loves me. *She* cannae help it Ah'm in the Home. It breks her heart, she says. My Mum's a *nurse* — a *night* nurse,' she specified, implying that it is more noble to nurse by night than by day. *'And* Ah've a big brother Douglas he's twenty he's in the army . . . *Ah'm* no' like that puir Billy in the Home that's aye runnin' awa' an' disnae ken whaur he's gaun and ran awa' last Monday again but they caught him on the beach an' he was greetin' a' nicht the next day,' she brought out all in the one breath, pride in herself blending into a confusion of pity and admiration for Billy.

'Have ye nae Dad then?' Stella interrupted, inexorably putting her finger on the weak point.

There was a long pause before Roberta replied: 'Och of *course* I've a Dad! What d'ye think Ah'm *are, a orphan?'* But she blushed, and Stella saw it from the corner of her eye:

'What for are ye in the Home then?' she challenged, but with an uneasy consciousness of sadism, which she cursed somewhere at the back of her mind: developing self-awareness was as much a burden as developing breasts, and just as inappropriate.

Roberta looked desperately off to the side, straining against the truth to remember the answer she'd been coached to give. At last she faced Stella triumphantly '. . . It's a secret!' — relief and satisfaction shone in her broad face, and her sudden smile made it round and simple as the sun.

Stella was nonplussed. This was plainly not the usual, ritual coyness calculated to raise the value of the confidences to come: it was an answer absolute in itself. As she gazed at Roberta and tried to smile back, she felt a pain that was mistily familiar, and almost unbearable, like some dead part of her feelings coming to life again, all pins and needles. She could only mutter 'Is it, eh?' and turn to questioning her about life in the Home, a mystery to outsiders like herself, seeing how most of the Home bairns were too ashamed of themselves for being cast-off to speak about it, and anyway too overwhelmed with the details of survival to notice a pattern.

Before they parted she had promised not to call Roberta

'Bubbles' any more. On the way home she was aware of the new soft self as if it were a child who'd been dumped on her doorstep, not wanting it but unable to refuse it. It felt like a weakness, an old long-forgotten weakness, and during the whole of that evening she tried to grasp and define it, but she couldn't get it to come far enough forward in her mind; it was like a loose first tooth that is deceptively mobile on the surface, but takes weeks to worry out. Eventually she shrugged it off: 'Ah think ma tits is saftenin' ma brain,' she complained to Sheila in bed that night.

'What brain?'

More than a week passed before they became confidential enough for Roberta to tell her secret. In that time their friendship had grown to the point where Stella gave Roberta the runt of her playtime apple — a gesture of commitment, for apples would be eaten, seeds and all, right down to the stem then. And she had steadily overcome her fascination with Roberta's snotters, except when they inflated and kept her in a suspense of betting with herself whether they would burst or not.

On the day Roberta told her the secret they were extra close because they'd both just had the belt from the teacher, Stella for the broad impatient 'Whaat?' instead of the polite 'Pardon?' they were trained to say; Roberta for blowing bubbles through her school milk. They drew together in a far corner of the playground like a pair of pariahs, and braved out the pain:

' 'S the first time Ah've had warm hands this week,' Stella muttered ruefully, pressing her stinging palms against the grey frosty stones of the wall. That delighted Roberta:

'Me an' a'!' she laughed, following suit. 'Ah'll have tae blaw through ma milk every day!'

'Then they'd call ye "Forever Blowing, Bubbles",' Stella ventured, and they both burst out laughing. '. . . Aye,' Stella went on, echoing in a drily rueful tone the words of the local milkman about his fractious horse, giving a nod in the general direction of the classroom, 'it doesnae tak' much tae get the auld bitch roused!' — and moved her hands to another stone. She was instantly diverted by the realisation that she'd made perfect prints, melting the frost on the stone. She pointed this out to Roberta, and they began to lay the prints of their burning hands on as many stones as they could, till the fever died down, and they started to stick on the frost.

'Hell, Ah'm freezin' noo!' Roberta exclaimed, hawing urgently on her hands.

'I've discovered a cure for cauld hands,' Stella boasted.

'How?' Roberta demanded, shaking her raw hands in front of her.

'Stick them down yer belly,' Stella replied cockily, doing so, and suppressing her gasp of shock. At that time she was in a constant ferment of secret experimentation like an alchemist during the Inquisition, and would suffer anything gladly for science. As soon as she got her breath back she went on, exasperated, 'Your belly is ay too hot in any case. It's *ridiculous* tae me, tae have such a hot belly and cauld haunds!'

'Ye're richt,' Roberta nodded, deferring to Stella's superior intelligence, and thrusting her own hands under the waistband of her skirt. She too suppressed the shock, but she couldn't suppress the watering of her eyes, nor the flow of snotter, which raced a sudden half-inch over the ledge of her upper lip. Grateful for such loyalty, Stella waxed magnanimous: 'Now Ah'll get ye a lollipop,' she announced.

'Ye've nae money,' Roberta said, but in a voice full of faith.

'Who needs money? "The best things in life is free!"' Stella rejoined, quoting her father, unconscious of the innuendo with which he was accustomed to use the phrase, leering at her mother. 'Follow me.' She strolled over to a large puddle, stove it in with her heel, stooped, and handed Roberta a big shard of ice like a broken window-pane, took one for herself, and began to lick it. She'd done this often on her paper-round in the early morning, when nobody was around to tell her it was dirty, and had herself half-convinced it was as good as ice-lollipops any day.

As they licked ostentatiously, Stella lectured Roberta on Nature's Bounty in the manner of their teacher telling them about the products of the Scottish economy. Both impressed by the theory, they sucked at the ice all the harder, till they were visibly shivering with a chill which they tried hard to shrug off, as a triviality in the face of the alternative of independent survival. It was important to them, who felt themselves such a burden on their parents.

But inevitably, one of the Mother's Boys, in scarf and sheepskin mitts, sauntered cosily up to them and sneered:

'Prodibly a *dug* peed in that puddle!'

Of course, it had occurred to Stella — very little that was filthy escaped her — but she had dismissed the thought with a haste that amounted to superstition. Now she dismissed the boy just as fast, with words she'd been saving for him ever since she'd heard them. Half-turning away from him, she snarled out of the side of her mouth:

'Fuck off, Jessie!'

'I'll tell the teacher you said that!' he shot back, overjoyed. 'You'll get the belt again!'

Before the words were right out of his mouth, Roberta's long arm flashed out from behind Stella and caught him by the scarf. Stella stepped aside as Roberta pulled him to her, so close that he had to angle his head back to avoid her bust, which had acquired an Edwardian fullness with the wind plumping out her jacket. Her knuckles were under his chin, and, glowering down at him with a thuggish expression that scared even Stella, she rasped:

'Try it, that's a' — just try it!' and pushed him abruptly away. He ran backwards for a few steps before he turned tail and hurried back to his cronies.

'Where did ye learn *that?*' Stella asked, impressed.

'In *ma* school,' Roberta swaggered, 'we *kill* cunts like him,' and closed the subject.

Stella at once appreciated with relief the benefits of having Roberta on her side, not giving a damn: 'One for all and all for one!' she cried, slapping her on the back.

'Aye!' Roberta grinned, herself relieved to find that the techniques of the other school worked here too, and appreciating the illusion: 'We'll be the Three Musketeers!'

'But there's only twa o' us,' Stella objected. Roberta's face fell.

'We could be blood brothers, though,' Stella went on, bright with the idea.

'Like in the pictures?'

'Aye!'

'How?'

'How!' Stella mocked, raising her hand in an Indian salute.

'Naw — *hoo?*' Roberta persisted, brushing frivolity aside with her emphatic Doric.

'We cut oor wrists and let the blood run thegither,' Stella explained, patiently patronising.

'Aye aye — ' Roberta was straining at the leash, ' — but *how?* How will we cut our wrists?'

'We need something sharp. . .' Stella muttered, looking about speculatively, till her eye lit on the beer-bottle top fastened to Roberta's windcheater like a badge, her only ornament. She pointed to it: 'That'll dae, tak' it aff.'

Roberta unzipped the jacket far enough for Stella to get her hand in to scrape the cork disk out of the back of the bottle-top; catching it as it fell off, Stella handed it to her: 'Come on then, it's your badge, you go first!' she urged.

Roberta pulled up her sleeve to show a chubby fair-skinned arm, goose-pimpled and bluish with cold. She touched the inside of her wrist with the bottle-top, and looked at Stella, ' — like this?'

'Aye.'

'But ma Mum says folk dies wi' cuttin' their wrist . . .'

'No' wi' just a wee *nick!*' Stella was incredulous.

'You dae't first then,' Roberta grumbled, handing her the bottle-top.

'Oh well!' Stella grabbed it impatiently, 'look noo!' — and pressed it hard into the back of her bared wrist, screwing the serrated edges round till a drop of bright blood sprang up, like a red berry appearing suddenly through snow. They both gazed in admiration till it began to congeal. 'Quick! You tae!' Stella urged, for she didn't want to do it twice: she already felt weak at the knees.

Roberta did the same with the badge, but her skin must have been thicker because, screw it into her arms as hard as she might, nothing happened. 'Never mind,' Stella consoled, seeing her crestfallen with failure, and red in the face with trying, 'we'll just pretend, see — ' and she crushed the little round berry blood on her arm against Roberta's.

Roberta was thrilled: 'Ah'll never wash it aff,' she said reverently.

'We're blood brothers now,' Stella announced, imitating the solemnity of Jeff Chandler in *Broken Arrow* and warm again with the sense of achievement.

They went back to the corner, played out, and lounged against the wall feeling mature and significant. For a while nothing was said. Stella looked on at the other children's games as if from a great height, and Roberta seemed lost in thought. Finally she began with great deliberation, 'If we're blood brothers I could tell ye ma secret about ma faither noo. . .'

'I wouldnae tell a soul,' Stella assured her automatically, too sated with significant action already to take it very seriously.

'Well it's aboot ma — ma faither . . .' Roberta hesitated again, discovering how hard it was to put it into words, '. . . well, like, he's no' ma real faither, ma Mum says. Ma *real* faither's . . . awa'.' Here she paused again, puzzled, as if the vagueness of it was striking her for the first time. Stella said nothing, but her mind raced with the possibilities. Roberta faltered on, 'This is ma — ye ken what Ah mean — *step*faither,' and abruptly shut up, and looked at Stella for a response. Stella thought this was the whole secret, thought she read the meaning in Roberta's troubled face, and tried to help,

'Was he cruel tae ye, ye mean? Like Cinderella?'

'Naw, no' like that!' Roberta snorted, scorning the juvenility of Stella's imagination, gaining impetus from her own scorn to get her story out: 'What he did was — well, ye ken my Mum's a night-nurse at the hospital, and she goes oot at night? Well . . . he like — he used tae come intae ma bed when ma Mum was at her work, ye ken, and kind o' — ye ken — feel me up like — ye *ken*!' She emphasised this verbal nudge with a physical one, and looked at Stella, white-faced. Stella only nodded her on, reassuringly unshocked: 'Fine Ah ken!'

Taking a deep breath at having got over the worst of it, Roberta summed it up: ' "Interferin' with me," the polis says.'

'The polis!' Stella was off the wall like it had suddenly grown spikes. 'How did the polis find out?'

'Ma Mum telt them,' Roberta replied, nodding securely with the rightness of it. 'She got awa' early one night frae her work and found him in ma bed, and she just ran oot, just like that, and brang back the polis!' She was as proud as if her mother had rescued a strange baby from a burning house.

'And what did the polis dae?' Stella could hardly believe her ears. This was a story that even adults would keep secret.

'They took him awa' an' put me in the Home.'

'Why? Why did they put you in the Home if he was awa'?'

The question had clearly occurred to Roberta too, for she immediately shook her head, 'Ah've nae idea.'

'Maybe since your Mum's a night-nurse,' Stella suggested, 'or in case he came back.'

'Oh aye! Right enough! Ah never thocht o' that!' Her face lit up. 'In ony case it'll no' be long afore she has me back, my Mum says.'

The bell to return to classes was ringing through the last part of their conversation, and everyone else had lined up to file back in. The blood brothers reluctantly bestirred themselves and joined them, Roberta in front, a big stolid figure, square-headed in the Home's standard delousing haircut. Stella gazed at her back and for the first time in her life was conscious of compassion, that aching, lonely bewildered feeling, like the universe is too big and we're too small, that has nothing to do with childhood.

Weeks passed, and Stella never told the secret. Every day Roberta had something glowing to say about her mother: she had got a letter from her about how much she was missing her; she had visited her at the Home and brought her pear drops, and had cried and said how much she missed her — that was always the theme. It disturbed Stella in a way that she had to avoid thinking about, that Roberta's mother, who had let her be put in the Home, should be so tender and demonstrative, while her own mother who was so possessive as not even to let them have tea at their friends' houses, constantly girned about what a terrible bind her bairns were to her. Gradually, Stella began to picture Roberta's mother as a coarser version of the Dorcas in the adverts for sheets, a benign unwrinkled smile, a nurse's cap, and soft white hands.

One Monday morning Roberta came to school full of herself. She had been allowed home for the weekend because her mother was off work, and she had been pampered the whole time. She itemised every gesture of her mother's care to Stella with all the leisurely relish of a gourmet in a Colditz recalling a meal at Maxim's, and Stella for her part listened as cooperatively as the beggar at the Barmecide's feast.

'*And* I slept in ma Mum's bed *and* my big brother's hame frae the army and he's got a microphone!' she exclaimed, with the air of having saved the best for last.

'A *microphone*!' Stella was too bewildered to find the appropriate response.

'*And* he let me sing intae it,' Roberta went on oblivious, thrilled with the sophistication of it all.

'But what's he daein' wi' a microphone?' Stella knew she shouldn't ask, but she couldn't help herself.

'What d'ye mean, what's he daein' wi' a microphone?' — Roberta saw nothing strange in it.

Stella couldn't begin to explain: her experience of microphones was confined to the one they used for the open-air concerts in the glen in the summer, that could be heard for half a mile in any direction, and she knew that Roberta's mother only had a three-room flat in a tenement near the docks. She just contented herself with repeating 'What's a microphone for — in the *hoose?*' She couldn't see Roberta in show-business like May.

'Tae sing intae, for Godsake!' was the exasperated, dismissive reply. Brushing Stella's unexpected ignorance aside as if it were a temporary aberration, Roberta went on with a well-rehearsed casualness, 'My Mum's coming to see me at the school this week, but she says I've no' tae tell them at the Home.'

Stella looked forward to this almost as much as Roberta did, and when the word was spread round that Roberta had a mother, who was coming to see her, her status rose. Every day, as soon as the playtime bell rang, she and Stella high-tailed it to the main gate, where they waited and watched like refugees till it was time to go back in.

After three days her mother appeared. Stella couldn't believe her eyes: a wee leathery-faced, over-powdered woman like a turtle drying out after a mud-bath, cracked and wizened and harrowed. Not only was she not like Dorcas — she wasn't even like Roberta: standing together they reminded Stella of the picture in her Nature Study book, of a mother sparrow feeding a baby cuckoo.

When the mother spoke it was even more like the picture. Wiping her eyes with her knuckles she asked kindly, in a piping voice, 'Are ye cauld, hen?'

'Naw, Mum!' Roberta boomed in a voice that made her sound like a laird with a log fire at his back.

'How are ye gettin' on, hen?' she then asked, as anxiously as if Roberta had just come out of a sanatorium, and she hadn't seen her for months. Stella moved away, conscious that her presence was a constraint.

Roberta was sad when she got to her line to go back in, and kept repeating 'My Mum's missin' me,' all day. She told Stella that her mother was coming back next day, with a flask of tea to warm her up. Stella didn't go to the gate with her then, but stood watching from her corner while the mother poured the tea and Roberta drank it. She wondered why her mother whom her dad told her was as near perfect as a mother could get never thought of bringing her and her sister a flask of tea — but without envy, for she had been brought up to believe she was much luckier than everybody who *wasn't* her mother's bairn, and if Roberta wasn't one of those 'Millions starving in the Sahara' who would, according to her mother, 'count themselves blessed with the half' of what she, Stella, got, then she was the next best thing. Now to watch Roberta getting a treat she herself, shivering in her windcheater, would have sacrificed most of nature's bounty for, relieved her of that guilt.

Yet she had to struggle not to feel like a poor little rich girl when Roberta's mother took a hankie from her message-bag, wiped her own eyes, and passed it to Roberta to wipe hers. More so when Roberta offered it back, and her mother shook her head, saying something, and Roberta blew her nose on it and put it in her pocket. Bess had a lot of hankies, but she kept them ironed in a drawer with empty scent-bottles. Stella had never seen her using one, and at the height of their winter colds, when the torn sheet supply was used up, her mother washed dusters for them rather than part with a *real* hankie to a mere bairn. Looking on, Stella could understand Roberta's devotion.

After the hankie had been passed, Roberta and her mother stood together in what seemed from Stella's distance to be a sympathetic silence, gazing up the road away from the school, marooned in a crowd of raucous bairns, as patient and forlorn as cows in a sodden field.

Roberta's silence persisted for the rest of that day, and although she must still have had the hankie, she didn't use it again, but returned to her original snottery condition. When Stella finally asked her what was wrong she said, 'My Mum says it'll be longer than she thought before she can get me back, an' she doesnae ken what she'll dae withoot me.' Then Stella fell silent, too, for Roberta's loneliness fell on her.

The next day Roberta's headaches began. She sat listless all day in school, and stood listlessly about when she was outside. Stella moped with her, and in the afternoon stole aspirins from home for her. She even told Bess that Roberta's mother wanted her and couldn't get her, but her mother just looked knowing and said, 'Aye, weel, there'll be things there *you'll* no' ken aboot!' She had hoped her mother would be outraged and go to the Home and complain, for Bess was always on about the sacredness of mother-love, and it was plain as could be in Stella's mind that Roberta's mother had that kind of love.

In the middle of the next week Roberta's mother reappeared, and again they stood like refugees, saying little, Roberta drinking her tea. When she came back over to Stella before returning to the classroom she was more her old self: she said she'd told her mother about the headaches and her mother had promised to bring pills to help them, better than she got at the Home, 'for my Mum's a nurse and she *kens* aboot thae things . . . But I've no' tae tell anybody,' she added, 'I'm only telling you because you're my blood brother.'

Sure enough, next day her mother came and brought the pills. From her vantage-point in the corner Stella not only saw her giving them to Roberta, she saw the pills themselves, they were so big. 'My God, Roberta,' she whispered to her in the lines, impressed, ' — if thae pills doesnae help ye, nothin' will — they're big enough tae cure a cuddy!'

'Aye!' Roberta laughed, proud as Punch, 'because my Mum got them *special* at the hospital!' Stella laughed too, with relief.

About half an hour later Roberta fainted in the classroom, and wouldn't come to. The headmaster and the janitor, the only men in the school, carried her out between them, sweating and staggering with the unaccustomed effort. Her face was pale and peaceful, but the clumsy way they handled her body and tried to rush with it made Stella's blood run impotently mad, for she knew that if Roberta had been one of the well-brought-up bairns with two parents and a home to go to, they'd have tried harder, and left her dignity. As they stood waiting for the teacher to open the door, distaste written all over their faces, they let the body sag in the middle, so that Roberta's backside touched the floorboards. Stella couldn't bear it. She jumped up to her feet and shouted, 'For *God*sake watch what ye're daein'!' The headmaster went red to the crown of his bald head and shot her an angry look, turning impatiently to the teacher, 'Come *along* Miss Bruce — open the door!'

As soon as they'd gone, the teacher whipped Stella out and belted her, twice on each hand, with an intense, long-in-the-gathering spite. Instead of going back to her seat straight away, Stella stood for a few seconds confronting her, not knowing what the look on her own face was, not knowing what to do, but needing to do something. The teacher hovered over her, trembling with rage, shoulders hunched up and nose white and beaky, like a bird of prey: 'Get back to your seat girl!' she squeaked, hysterical with embarrassment. Still Stella paused, unable to accept it, fighting an overwhelming urge to slap the teacher's ear and once and for all put an end to the undignified farce of school life. But the moment passed with the hesitation, and she went back to her seat, desperately controlling the tears of anger that were rising, and would be taken for tears of pain or humiliation by the rest.

She remained openly doing nothing, furtively cooling her hands on the iron legs of her desk, till the lunchtime bell rang. When she got out she thought she could never go back, and that afternoon instead of returning to school she walked on the beach, trying not to feel humiliated, wondering where to run away to, but giving up in the end and just letting the wind blow the passive tears into her hair, till it was time to go home.

She cadged the next day off school by getting up early and rubbing talcum powder into her face, then telling her mother she had 'a splitting headache' and had been 'as sick as a dog' through the night. In the middle of the morning, with the housework done and the current infant put into the lobby in her pram for a nap, her mother sat down to read the local paper, while her father, who was on a late shift, sat at the opposite side of the fire reading his western.

'Oh my God! Will ye listen tae this, Wull!' her mother suddenly exclaimed, folding the paper excitedly, to hold it easier for reading; ' "A man appeared before the sheriff's court on Tuesday, charged with indecent assault on a minor. Thomas McMann of 17 Sunrise Buildings, Abervale, admitted the offence against the ten-year-old daughter of his common-law wife, and was remanded in custody" — d'ye ken the man?' Her father gave a negative grunt.

'The dirty pig! Tae a ten-year-auld bairn! I wonder wha he is?' Bess went on in delicious outrage.

'Mind what ye're sayin' wi' Big-Ears owre there,' her father grumbled, not at all interested.

'Och, she disnae ken . . . Sunrise Buildin's — is that by the dock?'

'Aye.'

'Imagine, a ten-year-auld bairn! What was her mother daein', eh? Whaur the hell was she?'

'Och, likely it was some hoore's bairn,' her father replied, as if it were a commonplace thing and not worth getting worked up over. 'The mither would be oot hawking her mutton at the docks wi' the boys off the ships, an' the faither would be trainin' the bairn at hame.'

'Ye think so?' Bess was naïve and deferential. 'Is that what it would be?' Then in a burst of suspicion: 'How d'ye ken that?'

'Ach, Bess, Ah'm a man and men get tae ken thae things.'

'Aye, Ah suppose so . . . Is there a lot o' that?'

And they went on discussing it, oblivious of Stella sitting over on the settee pretending to read her comic.

She knew what her father meant, and she didn't believe him, but all the same it was as if she'd swallowed cold lead, that that was what everybody would think of Roberta, and that the things her father was describing could be true of anybody. She wished passionately that she wasn't a woman and went to the bathroom, got down on her knees, leaned her elbows on the seat facing the cistern and prayed, 'Dear God, turn me intae a laddie. Ah cannae face it,' over and over again, till she found she was sobbing and her mother was knocking on the door to get in.

She kept that prayer up desperately in her head all day, and went over it that night in bed with a vehemence that was nearly anger. She didn't really expect to wake up a boy, but she hoped against hope she would. It was the first thing she looked for in the morning, and when she found she was the same lassie as yesterday, she only shrugged bitterly — one more proof in a long series, that God didn't exist. 'Huh! OK! We'll see!' she threatened Him, and got up. '. . . But a' Ah have tae say is this,' she continued to address Him as she sat to do her morning pee, 'that Ah dinnae think anything o' ye, God, nothin' at a' — *anybody* could dae a easy job like yours!'

That day she went back to school, burning with a sense of shame and defeat. All the way down the road the tears were still at the back of her eyes, making her own self intolerable to her: tears for any reason were a weakness; tears for Roberta were worst. Yet again the image of her, howfed out of the classroom like a carcass into a butcher's, floated into Stella's mind and her eyes filled, and she felt herself diminished. The world with its close wet buildings and its raw salty morning smell felt as coldly and crudely fuctional as a public lav; she couldn't bear it and despised herself for going on in the old way automatically to school, for not knowing what gesture to make, for being as insignificant as a dead cat.

Then Roberta didn't turn up. At playtime she got hold of Billy from the Home and asked him about her. He shrugged: all he knew was they had taken her to hospital and let her out again, and she was in the sickroom at the Home. He didn't know what was wrong with her.

That afternoon there was a knock at the classroom door, and a man appeared. He was in his fifties, well-to-do, with a heavy overcoat, a Paisley scarf, and wavy iron-grey hair. The wavy hair was a signal to Stella: all the boys she knew with wavy hair were mothers' boys, whom she could picture standing patiently and pawkily innocent at their mothers' knees to get their waves pressed in, then they came to school and pretended to drop pencils and felt up your knicker-leg under the desk. Even the doctor who gave them their school medicals, and who always kept his hands a few goose-pimply seconds too long down your knickers, had red wavy hair; so did the greasy grocer in the corner shop, who invited the young women into his back shop when there were no other customers in. And sure enough, the first thing the man did was to begin a confidential chat with the teacher, charming her with a predictable smoothness, while she blushed and simpered and patted her perm with a chalk-dry hand. The bairns stared at their teacher's mating behaviour like tourists watching a snake-charmer: incredulous, repelled, and fascinated.

Finally, the social rituals over, he turned to the class, and in a fake-jovial tone which reminded her of the hated and hating school janitor playing Santa Claus at the Christmas parties, greeted them. 'Hello boys and girls! Do any of you know who *I* am?' Behind him the teacher tried to look benevolent and threatening at the same time. A hand went up to the half-mast position, in the front row. The man took his time noticing it, then said, 'Who am I then Billy? Billy, is it?' Looking at the laddie and recognising him, but not seeing him, like a social worker.

'It's Jimmy,' the boy answered, as dourly as he dared, 'and you're Mr McBain.'

'Aha!' the man exclaimed mechanically, as if responding to an enthusiastic answer, and went on with his performance: 'and do you know what I do?'

'You come to the Home.'

'Yes!' — with disappointment and an effort at patience — 'I'm Uncle Sandy who comes to the Home! And what do I do there?'

'Ah dinnae ken,' the laddie mumbled, his chin on his chest, hating the spotlight.

'I'm the man who painted the pictures in the dormitories. Did you know that?' he asked, with a self-satisfied glance towards the teacher, who responded with an appropriate smile of admiration, and blushed again. He went on, 'The pictures that scare you and make you shut your eyes and sleep at night,' and gave a grin that was a strange mixture of benevolence and sadism.

Stella was stunned. As soon as the words were out of his mouth she was asking herself if that was really what he had said, and refusing to believe it.

'*Do* they make you sleep?' he persisted.

'Aye,' said the boy in a dispirited voice.

The whole class was shuffling uncomfortably, on the edge of fear: what new authority was this? They knew he wasn't the dentist or the doctor, but he had the same air of contemptuous power. He appeared to relish their suspense for a moment or two before he came to the point: 'You all know Roberta McLusty?' There was a silence and a sudden relaxation of the atmosphere as they all took it in and realised that they weren't to troop out for some unimaginable investigation; that it wasn't the dreaded school psychiatrist who would be able to read their minds getting round to them at last. The man assumed a gravely paternal expression: 'Has any of you seen Roberta take anything recently — any pills or aspirins, or anything like that?'

Nobody answered, although just about everybody must have seen her mother give Roberta the pills. Stella instantly added two and two.

'Nothing? Nothing at all?' He waited.

Stella glanced at the teacher, and caught her looking at her, coldly meaningful, and was afraid she was going to single her out, but she didn't.

'Nothing at all now? You're sure?' the man probed, asking his question louder, as if they were a bunch of deaf idiots. And indeed, they had all taken on a glazed, simple-minded look.

He waited a few seconds more, scanning the class with increasing disdain, then turned back to the teacher. They muttered in secret again, while thirty-nine pairs of ears strained to overhear, and finally he shook hands with her and left without another word to the class.

The mystery preoccupied everybody for the rest of the day, except Stella, for she knew that Roberta was OK or they wouldn't have let her out of hospital. She was struggling with trying to figure what the man meant about the pictures: his innuendoes seemed to confirm her doubts that any alternative to home would be worse. She felt isolated and insecure, and longed to grow up overnight like the beanstalk, to be free of her tension of dependence on an adult world that for her was always divided between the kind people, who were impotent, and the powerful people, who were full of sudden inexplicable sadisms. She wasn't absolutely certain which category Roberta's mother came into, but it didn't worry her much, because she knew without having to work it out that sure as guns are iron, if Roberta's mother had wanted to kill her, Roberta would have wanted to die.

Next morning at ten o'clock the headmaster led Roberta into the classroom, put her in her seat, and after a brief word with the teacher, left. Not until the teacher was preoccupied with explaining long-division to the huddled masses at the front did Roberta get the chance to communicate. She turned a blank, flat face in Stella's direction and husked, 'Ah've went blind!'

'Ye've WHAAT?' Stella yelled, before she could stop herself, and was instantly summoned out and belted. But she hardly noticed the teacher or the pain, her head was so full of Roberta's stirring news.

At playtime Stella guided Roberta out, and waited to hear her story. It was disappointingly short, and Roberta was inexplicably defensive: 'When I came to that day I couldnae see a thing an' Ah've been like that ever since,' was all she offered.

'What's it like?' Stella asked, ignoring the sullen tone.

'Awfu' dark, like night,' Roberta answered promptly, well-used to describing it already.

'Was it the pills your mother gave ye?' Stella pursued as casually as she could, trying to disguise a burning curiosity.

'The *doctors* said it was pills, but I didnae tell them my Mum gave me some. They gave me jags an' a stomach-pump an' a'thing,' she replied, steering the conversation away from the danger-zone.

Stella understood and cooperated: 'Will ye be blind forever? What's a stomach-pump?'

'Tae clean ye oot. Naw — the doctor said I could see again if Ah wanted tae. It was sair.'

'Could ye?'

'Maybe.' Roberta refused to commit herself.

'But why would ye no' want tae *see*?' Stella couldn't understand it.

'Ah dinnae ken.' Roberta didn't understand it either, and didn't want to try: she shrugged irritably and walked away from Stella, to join a group from the Home.

After that, as days of her 'blindness' passed, and Roberta made mistake after mistake that gave her away to everybody without ever admitting her bluff, Stella's admiration for her grew. Yet despite her willing complicity, and even standing up for Roberta when the others caught her out, Stella couldn't penetrate the world into which Roberta had withdrawn. Giving nothing and feeling nothing, it was as if she were in some kind of invisible protective bubble. At first Stella was hurt, but eventually she was just plain bored. Determined at last to bring things to a head, she said peevishly one day to Roberta, 'You can tell *me* what it is, surely — are we blood brothers or no'?'

'No' noo — Ah've got ma *period!*' Roberta snapped, cruelly impatient, 'Ah'm a woman noo, ma Mum says.' She sank into an aggressive silence, started to speak, hesitated, then blurted, 'Ah cannae play at games!'

Stella was impressed, embarrassed, and put down, all at one time, and became equally aggressive: 'Why no'?'

'Och, it's *what ma Mum says,*' Roberta emphasised, grimly dogmatic.

Stella changed her tack: 'Have ye seen your Mum?'

'Of coorse she visited me in the hospital,' Roberta sniffed.

'An' what? When will she tak' ye back?' Stella didn't try to hide the needle in her question, but Roberta wasn't to be drawn. She gave no answer at all, and stood stubborn, holding her face up, expressionless as a boiled egg. Stella walked away after a minute or two of this, hurt and bewildered. She didn't speak to Roberta again.

At the end of that week Roberta left school for good. On the Monday following the teacher cleaned out her desk. She dropped all the bits of private junk into the bucket, and, tearing out the unused pages of Roberta's jotters, announced, 'We'll be able to use these for scrap.' She gave no explanation more than that. Once again Stella sought out Billy at playtime. He stuck his hands into his trouser pockets and looked unhappily away over Stella's shoulder, as if into the foreseeable misery of the future: 'Her mother's took her hame and gi'ed up her wark an' she's a' right noo. She wasnae blind at a'! She just did it tae get her mother!' he exclaimed in a tone of incredulity, that also hovered between envy and disgust. 'Christ! Ah wish if Ah had a mother tae come for *me!*' he added passionately, kicking out at the gritty playground, and turning abruptly away.

Stella went over to her corner and, to stop herself from wondering why she had echoed Billy's wish in her own heart when she already had a mother, she began to brace herself to face the teacher that afternoon in the gym.

CHAPTER 7

Change of Life

'Nae dochter o' mine will stay out past nine o'clock on the Sabbath!'

'But Mum, ma *watch* was slow!'

'Watch? Watch this haund!' — Sheila got a resounding smack on the face — 'That'll learn ye tae *watch yer step,* madame, as long as ye're livin' in *my* hoose! Just get right upstairs tae yer bed, an' think yersel' lucky I dinnae hit ye again!'

Stella, lying upstairs in bed, cringed. The obsessive vindictiveness with which her mother had kept looking at the clock since nine that evening and muttering repeatedly to herself, 'Ah'll give that wee bitch her come-uppance this bonny nicht, see if Ah dinnae. . .' had bewildered and frightened her. She was glad when she was told to go to bed herself, but had lain uneasily waiting for Sheila's footsteps ever since, clinging to her in her heart. Sheila at least was the devil she knew: their mother was getting stranger by the day. By the time Sheila came upstairs to the dark bedroom and had changed into her pyjamas, Stella had worked herself up to a pitch of sentimentality; she was feeling that herself and Sheila were like the Babes in the Wood, defenceless.

'Did she hurt ye?' she whispered to Sheila as she got in beside her, and then suddenly she alarmed herself by bursting into tears.

'What are *you* greetin' for? *You* didnae get hit!' Sheila demanded indignantly, cheated of the bitter privacy of the occasion.

Stella couldn't answer the question: she didn't know herself. She only sobbed: 'Was it sair?'

'Was it *sair?*' Sheila was incredulous. 'Christ, what's up wi' *you?*'

'Ah dinnae ken,' Stella sobbed, pressing her lips together and desperately trying to control herself, "Ah cannae help it!'

'By God you're a guid ane!' Sheila exclaimed, ' — Ah get a thick ear an' you greet! Ye're nuts!'

By this time Stella was in full, childish flood: 'Hoo . . . Dae ye . . . hoo-hoo . . .'

'Dae Ah hoo-hoo what?' Sheila mocked, impatiently and Stella began to laugh in the middle of her tears, and in the process came to herself.

'Oh for the love o' God,' she giggled. 'Ah think Ah'm slippin' ma cogs!'

'Weel Christ Ah wish if ye'd slip them in yer *ain* time!' Sheila exclaimed, and they began to giggle helplessly.

'You lassies tone doon or Ah'll be through tae yez!' came their mother's irritated growl from the next room, where she was getting ready for bed.

'God forbid!' Sheila whispered sarcastically, and they were off again, Stella sticking the corner of her pillow in her mouth to suppress her noisy laughter, and Sheila muffling her face in the sheets. After a few seconds Stella whispered, 'Ah hope she doesnae come through — Ah couldnae staund it tae see her in her knickers an' vest an' her teeth oot!'

'Aye . . .' Sheila agreed, '. . . she's like the Creature from the Dismal Swamp!' and they choked with malicious laughter.

'. . . clutchin' her fanny as usual. . .' Stella added, for this mysterious habit of her mother's fascinated them both. 'As if it would drop off,' they used to say. Their laughter intensified.

Another growl from the next room quietened them down, and Stella whispered, 'What the hell's wrang wi' her, anyway? She never used tae be as bad as this!'

'Christ knows — Ah think it's the change o' life, but she'll no admit her age tae anybody — Ah think she's forgotten it hersel' — she's been thirty-eight for the last five years at least . . .'

'Aye . . .' Stella agreed, and hastily asked: 'What's the change o' life? "Change o' life"? What is she changin' intae?'

'An auld bat by the looks o't!' Sheila whispered promptly, and there was more stuffing of sheets and pillows into their mouths.

Between giggles Stella added ' — or the Creature from the Dismal Swamp!'

'Och cut it oot or Ah'll pee the bed!' Sheila urged, half-serious. Gradually they subsided, then came up for air, and Stella persisted.

'But what *is* the change o' life? — Ah've never heard tell o't!'

'It's somethin' women get in their forties. They get a' moody an' weird for awhile, afore they settle doon tae auld age,' Sheila explained, curtly with a trace of self-pity. Then, on an afterthought, as Stella digested this, she added, 'Christ Ah think you've got it tae — ye've been gey funny lately!' and sank into gales of open belly-laughter.

'Me?' Stella was caught between amusement and alarm. 'But ah'm no' eleven yet!'

'So ye say,' Sheila stuttered out, 'but . . . but . . . ma Granny aye said ye were auld for yer years!'

This, accompanied with infectious hearty laughter, was too much for Stella. She laughed out loud too, till the tears ran down her face.

They could hear their mother's bare feet pounding on the linoleum as she ran through to settle their hash, but they were helpless. She stamped in, the light of the hallway behind her. They raised their heads to look, and seeing her not only in knickers and vest, clutching her fanny with one hand as predicted, but also with a headful of flat steel curlers and her teeth out, fell back writhing with laughter.

'What the hell's gotten intae you wee buggars?' she fumed. 'Is one skelpin' no' enough for ye in a day?'

'It's me, Mum,' Stella gasped, 'Ah'm hae'in' bother wi' the change o' life!' and even as her mother flailed at the bedclothes, under which they had immediately buried themselves for protection, they roared and laughed.

As soon as she had gone and it was safe to come up for air, Stella asked, 'But what for *does* she clutch her fanny like that? Is it the change o' life then?'

'Christ knows . . . dae you clutch yours?' Sheila asked wickedly.

'Aw come aff it!' Stella moaned.

125

It was the school holidays, and Sheila, who was due to leave school the following Christmas, had got a job in a summer café on the beach. Stella had nothing to do, and used to follow Sheila to work every day, and hang about on the beach with a library book, to avoid being roped in to help with the housework and the younger ones at home.

Now that Sheila had some money of her own, she had begun to buy herself clothes and make-up, and pursue the boys in earnest, taking full advantage of the chances her job in the café gave her to meet the summer holidaymakers. Stella watched all her sister's ploys with scientific detachment, helping when she could by covering up for her with their mother. Since the break with Roberta she had tried to draw closer to Sheila, and Sheila used this unexpressed but obvious need to exploit Stella with all the ruthless egocentricity of an adolescent.

That was how Stella became, as their married older sister put it, 'a martyr to the whims of the Beauty Editor of the *Woman's Own*'. Sheila wanted to try every beauty tip in the magazine, every week, but she didn't want to suffer when they went wrong, so she enlisted the almost masochistically willing Stella as official guinea-pig, and boasted casually to her friends, 'What's the point o' keepin' a dog an' barkin' yoursel'?' With slavish obedience, trying to find her way to her sister's heart, Stella had lain on the bathroom floor with cotton-wool pads soaked in cold tea on her eyes for the best part of two hours, with every member of the family coming in at one time or another to pee, and stepping casually over her. At the end of the experiment — which was when Sheila had finished listening to the radio, and remembered her — it was discovered that whether or not her eyes actually had the promised sparkled was irrelevant, for, so strong was the tea Stella's family brewed, that she looked, as she said, 'like a bloody lemur!' The next major failure was a home-made face-pack, which again Sheila left on her too long, so that the top layer of skin on her face peeled off, and for a week it was nipping agony for her to go outside in the cold air. The rawness of the early mornings when she did her paper-round made it so painful her eyes watered, till her cheeks were covered in hacks, and she had to be constantly reassured that she would regain her schoolgirl complexion (a treasure she had discovered she had by reading the *Woman's Own* herself to keep up with Sheila) and wouldn't as she feared, 'end up with hectic strawberry cheeks like the farmer's wife up the road'. She saw it all as the price she had to pay to belong to Sheila's world.

But now, since the Sunday incident, all that suffering had been in vain, for her mother had decreed that Sheila was to go nowhere in the evenings in future without Stella. It would take them back to their childhood, when Sheila had always to have Stella with her wherever she went, and they had both suffered, Sheila at having to keep an eye on a wild wee sister, and Stella having to sit through every sentimental musical Hollywood made. There was a puritanical streak in Stella that made her detest the frivolity of the musicals, and a complementary streak of Scottish realism that balked at the way people burst into song in what were to her the most incongruous situations. She didn't want Sheila socially, she just wanted her as an ally at home. Now that their mother was so unpredictable she needed Sheila more — Sheila was the last straw to which she clung; with growing consciousness since the Roberta episode, and since she had got a poetry book out of the library and read Stevenson's 'Home no more home to me. . .': it had struck her to the desolate core, and made her desperate: she couldn't face that feeling, yet it was in her, and she knew it.

So Stella argued bitterly with her mother's decree, but the more she argued the more her mother insisted. Sheila said nothing at the time. When her day off came, and she came downstairs in full battle-dress to go out, her mother instantly demanded, 'Where d'ye think *you're* goin', a' dressed up like a horse?' — adding, in a bitter parenthesis, ' — an' me wi' hardly a rag tae ma back'.

'Out wi' my pal,' Sheila answered, airily, straightening the seam of her fully-fashioned nylons.

'And *Stella.*' her mother snapped back.

'And ma Granny!' Sheila exclaimed, as if the whole idea was an outrageous joke.

'You don't take a step out that door without Stella,' her mother said, flat and final.

'Aw now Mum! Ye cannae *mean* it!' Sheila pleaded. 'Ma pal willnae want *Stella* there! Have a heart!'

'Stella, get your jacket on, you're goin' out wi' your sister!' was the only reply. Stella rose and put her jacket on, while Sheila fretted and fumed. Her mother took one of each of their arms and marched them to the door, put them out, and with a humorous, knowing 'See an' enjoy yersels!' shut the door behind them.

Stella's house of cards collapsed as soon as they were out the gate, for Sheila turned on her, snarling, 'You! you wee pig! You could've said you wouldnae go!'

'But then *you* wouldnae get either!' she protested.

'Ah — so ye say — you just let her dae't because you're jealous o' my fun and nosey about where I'll be!'

'No' me! I couldnae gi'e a *damn* where you go or what you dae!'

'Ye've nae friends o' yer ain, so ye think ye'll cash in on *my* act,' Sheila said, with deliberately cruel contempt.

It was the ultimate humiliation, which Stella had known would come. She hadn't known how she would react to it, and it was her own reaction she had dreaded; judging from her recent weak sentimentality, she had foreseen that she would be abject, forced at last against all her nature to beg. Once she'd done that, she thought, she was a goner; if she couldn't stand on her own two feet she wouldn't survive. It was with tremendous relief then that she felt her temper rising, and turned on her sister and said, between clenched teeth: 'Ma mither says I've to go wi' ye, and *I'm goin'* wi' ye, whether ye like it or no' — put *that* in your pipe and smoke it!'

'Ah'll run awa' frae ye!' Sheila tried.

'I can run faster than *you*, wi' your high-heels,' Stella sneered, disdainful and doggèd.

'Ah'll no' let ye visit me at the café . . .' Sheila blackmailed.

'Stick your café up yer *erse*, you shit!' Stella instantly responded, disgusted.

'Ah'll no' let ye cuddle intae ma back in the bed . . .'

'After this, Ah wouldnae touch ye wi' a ten-foot tarry *bargepole!*' Stella lashed back, and felt she meant it, and was delighted with herself.

Sheila walked faster, away from her, Stella caught up. 'Aw, fuck off, will ye?' Sheila roared, beside herself with frustration.

Pawkily, Stella said, 'Ye're awfu' desperate just about meetin' a *pal* . . .?' and let it hang in the air.

Sheila's resistance collapsed all at once, and she became persuasively confidential, 'OK, Ah'm meetin' a fella — if ye dinnae tell oor Mum, and ye behave yersel', ye can come.'

'Ah wouldnae *think* o' tellin' Mum — but I'm no' comin' tae be treated like a *dug,*' Stella bargained.

So they went down the road, negotiating terms, and as they talked Stella began to suspect that Sheila was, somewhere, and for reasons of her own, not entirely annoyed that she was coming too. When they came to the concert-hall, where Sheila was to meet the boy, Stella saw why: it wasn't a boy, it was a man, in his early twenties. In the process of their greetings and introductions, it became plainer to her that Sheila was beginning to actually admit to herself that she was glad she'd brought Stella, for her apologies to the man sounded entirely false.

Then there was really embarrassment when Sheila said to him, 'Do you mind . . . eh . . . you see . . . eh . . . I've only got two complimentary tickets . . . I didn't know I'd have to bring my wee sister, and I'll have to use one of them for her . . . I'm awfu' sorry . . . can ye buy yer ain?' Stella's cheeks burned; she looked away, but she instantly forgave Sheila everything — '*that* shouldnae happen tae a *dug,*' she thought, picturing the scene in the café where Sheila had met the man, and him asking her to the show, and her boasting that she had complimentary tickets, and now he was having to pay himself in. She looked at Sheila as the man went to get his own ticket: she too was as red as a beetroot. There and then Stella resolved to be as good as gold for the rest of the evening; she would be so good she'd be *invisible.*

After he'd got his ticket the man went over to the sweets kiosk and came back with a quarter-pound box of chocolates, and handed it to Sheila with a pleasant smile: 'What about your sister, what does *she* like?' he asked, mildly, not at all, to Stella's amazement, irritated.

'Oh thanks,' Sheila whispered, and Stella knew she was relieved at this proof that he could afford his ticket. Then 'Oh my wee sister's no' hungry — she's just had her tea!'

The man accepted this, and without further ado they went into the hall. Stella understood that Sheila wouldn't let him spend any money on her.

They sat down, the man first, then Sheila, then Stella at the end of the row. Until the lights went down Stella studied the other people coming in, leaving Sheila and the man to talk in peace. Shortly there was a roll on the drums which ended in an ear-splitting clash of cymbals, the curtains rose and the show was on. Stella had never been to one of these beach concerts; Skelf was the end of the line for tired old pros in the summertime, and the concerts were attended almost exclusively by older people who could endow the acts with the glamour they lacked through memories of better pre-war days. She anticipated that it would be like the Hollywood musicals without even the interest of the plot, and sat back with an inner groan, ready to withdraw into her daydreams.

But as soon as the dancers came out, tapping and pounding the boards, larger than life, she was drawn in: they were *real* people — much *realer*, she thought, than Fred Astaire and Gene Kelly and Jane Powell and Vera Ellen — they were all women, for a start: it had always particularly offended Stella to watch men pussy-footing all over the stage in the movies. Not a solitary man in her experience had done anything like that, or was *capable* of doing anything like that, and she thought Fred Astaire and Gene Kelly were silly asses, 'Jessies' was the word in her mind. But this was different: women crowded together, with thighs like Charles Atlas, lines of intense concentration and beads of sweat already breaking through their solid orange make-up, as they hoofed their way through 'There's No Business Like Show-business', singing wheezily but with genuine smiles of achievement on their faces, a sense of glamour. The pounding of their heels to the drummer's tempo, and the creaking of the boards, the warm lights, the intensity of the strange mixture of smells, the sheer laboured physicality of it all, gave Stella the same sense of warm, comforting animal intimacy she'd had one Friday night when she'd taken a walk to the farm and helped bring the beasts into the barn for milking. There, too, with the kerosene lanterns and the bustle; the steaming breath of the cows: their overwhelming sheer bulk and strength, jostling one another and the heat of them huddled together; then their restless rhythmic scraping of cobbles; the clank of the pails and the hiss of the udders when they were milked, had filled all her senses and taken up all her attention, with its simple here-and-now physical reality. She sat back, glowing, and forgot all about Sheila and the man.

The comedians and the stars were all human beings like herself; they spoke with broad Scots or local English accents, too; they performed sketches that weren't at all funny, but they were of familiar scenes, with familiar characters, plain and even uncouth — in all her reading and picture-going, Stella hadn't had anything like the inexplicable, intense pleasure she got when she saw one of the actresses in the character of a schoolgirl, demand a 'jelly piece' in a broad Glasgow accent. And then there was humour, too, in the way the actors and actresses, mostly as plain-looking as Co-op pies, tried with desperate finesse to indicate that they were only acting in these scenes, that in reality their own lives and personalities were glamorously, fastidiously, far removed from it: these were supremely human, plain folk trying to look like fancy folk acting plain folk; like battered old tramps hanging on to moth-eaten patchy fur coats, it was human vanity at its most lovable. It was a new magic to Stella.

She was still lost in it when the interval came, until Sheila nudged her in the ribs with barely concealed impatience: 'Bill says, are ye enjoyin' the show?'

'Eh? Oh *aye!*' she responded fervently.

They laughed. 'Next thing she'll be wantin' tae be an actress . . .' Sheila commented.

'No' me — Ah havenae the glamour an' Ah ken it,' Stella replied self-deprecatingly, and they laughed again, but kindly, and Sheila gave her a chocolate. Never mind it was the Coconut Ice, which they both hated, Stella appreciated the gesture like God and the widow's mite.

'Would ye like icecream?' the man asked Sheila.

'Yes please,' she answered demurely.

'And yer sister?'

Stella was about to nod when Sheila kicked her foot and said, 'Oh no, my sister doesnae like icecream — but she'll go and get it.'

He handed over the money, and Stella fought her way to the queue, and dodged her way smartly to the head of it to buy the icecream. Back in her seat, she immediately lapsed into invisibility, content to wait for the second half.

In the second half she became absorbed in the sets, and the rude mechanics of the changes, as the action and lights on stage became like emotional wallpaper, warm and homely and Christmassy. She was deeply impressed by the barefaced boldness with which the scenes were changed, by the bravura with which the backdrops were unrolled like the oilcloth maps for the school geography lesson, and everybody instantly accepted that they were in a country garden, or at the seaside: it was all make-believe, but open make-believe, not the Hollywood stuff that tried to pass for real. Every time a backdrop got stuck, or fell too fast with a thump, Stella's heart opened out just a little bit more to the whole enterprise. And to see adults playing 'let's pretend' like children was profoundly reassuring to her — it was the first clue she'd really had that their world wasn't entirely alien to hers. This, too, was more honest, for she saw them acting every day and not admitting it, and that more than anything sickened her of their world. She sat wide-eyed, soaking the whole experience up through every sense and impression.

But she was let down when the star came on, an accordian-player. The whole atmosphere changed; the lights went down a spotlight focussed on him as the inside curtain rose after the comedians bowed off, and the audience went silent. He was dressed in full tartan, youngish compared to the rest of the performance, and stern-faced with the seriousness of the artiste. Stella instantly recognised that here was an ordinary self-deceiving adult, the reverential atmosphere in the audience told her that as much as his appearance. 'Buggar it, here we go!' she thought, leaning back and gazing up into the darkness, detaching herself totally. He began to play 'There's a long long trail a-winding,' and she thought 'Christ, Ah hope it's no' *too* long!' and turned automatically to share the humour with Sheila. Then she discovered that Sheila was holding the man's hand and had herself entered into the sentimentality of it all, gazing romantically at the accordionist. 'Love a bloody duck!' Stella thought, scornfully, and looked a second longer, just long enough to get a warning sideways flash from Sheila's eye: Sheila had read her thoughts. She instantly looked back at the stage, where the accordionist was playing mournfully and sentimentally on, and contented herself for the rest of the time with unspoken sneers: 'God help us!', a melodramatic 'When will it ever *end?*'

*against
sentimentality*

learned from the movies, and 'Stop, it's too much, ye're breakin'
ma heart!'

There was wild applause and patriotic cheering at the end of the
tune, and the stern performer, mollified by the appreciation, conceded a community-singing of 'Ma Granny's Hieland Hame'.
Unable to look at the hypocrisy on the stage, and unable to look at
Sheila, for she could hear her nervously joining in the singing with
the man, Stella looked across the aisle to the other folk in the audience. They were all swaying in their seats, and singing gently,
completely taken in. One big fat downtrodden woman that Stella
knew from the paper-round actually had tears in her eyes, and the
sight of her stabbed Stella to the heart. 'Oh please Missis, dinnae
greet for *that!*' she begged in her head, 'No' for *that*. Your Granny
didnae ha'e a Heiland Hame, and ye've never seen heather *bloody*
bells in your life, like masel'. Dinnae greet — *fight!*' She didn't
know what she meant herself, but she looked back at the stage
where the accordionist was basking in the audience's sentimentality, and she hated him like poison for his patronage.

He finished his act with 'The Last Post', for which he stood up
and gazed poignantly, nobly, into the middle-distance. There were
sighs of genuine sadness from the audience: memories of the war
seemed to rise like ghosts in the hall, and Stella was torn between
succumbing to their decent sentiment and hating the accordionist
even more for his manipulation. After a minute she had learned to
live with both feelings, letting her heart go with the people round
her, and criticising the star as hard as she could. As he turned his
head to the side and tilted it upwards, bracing his body against his
instrument and standing feet firmly apart trying to look like a War
Memorial, she thought, she was suddenly struck by his resem-
blance to a constipated dog: the same sad liquid eyes with a tinge of
desperate awareness in the whites: the same clenched-teeth set of
the jaw, the same trapped rigidity and concentration. She relaxed
— it was revenge enough.

All the same she was glad when the comedians came back on.
Then, to exorcise the bad spirit she looked back again at the fat
woman. This time she was laughing helplessly at a coarse joke, and
Stella's spirits rose to exultation in relief. She enjoyed the rest of
the show like she'd never enjoyed anything in her life. She felt as if

133

they were all inside a magic lantern, the actors and the audience both.

Outside again, the man said to Sheila, 'Would you like to come for a drink in the café?'

'Oh,' Sheila hesitated, embarrassed by this lavishness. She'd only ever been out on dates with boys with no money before.

Stella stood to one side, shuffling her feet and impressed out of her mind — chocolates, icecream, a drink — 'God Almighty! Ah think Ah've died an' went tae Heaven!' she thought with just a touch of self-mockery.

'Oh come on,' the man urged, not knowing why Sheila hesitated, ' — it's early yet!'

'. . . if you're sure it's no' too much. . .?' Sheila still hesitated delicate.

'Eh? No, no! I like tae treat a lassie when I tak' her out!' he asserted, smiling.

'OK then,' Sheila agreed, ' — but no' *my* café?' and they moved off, Stella in train, studying the man who in his generosity was almost a new species to her:

'A' that, for *nuthin'!*' she exclaimed to herself, shaking her head . . . men were weird, and bigger-hearted than women.

They walked along the promenade to a café, and went in. Sheila and Stella sat down on the rickety chairs, Stella not pulling hers in to the table as Sheila did. The man hovered till they had settled, then said to Sheila with a twinkle of self-congratulation at his relative sophistication:

'A milk-shake a' right for ye?'

'Oh aye!' Sheila exclaimed, not hiding her gratification.

'An' yer sister?' — he nodded in Stella's direction.

Stella hastily said, 'Oh no, nothin' for me, thanks — Ah'm no' thirsty!' and Sheila added, with equal haste, 'She doesnae drink much at a'.'

The man walked over to the counter, and Sheila gave Stella a silent nod of approval. He came back with two milk-shakes and a glass of lemonade for Stella: 'Surely ye'll manage *that,*' he said, pushing it over to her.

'Thank you. You shouldnae have bothered,' Stella said meekly, restraining herself from seizing the glass and gulping the drink down in a oner: it had been hot in the hall. She waited till the man and her sister were on their second draw at their straws, before she lifted her glass self-consciously and took a modest sip. They were finished with their — to Stella — huge milk-shakes while she was only half way through her lemonade, and sat gazing into each other's eyes like film stars. To have to sip was exquisite torture to Stella, to have to sip and pretend she wasn't there strained her to the limits of endurance. She was glad when they at last stood up, and the man said to her, 'Hurry up and finish, we're goin',' for it meant that she could take the last third of the drink in one satisfying thirst-quenching gulp. As she was rising she noticed that Sheila had left half an ounce of milk-shake in the bottom of her glass. Concerned, she pointed it out: 'Sheila, you've no' finished yours!' Sheila gave her a killing look, said with synthetic sweetness, 'Oh, it's a' I could manage,' and turned a shy little female smile on the man. Stella still hesitated half-risen from her seat, her backside sticking out like a duck. They had turned away to go. She struggled with temptation, and, giving in, stretched out her hand to Sheila's glass eyeing their backs warily. But Sheila had read her mind again and looked round, flashing her a 'Just you dare!' look. Stella returned an 'Oh well, you know it was worth a try' shrug and ruefully got up and followed, not without a jealous glance over her shoulder.

When she got outside the man was saying, 'What about the shows? They're still on . . .' This time Sheila's still childish passion for the shows overcame any notions of delicacy. Or maybe it was she had conquered him with her eyes in the café, and had confidence now. Anyway, she instantly agreed, 'Oh aye!', and they walked towards the bright lights and blaring music, an overawed Stella trailing in their wake. '. . . How could anybody have that much money? Maybe he's a bank robber. . .'

Although Stella didn't get on any of the rides at the shows, it was enough for her to be there so late at night, and anyway she often came just to watch and listen — she was born to window-shop, and she knew it. She stood enthralled, still with the magic lantern feeling on her, for the showmen with their dirty faces looked like actors in the gaudy carnival lights, and moved about sure-footed among the dangerous, powerful machinery with breathtaking bravado; and the music was still brash and larger than life, and went through her with a tawdry poignancy, so great was the contrast between the words of the songs and the volume of sound, yet so well did the words and their rhythms suit the actions going on all around. There was something right to her about listening to the aggressive misery of 'Love Oh Love Oh Careless Love' while watching the frustrated violence of the dodgems, which could be made to bang into one another, but never quite hard enough. She watched Sheila and the man have turn after turn, with an irony almost maternal as Sheila screamed and clung to him.

This was the same Sheila who only last Easter had always insisted on driving the dodgem, and had scared her, Stella, half to death with her boldness . . .

At last it was over, and they walked up the road, Sheila and the man in front, hand in hand, and Stella behind, self-conscious, straying out to the side now and again like a family dog, impatient with their slow pace. They came to a corner not two hundred yards from their own house, and Sheila said, 'Wait for me round the corner, I'm going to say goodnight to Bill.'

'But we're no' hame yet,' Stella objected.

'Bill lives just down there,' Sheila answered, nodding in the direction of a tenement block.

'There? Where?' Stella was curious; she knew everybody who lived there.

'With the Finnegans,' Bill answered, forestalling the impatient reply which Sheila was spluttering over in an effort not to swear.

'The *Finnegans!*' Stella was shocked. The Finnegans weren't so much a family as a tribe; there were fourteen of them in a four-roomed house, and they looked and lived like a colony of monkeys — all reddish-brown-haired and thickly freckled, and going in and out of their house as often by the windows as the doors. Stella's first thought was to wonder by what miracle he managed to come out of there with money in his pocket and his suit not only intact but well-pressed. 'The Finnegans!'

'*Round the corner!*' Stella was peremptory, seeing that even *his* remarkable *savoir-faire* couldn't save him from being embarrassed at Stella's open-mouthed incredulity.

Stella went away round the corner and waited, muttering to herself, 'Oh moosh-ity, mooshity moosh, hurry up an' get on wi't!'

Eventually they emerged and, saying nothing more than a quiet 'Cheerio,' went their separate ways. Stella ran to catch up with Sheila, who had begun to hurry at last, it was so late. Her first words were, 'Does he really live wi' the Finnegans?'

'Aye,' Sheila answered, obviously puzzled herself.

'Whaur will he *sleep?*'

'God knows, eh?' Sheila was rapidly becoming sheepishly embarrassed; if she'd known he lived with the Finnegans she wouldn't have dreamed on going out with him. 'But he's only a visitor . . . he says he's got his own room . . .'

'*They've* got a bloody neck, advertisin' for payin' guests! Christ, if *he's* got a room tae 'msel', whaur the hell's a' the Finnegans sleepin'?'

'Search me!' Sheila laughed.

'Why? Have ye yin in yer bag?' Stella returned quickly.

They walked along thinking for a few seconds, then Stella broke in again with: 'It must be like the Ball o' Kirriemuir, eh? — "There was Finnegans in the haystacks, there was Finnegans in the ricks" . . .' she chanted.

' "An' if ye lifted oot the mortar ye'd ha'e Finnegans in the bricks"!' Sheila added, and they burst into gales of laughter all the heartier because of the release from their social straitjackets.

They were late in coming in, but Stella was master of the situation. As soon as she got in the door, as she was taking off her coat, she complained to her mother: 'Aw look Mum dinnae mak' me go oot wi' Sheila again tae her mouldy pals — they did nothin' but hoach about listenin' tae Eve Boswell an' talkin' about laddies a' nicht! I'm no' goin' back, no' for love nor money, an' that's that! Forbye, we got nowt tae eat an' Ah'm stervin' can I get a piece on cheese?' The last all in one breath, an insidious bit of flattery implying that her mother was more generous than the friends'.

'Aye, hen,' her mother said, sympathetic, and went to put the kettle on, saying only to Sheila, 'Ye micht have done somethin' tae entertain the bairn — she didnae *ask* tae go wi' ye, after a'.'

That night Stella hardly slept a wink, stirred to the bowels with excitement at the new and vivid picture of the privileges of the grown-up world, suspecting them, too — wondering why on earth a bloke would spend all that money on Sheila for nothing. At one point she turned her head to Sheila at her back, who she sensed wasn't sleeping either, and whispered, 'Why *would* a fella spend a' that money on ye, Sheila, for nuthin'?'

'For the pleasure o' yer company,' Sheila answered promptly, straight out of the *Woman's Own.*

'And why did ye leave yer milk-shake?'

'It's ladylike no' tae finish a' thing.'

'*Ladylike?*'

'Tae show ye're no' a greedy pig like you,' Sheila whispered, giving her a push with her foot to her own side of the bed, for she'd been quietly edging into the middle, ' — move owre!'

Stella lay still then, and thought yearningly of the milk-shake: she'd never been so close to a milk-shake in her life before, 'Ah'd ha'e gi'en ma richt *airm* for that milk-shake!' she whispered fervently, and her belly rumbled loudly as if to second the motion.

'Oh, it was great!' Sheila exclaimed, taunting, ' — creamy an' smooth an' *delicious!*' — she smacked her lips — 'yummy! It jist *slid* doon!'

'Lucky devil!' Stella muttered, consumed with jealousy.

'. . . *slid* doon! Fu' o' icecream it was! An! *chocolatey* — ? !' Sheila taunted on.

'Shut up! Ah cannae bear it!' Stella moaned, clutching her stomach and drooling. 'It's almost worth havin' a boyfriend an' lettin' yersel' get mooshed for!'

'Was you watchin' us frae the corner ya rat?' Sheila instantly exclaimed.

'Gadsake no! I was just thinkin' I believe I could staund even kissin' if there was a milk-shake in sicht . . .' she yearned.

'Weel, ye'll ha'e a while tae wait afore anybody wants tae kiss *you*, let *alone* buy ye a milk-shake, so shut your weary peepers an' sleep . . .'

Stella's spirits ran high for a week after, with looking forward to growing up. She ignored all her mother's moods and sournesses as being just peculiar to her mother, and drifted away down the beach every day, haunting the café, only going home for lunch and tea. One day she came back from lunch to find Sheila and the manageress in the froth of excitement.

'A man was just in, just this minute, and had a cup o' tea an' gi'ed me a three-bob tip!' Sheila exclaimed with shining eyes.

'Ah dinnae believe ye!' Stella scoffed: it was unthinkable.

'He was drunk,' put in the manageress, a plain woman in every way.

'Really?' Stella asked, 'Show me!' And Sheila held out her hand with two shillings and two sixpences in it. 'God Almighty!'

'Just for a fivepenny cup o' tea,' Sheila boasted.

'Why?'

'I think he fancied me,' she preened.

'He was drunk,' the manageress broke in again.

'Just like that?' Stella asked.

'Just like that — three bob!' Sheila laughed.

'Maybe he'd gi'e *me* something tae, if he's in the mood tae fling his money awa',' Stella mused, suddenly desperately greedy, and made for the door. 'What was he like? Where did he go?'

'Dinnae you *think* on it, a drunk man, a young lassie like you!' the manageress cautioned.

'A wee fella in's thirties wi' fair hair an' a red face, in workin' claes — that wey,' Sheila obliged.

Stella ran out and along the promenade till she saw the man, a little rolling bricklayer, burnt red by the sun. She came up behind him, and followed him at a slow pace to get her breath back. He was reeling from side to side of the pavement, but still managing to walk. 'Why should Sheila get a' the luck?' she thought, 'What's wrong wi' *me?* — I'll ha'e a bash this once!' and she came alongside him, then discovered she didn't know what to say. The man opened the conversation, however, half-turning his head and slurring out an over-friendly, nearly maudlin, 'Hallo dear!' Stella reckoned she could get away without finesse, and straightaway got down to brass tacks, 'Are you the man that was in the café there an' gi'ed my sister a three-bob tip?'

'Yesh,' he answered, then protested, 'Ah'm no wantin' it back!' shaking his head so vehemently that he had to lean on the putting-green fence to stop himself falling. The wattle-fence gave under his weight, and he began to keel gracefully over like the last moments of a sinking ship. Stella hauled on the arm nearest to her and righted him, 'Nae fear ye'll get it back! . . . min, ye nearly had yer head in the eighteenth hole!' He laughed, then became suddenly sentimental, 'Ish tha' yer shishter? A fine-lookin' lassie!'

'What aboot me? Ah'm no' bad masel'!' Stella was practically aggressive in her ham-handed effort at flirtation.

Without even looking at her, he said, 'Aye, you're a fine lash tae, hen . . .' and sunk back against the putting-green fence, while Stella sought desperately for what to say next. She pulled him up again, averting her head from the smell of drink, and he said, 'Thanksh dear,' lugubriously. Then he noticed her for the first time, and put two and two together: 'So ye are. How about comin' along the beach wi' me pet. . .?' He looked at her and she saw his eyes were as red as his face, and was revolted, but determined to soldier on. He continued, with a stiff leer which expressed itself more in the rolling of his eyes than in any movement of muscle, '. . . an' Ah'll show ye . . . somethin', an' let ye play wi't, an' gie ye money tae.'

'Aye, a' right,' Stella answered not understanding. 'But I'm thirsty — will ye buy me a drink first?'

'Surely!' he exclaimed, 'Lead the way!' She walked beside him, steering him towards the café where Sheila and the man had taken her a week ago, keeping her eyes on the ground to avoid the glances of passers-by, on the same principle that an ostrich buries its head in the sand.

They arrived at the café and he pulled himself together a bit, and stood back to let her in first, like a gentleman. She stood beside him at the counter as he said to the man serving, 'A cup o' coffee — awfu' black, son, will ye? An' gie the lashie here wha' she wansh. Wha' ye wan', darlin'?' He put his arm on her shoulder in such a way that Stella wasn't sure if it was fatherly or what, and she thought, 'I may's well be hung for a sheep as a lamb.' and said boldly, 'A milk-shake.' The man didn't bat an eyelid.

'Gi'e her a milk-shake, Jimmy,' he ordered, swaying on his feet.
'A milk-shake it is!' said the waiter with false gusto. 'What flavour?'

'Wha' flavour, hen?' the man repeated.

'A green one,' Stella said.

'One green milk-shake coming up!' said the waiter, mixing it.

The man swayed on his feet again, 'Would you bring ma coffee darlin'?' he asked pathetically, handing the man a ten-shilling note before stumbling over to a table. Stella collected the coffee and the milk-shake and the change, and, still with her head in the sand, took them to his table. He shored sugar into his coffee and, to her disappointment, pocketed his change. Ignoring the sound of him slurping his coffee, she concentrated on the milk-shake, drawing on the straw as long as she could till she felt her lungs would burst.

The man was reviving. He looked up from his coffee and leered stiffly at her again, the pale blue of his irises looking strangely cold and watery in his brick-red face: 'And after this we'll go along to the sand, eh? And I'll let you play wi' somethin'?' then he stuck his rough boiler-suited knee between hers under the table, and she suddenly got an inkling of what he meant.

Her heart stopped but she smiled, 'Aye,' pushing her chair to get away from his intrusive knee, and bending down her head, concentrating on her milk-shake to stall for time. But her very lips quivered on the straw, and she panicked, standing up suddenly and pushing her chair further back with a rasp.

'What'sh the matter?' he asked, in his sudden alarm betraying a clearer consciousness than before.

'Oh — nothing,' Stella faltered. 'I need the bathroom that's a' — I'll be right back!' She tried to walk casually out of the café, but she was trembling like a leaf from head to foot. Once outside the door she ran like the wind, feeling that her legs would collapse under her any time, and took refuge in the ladies' toilet across the road. She leaned over the sink, grateful for the coolness of it, and was suddenly foaming sick. 'Aw God, ma bloody milk-shake!' she thought tragically. 'One green milk-shake coming up a' right!'

When she'd come to herself she stood in the doorway of the toilets, waiting and watching for the man to pass, so she could feel safe. Eventually he emerged from the café, and she half-hid, watching to be sure of which way he went. He wasn't looking for her; he just lurched along the road in the direction of the beach. She stood outside, breathing deep. Gradually a thought came over her. On an impulse she ran across the road back into the café. Her milk-shake, half-finished, still sat on the table. She went to it and sat down and began to drink. After a few seconds she felt uneasy and looked up: other customers, who hadn't been there when she came in with the man, were gazing at her in some astonishment and disdain. She tried to look as if it was her right, but became acutely embarrassed, and got up quietly again, but this time couldn't stop herself from running out of the café and, indeed, ran half-way home before she felt she had shaken off those looks.

Once she had got her breath back she had no defence against the sense of black-burning shame that washed over her like a tidal wave. 'My God!' she thought in despair, 'I'm just rubbish! A scab on the face o' the earth!' She stumbled home, the tears blinding her, numb with self-disgust, thinking of herself as the most revolting scavenging hanger-on she'd ever heard of. Only her mother was in the house, the bairns were all out playing.

'What's the matter wi' you?' her mother asked, shocked at her begrutten appearance.

'Ah dinnae ken. . .!' Stella howled, and broke down completely.

'Eh — ye're a strange lassie . . .' her mother shook her head, bemused, but took a clean towel off the fire-guard and gave it to her to cry in. It was warm, it was a comfort, it had the fresh-air smell she associated with her mother's care, and she sobbed her sob out luxuriously. Then she got up:

'Where are ye goin' noo, Sarah Bernhardt?' her mother enquired, still rather stunned by the passionate performance, and worried about her.

'Just tae pee,' Stella answered. She went to the toilet and sat depressed, her knickers at her ankles. 'Sheila gets a' that — chocolates an' a' thing — for a kiss, an' I'm supposed to play wi' a dirty wee brickie's dirty wee dickie for a bloody milk-shake — what's *wrang* wi' *me?*' she tortured herself, and gloomily rested her head on her hands, staring at the gussett of her knickers because the navy blue toned in with her dismal mood. After a while she became aware she was staring at a few drops of blood — unmistakably blood. Her knickers still at her ankles, she hobbled out to her mother in the kitchen, 'Mum, look at me breeks — Ah think it's ma period, eh?'

Her mother had been sitting gazing into space with a shirt of her father's in her hand, ready to sew a button on. She put it down and peered at Stella's knickers: 'Aye, so ye have! Wait an' Ah'll get you a sanitary towel.' She got a sanitary towel then rummaged around in the sideboard drawer and brought out a wizened old sanitary belt, while Stella stood like a statue, trying to take it in that she had her period.

'Put this on,' her mother said, handing her the towel and belt.

'Ah dinnae ken how,' Stella admitted, feeling gauche.

Her mother looped the towel on to the belt for her, and Stella stepped into it then pulled up her knickers and went back to flush the toilet, still stunned. '*That's* why Ah've been so peculiar — like Roberta,' she thought, and came through and sat down on her father's chair at the fire, opposite her mother.

'Eh aye . . .' her mother sighed, '. . . I suppose you're a woman noo.'

Stella had a sudden insight. 'No' yet I don't think,' she said, with a quiet, fading hope.

Not hearing her, her mother went on 'Eh aye . . . it's gey early . . .' and trailed off into her own thoughts, putting her chin on her hand, and resting her elbow on her knee, gazing into the fire. Stella did the same, and sat there, unconsciously a young replica of her mother, even to the expression.

CHAPTER 8

Little Women

A week or two later, wee Mrs McCosh from the Salvation Army came to the door, asking for Stella. Her mother didn't invite her in, she treated her more like a pal of Stella's than like another adult. Stella was embarrassed, but wee Mrs McCosh was humble and apologetic with her mother, who quickly left them to themselves.

'Eh . . . Stella . . . Ah was wonderin' if you could help me out?' she began, uncertain of her reception and a bit harassed by having had to talk to Stella's mother.

'Aye! Of course!' — the longer Sheila worked the more dependant and useless Stella felt. 'What wi'?'

'It would be a wee bit money tae ye; it's just a wee job for one day on Thursday.'

'What daein'?'

'Ye ken I sometimes work for the Co-op . . . well we cater for trips now and again, and there's a couple o' buses o' auld-age pensioners comin' in for their dinner and tea, that was cancelled somewhere else.'

'I cannae cook,' Stella hastened to say, embarrassed.

'No, no! It's a' ready cooked, ye'd just need tae serve up and spread the pieces an' help wi' the dishes.'

'That's a' richt then.'

'It's at the kirk hall — '

'No' the bloody kirk hall!' Stella thought. She hadn't been back since she took change for her threepenny, and had developed a superstition about the place.

' — if ye'll come aboot ten. Ye'll be a' day though, mind! Till

144

about seven at night!'

'Will I get ma dinner?' Stella put in, anxiously.

'Oh aye, ye'll get that, an' yer tea tae — the store disnae stint ye!' Mrs McCosh was proud of her association with the Co-op, even though it was on a freelance basis, and straightened up an inch, 'And ye'll get at least seven bob for the day . . .' She had saved the best to last.

'By jings! Who'll be there?' No' the minister?'

'No, no, it's got nowt tae dae wi' the minister. It's a Co-op do. There'll just be me an' twa — three o' ma freends — wee Mrs Henderson frae the Army, ye minds o' her? Daft Georgie's mother?'

'Oh aye, I mind her fine — a nice woman. Oh, in that case, I'll maybe enjoy masel',' Stella warmed to the idea, the couthiness of the Salvation Army stalwarts coming back to her.

'And mak' a wee bit pin-money.' Mrs McCosh was beside herself with pride at being on the employing end of business for a change.

'Thanks a lot, Mrs McCosh. Who's organising it?' Stella asked, more to give the woman her due than out of curiosity, for she believed she already knew.

'Ah've been asked tae dae it,' Mrs McCosh announced — a brain surgeon asked to operate on the queen couldn't have spoken with a more fraught sense of responsibility, and the shadow of the burden crossed her brow.

'Well, Ah'll be there — Ah'll no' let you doon,' Stella reassured her, and the brow cleared.

'Ah thocht ye'd be aiblins owre guid for tae serve at tables noo Ah heard ye've gotten intae the Hige Skule. Ye must be a clever lassie!' and Mrs McCosh looked up to her, with a smile that was wryly comic.

'Me?' Stella was flattered, amazed, and humbled all at once. 'No' me, Mrs McCosh! Owre guid tae serve at a table? I'm just delighted to get the chance tae mak' a bit cash . . . oh aye, I'll be joinin' the *aristocracy* next month, but I'm still savin' up for my blazer,' she confessed, not sorry to do so though she heard her mother clearing her throat in warning from behind the kitchen door.

'Guid lassie!' Mrs McCosh said, with a look that congratulated her for the confession as well as the saving virtue. 'Ah weel, Ah'll awa' doon the road for ma man's tea comin' in. Ye'll mind Thursday?' and she started off down the path.

'Trust me for that!' Stella called after her, and shut the door.

Her mother was in the huff when she entered the kitchen. 'What have ye tae tell a' the family secrets for tae the likes o' Mrs McCosh? Noo she'll be tellin' a'body I cannae afford ye a blazer!'

'Well, ye cannae, can ye?' Stella said, puzzled.

'*Ah* ken that, an' *you* ken that, but does *a'body* ha'e tae ken it?'

'Och, come awa' Mum, Mrs McCosh willnae think twice about it, a woman that cannae afford a decent coat tae'r *ain back*!'

'Oh, whit Ah'm tae dae wi you God knows, oor Stella! The skule maister tells me ye're clever but for a clever lassie you're as thick as ma finger! Just mak' sure ye dinnae show yersel' up at this do, in front o' yer precious Mrs McCosh that thinks sae much o' ye! . . . an' her man no' sober twa days in a row . . .' she added, as if to herself, but for Stella's benefit.

'Ah'll need a pinny,' Stella said, ignoring the jealousy.

Ironing the apron on the Wednesday night, Stella realised that she'd never in her life served at a table; at home they had only one tiny kitchen table at which her parents sat, and the rest of the family took their meals on their laps, except for the youngest ones, who squatted on the floor with theirs. She got more and more nervous about it the more she thought of it, and though the thought that she'd be working with the Army women was a comfort in some ways, it was a drawback in others, for, it occurred to her, 'What will they think o' me that's supposed to be brainy, and hasnae a clue how to set a table or dish up the grub?' Her father was sitting near her at the fireplace reading his book, and she asked him, 'Dad, how dae ye serve tables?'

'How would Ah ken? Ah'm no' a bluidy nancy-boy waiter!' he laughed. 'That's women's work — ask your mother.'

'No but — how do you *think* you would serve tables?' she persisted, not wishing to ask her mother and get a long lecture covering the whole family history of servitude for three generations, and to have it pointed out yet again that for a brainy lassie she was thick as a brick.

'What tae hell's sae hard aboot shovin' folks' grub doon for them? Yere mither does it every day!'

'But in a polite way?'

'Wha's gonna be at this do? The Queen o' Sheba?'

'Pensioners just.'

'Pensioners?' he laughed. 'In that case I'd advise ye tae draw back your hand quick when ye put doon the plates, or they'll ha'e eaten it before ye can say "knife"! Auld folk's a lot o' gannets for their grub — ye should ken that — look at your Auntie Belle' — the last was said bitterly, part of his running feud with his aunt-in-law. 'They'll be so keen tae get it they'll no' notice if you just fling it on the table withoot a plate! — and ye'd better tak' earplugs if they're gettin' soup — how mony is there?'

Stella laughed, relieved: 'Twa buses.'

'Twa busloads. Gey near eighty!' he was enjoying himself, seeing her cheer up, '. . . an' no' a tooth among them, I'll bet!'

So it was a confident Stella that strolled down to the church hall in good time the next morning. The others were already in the kitchen at the back: wee Mrs McCosh, daft Geordie's mother Belle, Nellie Kinkaid, Cissy, and a girl of about fifteen or sixteen, tall and slim, fair-skinned and dark-haired, fine-featured, to whom Stella was immediately attracted. The kitchen was tiny, which Stella thought was typical of kirk hypocrisy somehow, and it felt a lot smaller than it actually was because almost every available work-top was laden with baker's trays full of bread and cakes and tea-bread, and stacks of plates. The four wee women, two shulpit and two brosey — the latter with their sleeves rolled up as usual showing their pudgy arms with the dimples at the elbows that made you feel that somewhere they had never grown up, and were chubby babies still — bustled about with a ham-handed practicality much as you would imagine Santa's gnomes would, touchingly willing, touchingly self-important, and murmuring inconsequentially among themselves the whole time. As the girl, busy too, slipped expertly around and between them, with a pleasant smile,

Stella was reminded of an illustration of *Snow White and the Seven Dwarves*. There was a clatter and jingle of boxes of cutlery being moved, and a kettle sung on the stove.

'Oh it's yoursel', Stella!' wee Mrs McCosh greeted her enthusiastically when she noticed her standing in the doorway. 'An' ye've your pinny — good lass!' Now the extra pair of hands was here, Mrs McCosh took a breather, and, hands on hips, surveyed her domain to see what she could find Stella to do. 'Ah'll tell ye what,' she suggested, as if suddenly inspired, 'mak' us a' a cup o' tea, there's a guid lass! The kettle's boilin', and the teapot's in the press wi' the cups and the tea. You'll get a bottle o' milk out the crate there . . .' she nodded towards the corner.

Stella immediately set to, squeezing through between the solid cushioning of Nellie's backside and Cissie's belly, and not able to step back, for the two of them took up the width of the kitchen. 'Ye're a pund or twa mair than ye need there, Cis!' Stella joked as she finally worked herself out and went to the cupboard.

'Och the doctor's aye puttin' me on a diet but it doesnae mak' a blind bit o' difference,' Cissie defended herself.

'That's because she has the diet then she has her ordinary grub,' Nellie commented, red in the face as she straightened up with the cake she'd just picked off the floor, 'I keep tellin' ye, Cis, that ye ha'e what it says on the paper the doctor gi'es ye an' no' a crumb mair . . . but no' Cissie — first she has the boiled egg an' the cracker, then she has her breakfast as usual — ye're an' awfu' case!'

'Help ma Hannah, what the doctor has on yon bit paper wouldnae keep a sparra alive!' Cissie complained.

'Ach, you an' me'll never be slim, Cis,' Nellie consoled, 'our bodies wasnae made for 't . . .'

'Onyway, ma man's happy — he says he likes a wumman he can get a grip o',' Cissie was defiantly confident.

'Ye neednae tell us that — we've the proof in front o' our e'en!' wee Mrs McCosh, leaning on the sink shaking with laughter at this time-honoured interchange, broke in. Cissie had eight children.

'Here's yer tea,' Stella interrupted. 'Whaur d'ye want it?'

'Just in oor hand, hen — there's naeplace to put it down,' Mrs McCosh instructed.

As Stella handed Nellie her cup, Nellie looked at the cake in her hand with feigned bewilderment, and turned to wee Mrs MCosh: 'Ah'll better just ha'e this masel', Isa — it's been on the floor an' God knows what germs it'll ha'e picked up . . .' But she waited for Mrs McCosh's OK before she bit into it.

Wee Mrs McCosh was magnaminous, 'OK Nellie, but we may's weel a' ha'e a cake if you're ha'ein' one — help yoursel's ladies, a handfu' o' cakes'll no' be missed . . . onywey,' she went on, knowledgeably, 'auld folk ha'e appetites like birds — they'll never manage a' this in a month o' Sundays. We'll a' be goin' hame laden wi' the left-owres the nicht!'

They reached out severally to the tray nearest them, and took a cake with assumed innocence, and in the course of the cup of tea, Stella was introduced to the girl, Morag, who turned out to be daft Geordie's mother's niece from Edinburgh. While Mrs McCosh was explaining the relationship, Stella caught sight of the look on Belle's face, pleased with herself for being able to produce such a fine-looking relation, but timorous about claiming the relationship herself. It gave Stella, with her newly-aroused womanly sympathies, a fleeting insight into what it must be like to be Daft Geordie's mother, and the protective instinct she had kept rigidly down after the rebuff by Roberta, sprung up now that her defences were lowered with these innocent little women. It was plain, too, that the meek quality of passive suffering that never raised its head in protest brought out a womanly protective tenderness in the niece, for she kept referring deferentially to Belle every chance she got — 'Isn't that right, Auntie Belle?' and, 'My Auntie Belle says . . .' Among all the chaff and banter of the teabreak, Stella studied them both with dark eyes, saying very little.

'Oh weel, ladies, back tae work or the puir auld sowels will have tae be waitin' wi' their tongues hangin' out for their dinner!' wee Mrs McCosh exclaimed eventually, pulling herself together with an effort as if she could have stood there all day, and unconsciously holding out her hands for their cups as if she were in her own kitchen and not the boss. Suddenly realising it, she made a privilege out of it: 'Ah'll just wash up the cups, Cis, if you and Nellie will put the tables up. Stella and Morag can start bringing down the cutlery, and . . .' she faltered, overwhelmed with this evidence of her own management abilities, scarcely able to believe her own ears, '. . . and Belle and me'll start settin' up the chairs.'

The bustle started up again, after a brief hiatus of laughter when Cissie and Nellie both tried to get through the kitchen door at one time. Stella followed Morag to the boxes of cutlery, content to take her lead, for it seemed Morag knew what she was doing. They lifted the first heavy box of knives between them, and edged through the door, not speaking to each other but listening to Cissie and Nellie's exaggerated grunts and groans as they lifted the heavy trestle-tables over from the walls.

'God helps!' Cissie was exclaiming as she and Nellie tried to lift one of the longer tables, and Stella and Morag were coming into the hall with the spoons. 'Ah doubt Ah'm failin', Nell — this one's owre much for me!'

'What's wrang? *Ma* end's a' richt . . .' Nellie enquired, exasperated, studying what Cissie was doing from the other end of the table. Then she said drily: 'Maybe if ye lifted yer foot up off the leg ye'd manage better . . .'

'Naw!' Cissie exclaimed, looking down and moving her foot. 'Mak' nae wonder Ah couldnae lift it — Ah was tryin' tae lift masel' an' a'!'

Morag and Stella collapsed with laughter, dropping the spoons with a clash that echoed through the empty hall, and holding their sides. 'Oh my God, Cissie, ye're too much for me!' Stella gasped, wiping her eyes with her apron. Morag, leaning against the door and laughing silently but helplessly, laid her hand on Stella's arm in agreement, and Stella was electrically conscious of it, her laughter abruptly tailing off. Nobody in Skelf touched anybody else casually; it always meant something. Stella slipped into a kind of daze, in which her heart seemed to heat up like a stove, and make her whole body glow; she blushed and couldn't hide it, but stooped to pick up the spoon-box in an attempt to do so.

As they laid down the last box with the forks, Stella, still burning strangely, looked Morag full in the face. Morag just smiled faintly, the same soft-eyed smile as Belle's, warm and self-deprecating. Stella had never had anything like tenderness from a woman before in her life, she had only seen it from a distance, and always between a man and a woman. She only knew one way to respond:

she fell in love. Her heart beat like a trip-hammer.

But it wasn't till they had rolled out the huge paper table-cloths over the tables that stretched the length of the hall, and were setting out the cutlery, that she realised that this was what it was. All the meantime she had been gone in a daze, only the slight, automatic part of her conscious mind working and preventing her from still standing there, feeling that smile. She laid out all the cutlery down her side of the table, then Nellie came over to set out the napkins and exclaimed quietly to her, 'Hey Stella! are you left-handed or what?' pointing to the cutlery she'd set. It was all the wrong way round.

'Oh God!' Stella blushed deeply. 'I'll sort it!'

'No, no,' Nellie laughed, 'I'll fix it as I go along wi' the napkins. Will ye help me wi' them?'

'Aye!' Stella agreed at once, grateful to her for not making her mistake public. Nellie took a paper napkin off the pile in front of her and began to fold it, 'I thought I'd dae it fancy, the way I learned when I worked in the hotel, just for the auld folk like, tae mak' it nice for them. Can you do it like this?' and she held up a napkin folded like a boat. She'd done it as quickly as she spoke, and Stella was deeply impressed:

'No! But if you'll show me again slow, I'll try.'

Nellie showed her and Stella said, 'That's marvellous, Nellie — real delicate!' and tried to do it herself. Nellie had to help her again and again for about five minutes till she could get it right and in the end Stella became as much impressed by her patience as by her skill. As they moved up the tables with the napkins her mind was working on two levels at once: 'I'm in love — *in love* for Godsake' — it hadn't struck her yet that it was with another girl, she only had an Alice-in-Wonderland astonishment, a new first strange sense of identity — and at the same time she was wondering 'What has Nellie's life been?' — trying to discern, surreptitiously, the Ghost of Nellie Past in the face of the woman working opposite her; the Nellie of some posh hotel with French service.

'Posh!' At first it seemed an echo of her own thought, till she realised that it was Mrs McCosh, standing behind her and looking with a satisfaction that was as proprietary as it was total, at Nellie and the napkins: 'That's a perfect touch, Nell — just *perfect!*

Wait'll the manager sees *this!*' she exclaimed, folding her arms on her chest and straightening her back 'Aye . . . good for you Nell — *we'll* dae the auld folks proud, puir sowels — the Queen hersel' in her palace willnae ha'e a better spread . . .' and she lapsed into a placid daydream where she stood, even, Stella guessed from her eyes, allowing herself to yearn for more scope. Nellie gave Mrs McCosh a look of indulgent understanding, intelligent and sisterly, and for an instant Stella could, clearly, see the ghosts of both Nellie and Isa McCosh Past, and even the might-have-been.

For the rest of the morning, till the pensioners were due to arrive, Stella threw herself into the work, fetching and carrying and learning as much as she could, with the enchantment of love on her, feeling magic and capable as Puck.

When the vanmen arrived with their huge cauldron of vegetable soup, and another huge cauldron of mince, and a steel box full of mashed potatoes, and started flirting with the women, she was jealously glad that Morag retreated into the cloakroom, but stayed herself by the kitchen, listening to their banter. As they left one of them noticed her and said in a loud stage-whisper, 'Watch yon terrible Mrs McCosh in there doesnae work ye tae death, hen — she can be an awfu' tyrant when she gets goin'!' then, whistling innocently, he swaggered away. Mrs McCosh was absurdly sensitive about it, shouting after him, the worst word of her belly: 'Ye — ye impiddent brute, ye! Wait'll Ah see you next!' shaking her little brown fist impotently, making the others, who had already begun to laugh at the vanman's words, hold their sides at the sight of her.

Even Belle shook a little with laughter, and Cissie said, 'Come awa' noo Isa, fine ye ken ye're nae match for 'm . . .' — and Nellie added, 'Aye, it's just us that's faird at ye!' and her great belly quivered like a blancmange under her tight apron with suppressed laughter, but they all sobered immediately when Belle broke in, 'Tak' nae notice, Mrs McCosh — you're the best boss that ever was.'

'Ye are that,' Stella seconded, and Mrs McCosh, who had been hovering between tears and temper, was soothed.

Morag came in then: 'I think I hear buses, Mrs McCosh!'

'That's it, girls — action stations!' Nellie cried, and Stella got a severe case of stage-fright on the instant, looking frantically about her for what to do, feeling as if her hair was standing on end.

'See if it's them, Stella,' Mrs McCosh commanded, coming into her own again.

Stella went out to the hall door and peeked out cautiously. The two buses had drawn up, and slowly but inexorably, the first wave of pensioners was teetering forward. She ran back to the kitchen as hard as if they had been a pack of wolves at her heels. 'Aye, it's them!' she exclaimed, wild-eyed.

'Settle doon, hen, they're no' wantin' tae eat *you,*' Nellie reassured smiling.

' — No' if ye get their grub tae them quick, onywey,' Cissie teased.

'Dinnae listen to her, hen,' Mrs McCosh offered a splendid example in herself of coolness in the teeth of the onslaught, for as she spoke the hall doors were thrown open to the wall and the distant rumble of feet and sticks was heard on the tiles. 'Ye cannae feed them till they're a' settled in,' and blasé, gave another stir to the mince.

Cissie got up and ambled to the kitchen door, craning her neck to look through the glass. As she gazed she said wryly over her shoulder, 'Ah don't know though, Isa — it's awfu' like Dunkirk oot there . . .' then, standing back from the door she whispered loudly, 'Stand by for inspection, troops — here comes the top brass!'

They all stood up giggling self-consciously, smoothing their aprons and clearing their throats. Daft Geordie's mother shrunk so far into herself, over by the cupboard, that she began to look like Rumplestiltskin, as if she might disappear altogether any minute. The door swung open and the organisers strode in, a tall, cadaverously thin man who had a grey face, and ulcers written all over him, and a stout woman with glasses, a thick herringbone coat, so well corseted that it looked as if all the fat on her body had been squeezed up to her bust.

They introduced themselves as Mrs McCosh came warily forward, and the stout woman said, heartily patronising, 'Everything under control my dear?'

'Oh aye, we'll manage,' Mrs McCosh said diffidently, but with a gleam in her eye for the *cognoscenti.*

'Right well — carry on ladies!' the woman waved an airy hand and rolled out — or appeared to roll out, for she walked without any apparent body movement at all. This fascinated Stella, who instantly got a picture of a pair of fat thighs squeezed up over her stockings and rolling off each other as they propelled the woman along. They heard her in the hall, clapping her hands for silence, while the shuffling and girning and mumbling of the hungry pensioners subsided into a dull roar, and Stella got the impression that the hall behind her was one great empty belly, rumbling for food.

Mrs McCosh began to ladle out the soup, 'You serve the heid bummers at the top table, Stella — you're the clever one,' she said, passing two full plates to Stella. 'Start wi' the man and wifie that was just in.'

'Aye, the boy looks like he could dae wi' a damn guid feed,' Nellie commented, while Stella stood in stunned disbelief, holding the plates and goggling at Mrs McCosh:

'Me?!'

'Aye — you're a smart lassie — on ye go before they start shoutin' for it.' Mrs McCosh urged in a voice that brooked no contradiction.

As she walked out to make her début, Stella's hands shook like leaves and the soup lapped up, scalding her thumbs till there were tears in her eyes; and the appreciative murmur of the pensioners sounded like a threat to her. The walk to the top table took forever, but she made it, and then to the centre where the organisers sat. She remembered the little she knew of manners and served the woman first, twisting round and leaning forward to give her the soup-plate that was in her left hand. As she straightened up she discovered that she'd forgotten about the other plate in her right hand, and had, in leaning forward, leaned that forward too, and split about a third of the soup on the woman's coat draped over the back of her seat. She quickly gave the man his soup, and ran back to the kitchen sucking her thumbs en route. Morag was still out serving, and Belle; only Cissie and Nellie were there, queuing up with plates for Mrs McCosh to fill. 'Oh Mrs McCosh!' she burst out, 'Ah've skilt the man's soup down the wifie's back when I was servin' it!'

'What did she say?' Mrs McCosh wasn't over-anxious.

'She disnae ken — it was on her coat on the chair . . .'

'Oh dear,' Mrs McCosh said, mildly, looking with private irony at Cissie and Nellie.

'Accidents will happen,' Cissie said, with a flat matter-of-factness that baffled Stella, and the three women looked at each other again.

'Ye're no' mad?' Stella was amazed, looking from face to face and finding mild blanks.

'Not at all! — the soup's no' strong enough to stain it onyway — forget it, hen,' Mrs McCosh shrugged, handing her two more plates of soup ' — on ye go an' serve the rest.'

There was an unusual silence behind her as she went back into the hall.

Such was the hectic rush to serve the pensioners, who ate ravenously, eyeing one another's plates jealously askance all the while, that Stella forgot all about love till it was time to take round the big tray with the cups and saucers for their tea, and was delegated to do it with Morag. Just knowing that Morag's hand was on the other side of the wire basket was enough to give her electric thrills up her arm at the other side. She didn't. want to speak to her; nothing relevant could be said; Morag anyway seemed to exude a companionable atmosphere, a friendly little island of silence drifting through that noisy sea of the sounds of old folks eating and drinking. Again Stella lapsed into a blissful state of subconsciousness, moving and doling out cups and saucers automatically.

After the last teacup had been filled, wee Mrs McCosh stood in the kitchen doorway, a satisfied woman, mistress of all she surveyed, and conceded, 'Well! The feedin' o' the five hundred can ha'e been nothin' tae *this!*'

'Puir auld sowels,' Nellie put in, 'they're like a flock o' vultures! No' one o' them refused a *thing*! The plates a' came back clean as whistles — they'll be easy washed.'

'That's mair than you could say for their jumpers though,' Cissie added, comic, 'for that's whaur the half o't went!'

'Aye . . .' Mrs McCosh was sympathetic, 'it's awfu' tae be auld like that an' no' sure o' the road tae yer mouth, puir sowels . . .'

'It's as weel ye put ours in separate pans though, Isa,' Cissie said, 'or they'd a' been awa' wi that tae, an' we'd ha'e had tae send out for fish suppers!'

'Oh fur sure ye've tae think o' a'thing in this job,' Mrs McCosh accepted the compliment as her due, and turned and came back in, 'Just put the gas on under it now, will ye, Bella?' and added in a rueful aferthought, 'Ah'm only sorry the Caterin' Manager didnae see it when it was a' set . . .'

After the pensioners had left, and the workers themselves had eaten, there was the long, soggy process of clearing up, and washing and drying all the dishes. The conversation was more subdued then, for they were all tired, and trying to save their resources for the afternoon tea in two hours' time. Sandwiches had to be spread with meat-paste, and again the two lasses were thrown together, Stella spreading the margarine and Morag spreading the meat-paste, with Belle at the end cutting the sandwiches into dainty squares. Belle and Morag spoke away quietly to each other, mainly about Morag's family, and in the course of their conversation Stella learned that Morag worked in Woolworth's in Edinburgh: she was neither depressed nor disappointed at this, but began to work out how she might manage to get to Edinburgh some day, to see her again — for Morag was only in Skelf for this one day. The rhythm of spreading the sandwiches, the warm glow of standing next to Morag, and the quiet hum of the women's voices lulled her till she was all but sleeping on her feet, for she'd been up before six that morning for her paper-round.

'Stella — Stella!' Mrs McCosh's voice at last penetrated her daze. 'Are ye dreamin', hen? Ah said Ah think that'll be enough. What d'ye think Nell? Twelve half-loaves among eighty-odd folk should dae, eh?'

'Aye well, ye'd think after the dinner they ate they couldnae be very hungry for an early tea,' Nellie calculated.

'Well if they are, we can ay spread mair,' Mrs McCosh decided. 'And anyway we have tae keep something back for oursel' tae tak' hame.' They all nodded, eager as children are to bring home some treat from a party. 'We've a right to our perks, eh? OK ladies!' She rose with a tired sigh, and, lifting a plate heaped high with sandwiches, led the way into the hall, 'We'll set the tables an' then have a cuppa oursel' afore the rush starts again.'

Once that was done there was a blissful half hour in which they all sat down and relaxed. Stella was glad of it, for her eyes were at the back of her head, and she was moving in a dream. Yet she was thoroughly gratified; she had held her own in a job with adults like Sheila, and she had a private life too, all to her own, like she suspected Sheila had, and surely God wouldn't interfere with any of that happiness, when it involved no demands?

The pensioners came back as hungry after their walk along the seafront as if they'd had no dinner at all. They devoured the sandwiches and looked for more. Mrs McCosh said, 'Oh well, they're entitled — Ah'll just keep back a loaf each for oursel's' — and so another heap of sandwiches was spread and served up. Then, to everyone's dismay, all the cakes were consumed, too.

'Help ma Hannah!' Cissie said, leaning against the wall and wiping her brow, 'nothin' that moves is safe in there! I believe if Ah laid ma hand doon they'd ha'e it slapped atween a piece before you could say "dicky"!'

'Aye, they're inordinate hungry,' Belle agreed.

'Some o' them's eatin' like they'd never seen food before.' Nellie chimed in. 'Did ye see yon auld boy at the front? If he goes on like that, Ah'm fear'd he'll ha'e an apoplectic!'

'Never mind him — the wifie next 'm was ferrettin' awa' a cake an' twa sandwiches in her handbag,' Cissie said.

'Never!' wee Mrs McCosh was shocked. 'The puir auld sowels! They must be on gey short rations at the home, eh?'

'Oliver Twist isnae in it!' Nellie exclaimed. 'It's criminal, Isa!' Mrs McCosh went to the door of the kitchen and peered into the hall, then turned back to them, sheepish: 'Look, it's a cryin' shame, puir auld bodies! What d'ye say we mak' the rest o' the bread intae sandwiches for them tae hae in the bus hame? We've five half loaves left, if you dinnae mind goin' hame empty-handed yersels' . . . it'd gi'e them an extra piece each . . .' she suggested, hesitating and ashamed to look at them straight.

'Och aye tae hell!' Cissie exclaimed, slapping her thigh and rising, then ' — sorry Isa, Ah ken ye dinnae like swearin' — but God helps! we'll be like that oursel's one day — let the puir auld bu — beggars ha'e a guid blaw-oot!' And she went and took her bread from its place of concealment, under her cardigan in her handbag. The others, including Stella, did the same, with mixed feelings of shame and pride.

'Stella hen,' Mrs McCosh said, 'go you down to the baker's shop and tell them Mrs McCosh sent ye tae get eighty wee cake-bags. We'll dae them proud!' she announced, throwing caution to the winds.

The pensioners were delighted. The old man who had filled himself nearly to bursting, rose and tapped the table with his stick loudly as the women, after handing out the individual bags, were retreating to the kitchen. Stella thought, 'This is where I find out what "apoplectic" is,' and held her breath. But he only proposed a vote of thanks, like a gentleman, to 'the good ladies our hosts'. Wee Mrs McCosh's eyes twinkled with tears of gratification, and she declared to the gathered assembly, 'It was worth it, tae see folk enjoyin' their meat!' Stella went to the bathroom and wiped her eyes on her pinny, overcome at their own generosity.

With the pensioners gone they had the hall to clear up again, and sweep — Cissie exclaiming as she shovelled up the crumbs, 'God helps, Nell! There's enough on the floor tae feed another bus load!' — and the dishes to wash and stack in big hampers ready for collection by the vanmen the next morning. It was nearly seven o'clock, but they had to wait for the Catering Manager to come with the wages. They all sat in the hall, with growing self-consciousness about waiting for money, except for wee Mrs McCosh and Belle, who were putting the last touches to the operation by mopping the kitchen floor. Stella, although she was paralytic with tiredness and thinking she'd have to crawl the last half mile home on her hands and knees, was sorry it was all over; partly because she wouldn't see Morag again — and she kept darting shy glances at her from the side, to fix her image in her memory — but partly because for once she'd fitted in, and had played her part in an adult world unobtrusively, and had felt *practically* useful. She sighed and crossed her legs. Morag turned to her. 'Tired, Stella?'

'Just a wee bit,' Stella admitted.

'Weel ye micht be, hen,' Nellie complimented, 'ye've worked like a black!'

'She has that,' Cissie agreed, rubbing her own leg sorely with a hand like a bunch of raw sausages, 'God helps! Ma various veins is killin' me! Ye maun ha'e tae cairry me up the road, Nellie . . .'

They all laughed, Stella most heartily, glad to have the spotlight off her, for she wanted to be treated as an equal. With the noise they made they hadn't heard little Belle emerge from the kitchen with the pail of soapy water from the floor, and she was trudging past them with it before Stella noticed her. She jumped up and went over, seizing the pail from Belle's hand: 'Here, Mrs Duncan, gie's me a haud o' that! Where's it goin'?'

'No, no, hen — Ah'll manage,' Belle protested, embarrassed, stretching her hand out for the pail. But she had looked like an exhausted pilgrim who discovers he's still only half-way to Mecca. Morag came up, 'Sit down, Auntie Belle — Stella and me will do it between us — you put your feet up!' and, covering Stella's hand with hers, she bore half the weight of the pail and began to move forward. Her hand was soft on Stella's, even with the strain of the pail, and Stella felt her day to be crowned. After they'd emptied it outside, she said impulsively to Morag, 'You're a nice lassie — I wished you stayed here all the time.' Morag only smiled curiously, not knowing how to answer, and Stella trembled a little at her own boldness — and with irrational hope.

They'd another half hour to wait till the manager came: 'Manage all right, Mrs McCosh?' he asked politely, and Mrs McCosh answered with unconcealed pride, 'Like clockwork, Mr Stewart! We gave them a *grand* spread!' and led the way into the privacy of the kitchen to get her money. Minutes later he emerged and left, and a minute or two after that, Mrs McCosh followed, having done some expertly rapid mental arithmetic in the meantime, and divided up the cash.

She handed Nellie and Cassie a pound and two half-crowns each, with the caution, 'Noo, dinnae you go spendin' that on yer bairns — gi'e *yersels* a treat for a change!' then, giving Belle the same, said to her, 'An' that goes for you tae Belle — ye spoil that Geordie o' yours an' fine ye ken it . . .' Then she handed Morag a ten-shilling note, 'You get less because you're younger, hen.'

'Oh no, I dinnae want paid!' Morag exclaimed, looking embarrassed at the money, 'I just came to be with my Auntie Belle!'

'Ye done yer work work an' ye deserve yer wages,' Mrs McCosh said flatly, inexorably fair, then added, with a significant inclination of her head towards Belle, who was taking off her slippers and putting on her shoes, 'What ye dae wi't's yer ain affair though . . .'

As Mrs McCosh was handing Stella her ten shillings, and saying with an amused smile, 'Ye,ll be a wee bit nearer tae gettin' your blazer now, Stella,' Morag was pushing her ten-shilling note into her auntie Belle's apron pocket, protesting against her confusion and recoil. 'Now Auntie Belle, you know I'm in a regular job and dinnae need it!'

'Eh aye — it's been a long day!' Mrs McCosh exclaimed, taking a deep breath of fresh air as she locked the hall door behind them at last.

'But I havenae half enjoyed it, Mrs McCosh,' Stella said, sincerely, 'Thanks a lot!' and they began to go their separate ways, joking only feebly now.

Stella went a bit of the way up the road, and turned back to look at Morag; she watched her retreating figure, taller and straighter in contrast to the tiny downtrodden Belle: they looked like Don Quixote and Sancho Panza, going home in the empty street, and she was filled with a warm, inarticulate gratitude for nothing and nobody in particular. Then she looked briefly down the other road, just in time to see Nellie and Cissie trudge heavily round the corner, their empty message-bags in their hands, with wee Mrs McCosh shuffling flat-footed in the gutter beside them, like a satellite, and she was instantly nostalgic.

'How much did they gi'e ye?' her mother asked, as she came in.

'Ten bob — no' bad, eh?' she held it up.

'Mind ye put it by for your blazer . . . have you had your tea?'

'Aye Mum. Ah'm knackered — I'm goin' tae my bed or I'll sleep in for my papers.'

'On ye go then — I'll bring you up a cup o' hot milk in a minute.' Something in the thin gangling figure, its curls clapped in to its head with the heat and sweat of the day, standing there with its ten-bob note in its hand, touched her mother. 'If only Ah hadnae so many bairns . . .' she thought. Then another thought, sadder, seemed to strike her, and she sighed, shrugged and got up to put on the milk.

CHAPTER 9

Women in Love

As the feeling of a justified existence wore off in the next few days, Stella began to want to be with the wee women again, to renew the sense they had given her that she was an asset, and to be at least vicariously in touch with Morag. But she wasn't sure if she would be counted grown-up enough to make social calls on her own, and hesitated, afraid to put it to the test. So she withdrew into herself, and sat for days on end with her head in her library books, sending out an atmosphere of deep adolescent gloom for about six feet in every direction. The sight of her eventually wore her mother's frayed nerves to the point of hysteria. One evening it all boiled up suddenly. Something came over her mother as she was washing the bathful of younger ones, and rising up abruptly, leaving them half-washed and bawling, she trudged through to confront Stella.

'*You!*' — Stella looked up, automatically, her head still full of her book:

'Aye?'

'*You!*'

'*What?*' Stella asked impatiently, dourly, anxious to get back to the oblivion of the story.

'Ye sit there wi' yer face trippin' ye, mornin', noon, an' night, wearin' ma nerves tae a frazzle, readin' yer brains intae train-oil an' never a hand's turn in the hoose will ye dae, is what!'

Stella was mute, hoping to let it run its course. Her mother advanced till she stood over her.

'Ah'm sick o' the sight o' ye, moochin' wi' yer face in a book — it's mair than flesh an' blood can bear; an' me trachled tae death wi' a parcel o' bairns.' A tear of self-pity ran down her mother's cheek, and fuelled her anger: she struck out and gave Stella a thick ear. 'Tak' that!' she exclaimed defensively. I'll show *you* a different road tae the well, my lady!' and heaving a deep determined breath, took her cigarettes and matches from the mantelpiece. She lit a fag and sat down heavily with a private sigh and a bitter, resolved face.

Stella sat opposite with her hand on her cheek, feeling her mother's fingerprints rising out of the flesh, dumbfounded, her own temper rising. She felt the slap to be a fair one as her world went, but still there had been an undercurrent to her mother's attitude that made her suspect she was bearing the brunt of other grievances that had nothing to do with her personally. That sense grew as she stared at her mother gazing into the black grate and smoking bitterly. 'What was *that* for?' Stella broke in, against the background of screams of fearful pleasure from the bathroom.

'For Ah felt like it!' the reply came with an aggressive sniff, a naked challenge from power to impotence, the cat and mouse tone of resentful motherhood that gave Stella a furious sense of undeserved humiliation. She eyed her mother cautiously, as she sat gazing again into the fire trying melodramatically to look like the innocent injured party, blackmailing an abject apology — cautiously, for she didn't want her mother to see her own expression which was one of burning resentment: 'Oh someday *someday . . .*' she thought to herself, recognising the blackmail, but didn't allow herself to think any further, for a swift, cartoon image of herself knocking her mother's head off her shoulders in one clean bloodless swipe rose up in her mind and gave her exquisite satisfaction. Then guilt followed, then a self-pity that echoed her mother's, then resentment of all the feelings that had gone before. She stood up suddenly. Her mother looked round, in full expectation of the usual apology, 'Well?' saw the resentment on Stella's face, and looked away again with injured invulnerable dignity.

'*Well*, I'm goin' out,' Stella said through clenched teeth, ' — why should I stay here and get dog's abuse?'

'Oh aye,' her mother shot back with sarcastic sweetness, 'on ye go — awa' an' enjoy yersel', an' leave your auld mither here wi' a parcel o' bairns, ye ungrateful little shit! Oot ye go!' The bairns in

the bath, hearing their mother's voice raised in anger, howled in the sheer insecurity of it — besides, the bathwater was getting cold too.

Stella put her coat on and her mother rose to go back to the bath-room with an, 'Aye, aye for *God*sake, haud yer wheeshts, youse yins. Ah'm comin' tae ye!' then as Stella opened the door delivered her parting shot, 'And you — I'll be glad tae see the back o' yer girnin' dial — aye, oot ye go, an' see if ye can find somebody else tae put up wi' ye — awa' an' bide wi' yer precious Mrs McCosh, for ye're worse than useless tae me! See if *she*'ll keep ye for *nothin'*!'

Stella's answer to this was to slam the door viciously behind her, shaking the whole house. But she didn't get away with it, for her mother immediately opened it again and roared up the path after her, 'And I'll see you about *that* when you come back, my bonnie lassie!'

Outside, she was glad of the gathering gloaming, for the cool air brought the handprint on her face into even greater relief, and she would have hated anyone to see it. She walked about for a while, cursing her mother under her breath. 'She goin' too far wi' this change o' life — she's gettin' beyond a joke!' She thought about what if she'd had Mrs McCosh for a mother, but she couldn't imagine it, and anyway she felt she was too old now, past needing a mother at all. But the night came down and she'd nowhere to go. She started to calculate how much she could pull in in a week if she had an afternoon paper-round as well, and could get a job deliver-ing for the grocer at weekends, and dismally trudged into the middle of the road to kick a stray tin can, so dejected at the realisa-tion that even then she couldn't keep herself, that she identified with the can, and, in a mood of self-hate, kicked it all along the way down the road, following wherever it landed till she found herself as if by chance outside Belle's house.

Just having come far enough in herself to contemplate inde-pendence gave her the confidence she needed to go and knock at the door. She brightened up, and forgave her mother, and thought to herself that at least she could feel more independent if she worked in the house, resolving to turn over a new leaf the next day. All this, not without some sense of making a bargain with Providence, as she waited at the door, hearing Belle's slippers shuffle along the linoleum of the lobby. When the footsteps got right up to the door she felt herself get as socially nervous as she used to be selling charity flags at the doors of the posh houses in Skelf, but when Belle opened the door and as natural as can be said, 'Oh it's you, Stella — come awa' ben — I'm fair glad tae see ye, I've just been sittin' wearyin' by masel' at the fire. Geordie's readin' his comics,' she laughed at herself.

'I was hangin' about at a loose end, and thought Ah'd see how you were gettin' on,' she said as she followed Belle along the lobby.

'Aye,' Belle understood, ushering her into the living-room, 'in ye go and sit down and I'll get a cup for ye.'

Stella was pleased and awkward at the prospect of getting a cup of tea like an adult, and all but swaggered into the room. Geordie, lying in front of the fire with a cardboard box full of comics, and turning the pages of one, looked up and grinned, a friendly Caliban, with his scruffy black hair, 'Hullo Stella!'

'Aye, Geordie!' she repeated, and sat down formally, on a kitchen chair away from the fire. Her first impression of the house was one of the bareness — there was only one small carpet, the one Geordie lay on, in front of the fire; the rest was faded linoleum and some sticks of junk utility furniture — and of warmth, partly from the fire, partly from Geordie's relaxed posture in front of it, partly from the homespun tweed-and-dirt smell that was rising from his trousers as he baked his backside which was almost on the hearth, partly from the gentle spluttering warmth of the gas mantle over her head, and partly from the wheezy singing of the kettle, drawn half off the fire, to one side of the hob. There were two cups without handles, a sugar bag, a milk bottle, and an open teapot on the grate. Stella thought this a wonderfully practical arrangement. Belle came quietly back in with another cup; and to Stella it seemed she took a dream-like time to reach the fireside with it. Belle did everything as slowly and gently as she spoke — even when she prodded Geordie with her foot to make him move so that she could get in to the kettle, it looked as if she did it in lead-soled diving boots. It reminded Stella of the Movietone newsreel of the Grand National, showing you the race in an underwater-slow motion, and she half expected Geordie to roll back, his hair waving out like seaweed disturbed, as the horses' manes did on those films. Instead he pulled back quickly, jerkily willing.

As she filled the teapot Belle said, 'What way are you sittin' across there, Stella? Draw into the fire, lass — dinnae mind Geordie here.'

'Oh no! It wasnae for Geordie,' Stella protested, 'I was just mindin' my manners!' Belle looked up at her in bewilderment, and Stella rushed on, 'You shouldnae bother wi' a cup for me, Mrs Duncan!' But she rose and sat on an old leather upholstered chair beside the fire. Belle was quietly pleased at the compliment to her importance in these manners, and prodded Geordie again with her foot, 'Sit up, man, and show yer manners when a young lady visits ye!' Geordie was in turn flattered at the suggestion that Stella was visiting *him*, and, on his best behaviour, got to his feet eagerly, drew the chair Stella had been sitting on into the middle of the group, and sat down as prim and still as if his limbs had been arranged by a Victorian photographer. Belle smiled approval at him and he grinned back with a special effort to keep his features within the normal bounds of expression. She set the teapot down on the hob to infuse.

There followed a silence which Stella immediately felt to be awkward — having got so far with their genteel comedy of manners, all three had shot their bolts, they sat with their hands folded in their laps as if waitng for the prompt-man to whisper their lines. She couldn't look at Belle, and tried to glance casually about, but stopped herself as she realised the action might be taken for nosiness. She gazed down at the hearthrug, but there was no pattern left on it. She looked slightly to the side, and saw Geordie's bare feet ingrained with dirt, and shifted her gaze, embarrassed. Belle appeared to be oblivious of the whole charade; her consciousness seemed to be only a dim, flickering occasional thing, perhaps through seeing too much reality. As she got over the sight of Geordie's feet Stella notice his box of comics, and remarked with a cheerful relief that seemed to herself to echo off the four walls, ceiling and linoleum, 'By jings! Geordie's got a wheen comics there!'

'Oh, he's weel spoiled, believe you me,' Belle rejoined, and as if this were her cue, she lifted the teapot to pour their tea, ' — everybody's ay gi'ein' him comics, aren't they, Geordie?' she turned to include him as she handed Stella her tea in a cup that had a handle, which flattered her again.

Geordie grinned widely.

'A'body's sure gui'd tae'm, I say,' Belle went on, nodding with some sternness at Geordie, indicating that he was to read a lesson in her words, and Geordie instantly sobered up, frowning with the effort to substitute proper gratitude for infantile satisfaction.

But Stella felt guilty. She had never been good to Geordie, she and Mrs Duncan knew it: she had been the devil that gave him tap-washers and assured him they were money, and sent him into the fruit-shop to spend them, one day on the way home from school. The girl in the fruit-shop, although she knew someone had put him up to it, had given him two bags of black bananas and a row. It didn't much assuage Stella's guilt to know that she had eaten as many of the bananas as Geordie, and had had a grim time with sickness and diarrhoea at school that same afternoon, for she remembered the sight of Belle marching through the school play-ground the next day at break, to complain to the headmaster about it. Stella had been called into his office later on after somebody had clyped, and got two of the strap followed by a moral lecture about 'those less fortunate than ourselves' which had left her burning with shame. This shame returned now, and Belle saw it, and looked both knowledge and forgiveness at Stella, and said, as if recalling the episode of the bananas in the same line as the examples of kindness. 'I mind you gave him some bananas yoursel', Stella — but the daft craitur had to go an' mak' a pig o'sel' wi' them — what a mess! I lost ma temper that day for once in my life — I was that mad Ah couldnae think straight!'

Geordie had no memory of it, but Stella relaxed at this magnan-imous absolution, and laughed: 'Aye, Mrs Duncan! Me tae — Ah suffered masel', for I ate as many as him — and I got the belt intae the bargain!' and Belle laughed, and the ice was broken.

Stella stayed for another hour, managing to slip in a question about how Morag was, but getting no satisfaction: 'My faimily's no' letter-writers,' Belle explained. When she left it was with a dozen of Geordie's comics — some excuse to come back — and a cocky feeling that socially she could hold her own with the best.

And when she got home her mother's wrath had cooled: she'd had a quiet time to herself, with the bairns in bed, and sat at the fire with a love-story magazine and a tea-plate of mashed cauliflower, a special supper treat which, because it was special, she ate with a knife.

The hesitant look on Stella's face as she stuck it round the door with a '. . . Mum?' amused her, and without another word said about their fight, she told Stella there was some cauliflower still in the pot if she wanted it. Stella smiled a half-rueful apology and stuck in.

Although she felt her mother's original outburst had been unfair, she appreciated the gesture, and didn't mention the slap at all to Sheila in bed that night. All she said was, 'Ma mother's gettin' weirder by the day,' and Sheila, viewing the two of them, both Stella and her mother, with the detachment of her own new world, commented, 'Then that's two o' ye, for ye're faur frae normal yersel'!' Stella turned over, not risking saying anything.

For the fear of being a freak was strong in her, the more she brought her crush on Morag into the daylight part of her mind. She did her best to repress her doubts about herself, and to take the whole experience like a fantasy, a fairy-tale, but she couldn't wholly succeed, and this underscored her restless discontent, which was beginning to take on cosmic proportions to her. Occasionally at night, more out of habit now than faith, she would silently demand, 'God, come on, be a pal, dae a miracle! — let me wake up in the mornin' a nineteen-year-old laddie in a well-paid job — I'd be as guid as gold the rest o' my days . . .' She had some slight hope that persistence might work when tears didn't, and she felt that maybe God might make up for all his years of neglect by one big dramatic generous act. The morality of her situation hadn't occurred to her at all, until one evening two or three days later she was idly reading an old *News of the World,* and came across a case of homosexual assault. It was late; her father, just in from his work, sat opposite her at the kitchen table, having his supper.

'What does "homosexual" mean Dad?' she asked, casually, perfectly inured to the shock horror revelations of Sunday papers by now.

'*Poof*,' her father answered with abrupt contempt, shovelling in a forkful of tatties and mince.

She knew the word well already; it was applied to any boy at school who fell below the standard of manliness. But the softness the word implied in school usage didn't go with the idea of assault, so she tried again: 'What's a poof?'

'A Nancy-boy — a disgustin' pervert! Shut up I'm readin!' She ignored the warning and still looking down at her paper persisted, 'Well, what's "homosexual assault" then?'

Her father looked up from the dual occupations of eating and reading and answered with a savagery not directed at Stella, 'It's disgustin'!'

'Aye,' Stella agreed, 'or it wouldnae be in the *News o' the World* — but what is it? Come on, Dad, *tell* me,' she urged.

'A man forcin' another man tae dae *yon*, ' her father snarled, as if it was too despicable for mere words, and in his tiredness and disgust not really noticing it was the eleven-year-old Stella asking.

'What for?' she was bewildered. There were enough women and more in the world, it seemed to her, without a man "needing" to rape a man.

'Because he's a *poof*.' Her father's savage tone provoked her curiosity. She persisted partly just for the rare pleasure of seeing him so worked up:

'But I thought poofs were like lasses?'

'No' them a' . . .' he finished his food and laid down his knife and fork, 'but they're a', every last one o' them, dirty rats! If I had my way I'd ken what tae dae wi' them!' He spoke with a vicious glint in his eyes, looking straight at her and striking terror to her heart as it dawned on her somewhere what this meant for her.

'What would ye dae Dad?' — swallowing her heart back down again, for it had risen to her mouth.

'I'd bloody *castrate* them!' he replied without hesitation, as if he'd been thinking about it for years, and waving his knife. 'Then I'd stand them a' against a wall and *shoot* the buggars!' still looking at her, still with a passionate, bigotted gleam in his eye.

Stella waited till his emotion cooled, and he got up to put his plate in the sink, and while his back was still to her, asked in the most casual voice she could, 'Are there *women* poofs Dad?'

'Aye,' he said, not interested in particular phenomenon.

Stella felt the blood drain from her as she looked at the back of him washing his plate and cutlery, his broad shoulders and cocky little male hips, and wondered why normal folk always had to be vicious about freaks. Not being able to deny her crush on Morag, feeling it to be a fine thing, she hated him, momentarily, and got up abruptly and went and was sick in the toilet, raging, 'God you *bastard,* you *bastard,* how *could* you? Is this your idea of a joke or what?' Her father, with his excessive admiration for the manly virtues, had made her believe that the highest thing a woman could achieve was to be like a man. She had done her best to live up to it — even then she carried two little india-rubber balls, one in each coat-pocket, for he'd told her that if she squeezed them as hard as she could all day, she would develop 'a grip like a man'. She was sick with betrayal: it was unbearable, as if he had fed her fat just to throw her to the wolves. She had thought he loved her and was bringing her up to succeed, but the truth was, he had been rearing her like any bit cattle, and teaching her tricks to amuse himself, to make up to himself, she thought, 'for the shitty son he never had'. And then she relented to God — it wasn't God's fault, 'But where the hell *are* you, God?' she begged.

Next morning she eyed her father from the other side of a great divide, and avoided speaking to him, noting that he wasn't even faintly aware of her silence. Her mother was upstairs making the beds, and Stella was tidying up the kitchen. Down on her hands and knees brushing the carpet, she allowed herself the passing relief of banging the hard wood of the brush off one of her father's ankles as he sat with the paper, checking off his horses.

'Here!' he jumped, 'watch where ye're goin'!'

'Sorry,' Stella mumbled insincerely, feeling wicked and wondering how Cinderella had stood it so meekly.

'Hey!' he exclaimed after a few seconds, while Stella was still on her hands and knees, reaching for the dust under the sideboard. She had a quick gloat, thinking he'd hurt himself again, then as he exclaimed again, she asked him what was wrong.

'Ah have a treble up!'

'A treble!' Stella jumped to her feet, thrilled out of her misery, and went to the bottom of the stairs to shout to her mother, 'Haw Mum! Ma Dad's got a treble up!' Her mother ran downstairs, even more excited than Stella: 'How much?' They both stood meekly by while he calculated:

'Thirty quid — give or take a few bob,' he announced airily, grinning from ear to ear.

'Thirty quid!' her mother shouted, 'thirty quid!' and sat down in her seat, while Stella was rooted to the spot in amazement, 'Put the kettle on, Stella! *This calls for a celebration!*'

Stella instantly complied, all sweetness in the hope that some of it would come to her, and she silently cheered her mother, who was saying, 'Get your jacket on, Wullie, and get down to the bookie's an' collect — I want tae see it here in my haund! Hurry up, I'm hae'in' a canary here!'

Her father had risen and taken his jacket off the back of the chair, but seemed all set to go into a peroration about his superior system with the horses, and how he knew these were certs, but her mother couldn't bear it: 'Aye aye — I'll hear it a' when ye get back, but awa' ye go an' get the cash in yer hand first! What a godsend!' she went on, as he obeyed, 'I'll get my coat for Senga Corner's weddin' after a'! Stella!' she bawled, as if Stella were three blocks away rather than right beside her, waiting for the kettle to boil.

'Aye — ' Stella answered eagerly.

'You an' me, me hen, will ha'e a day out in Edinburry, at C & A's, see if we dinnae, you betcha!'

'Really? No' kiddin'?' Stella was overjoyed.

'Just our twa selves, see if we dinnae! This very Saturday! When's Saturday?' she added in an afterthought.

'Tomorra,' Stella said, and sprang in the air and clicked her heels together with glee, making all the fire-irons rattle as she came down.

'Your Dad'll just have tae watch his ain bairns for once . . .'

'It'll dae him guid,' Stella nodded like an old wife.

She made the tea, and got her mother to promise to let her try on the hats 'just for five minutes' in C & A's — a great treat to her, though it embarrassed her mother; Stella thought there was nothing so absurdly funny in this planet as the sight of herself in the 'pawky' hats in C & A's, and she would put them on one by one with Sheila, each pretending to be the wife of some local worthy: 'Look at me — ' pulling a long face — 'I'm Mackintosh the chemist's wife' — gales of laughter. She smothered her mixed feelings about going into Woollies; she had to learn to hide from trouble.

As they sat drinking and planning and looking out the window far too prematurely for her father's return, the Co-op baker's horse and cart went by. Her mother drew out her purse from her apron pocket and handed to Stella: 'Tae hell wi' poverty — get us a cake, hen!'

Stella ran after the baker's cart, glad to get some physical release for her excitement. Geordie, who most days trailed along at the back of the cart, spotted her and got the baker to stop. She bought two cakes, forgetting to get one for her father, then, as the baker took her money she said on an impulse ' — And gi'e Daft Geordie a bag o' crisps.'

'What will yer mither say?' the baker asked, deeply suspicious, and giving Geordie, who had begun to caper about in anticipation, a crushing look.

'Never you mind what ma mither'll say,' Stella rejoined, 'here's the money, gi'e 'm the crisps.'

The baker shook his head but handed them over, and Geordie was so delighted he couldn't open the bag. Stella took them from his spastic hand and opened them for him, with, 'Tell your Mum I'm askin' for her, eh?' and dodged away back home, still eyed suspiciously by the baker, who shook his head slowly to Geordie and commented, 'Women!'

Geordie looked solemn for as long as he could, then pounced hungrily on his crisps.

The next morning, as soon as Stella had done her paper-round, they set off on the train; her mother, as eager as any young woman out for a day on the town, was at her best, like a good-natured older sister, and Stella responding for all she was worth, clung to her mother in her heart with the desperation of the condemned, for she knew that as soon she saw Morag again, and felt the thrill of love, she would be forever beyond the pale. As they crossed the Forth Bridge her mother gave her a ha'penny to throw in for a wish, and she threw it out of the window with all her might, wishing to be instantly made a laddie, or struck painlessly dead. Yet when they got off the train and her mother headed straight for Woollies for a cup of tea, she didn't protest — better get it over with. The more she thought of herself as a disgusting pervert, the more she saw her mother as innocent as Eve, and herself as old, wise in the ways of the depraved world, and she the more she thought that, the more she clung like a child. As they entered Woollies, Stella shivered and her mother said, 'I hope you havenae caught the cold on that draughty train,' and then when Stella wanly tried to smile she added, ' — a cup o' tea'll sort you out,' and Stella could have wept, burdened with the love that cannot speak its name.

As they made their way to the stairs at the back to go to the restaurant, Stella looked around carefully for Morag, and with growing delight, gradually realised that she had totally forgotten what Morag looked like. 'Christ, Ah'm cured!' the words exploded in her mind as they reached the restaurant, and she noticed her mother peching unusually with the effort of the stairs. She became all concern — in an 'if you treat me right I'll treat you right' attitude to God — and asked 'What's wrong Mum? — it's no' like you!'

'Oh, I need my tea,' Bess smiled dismissively.

The rest of the day was perfect, for Stella was overwhelmingly grateful to everything that moved for her release, and her mother, thinking that it was she who had brought about the transformation, was herself delighted. As they queued in Woollies to buy their tea before catching the train home, she commented to Stella 'What a helluva difference in ye, hen!' and leaning over her confidentially, said in a tone of rebellion, 'You see, you and me needs a bit brek tae — we hardly get our dials out the door frae one week's end tae the next — tae hell wi' the expense, you and me'll dae this mair often in future!' Then generously, 'You ha'e twa sausages Stella — you're a growin' lassie — and sausages is the boys! — ' she nudged Stella wickedly — then miraculously, 'What d'ye say we treat oursel's tae a trifle on the quiet? Ah've a helluva notion o' a trifle . . .' and she looked as yearningly at the cakestand as any child at a sweet-shop window, while Stella waited delicately for the outcome of her deliberations — 'Aye! Ah'm *ha'en'* a trifle, why no'?' her mother at last exclaimed, as the queue behind them grew restless with the delay, and put two trifles on the tray. One for Stella. Stella felt cherished, and when her mother sent her for two more, she floated to the counter on a cloud of sheer bliss, thinking, 'Heaven would be fu' o' trifles an' Woollies' beefy sausages!'

But the train wasn't half an hour out of the station before her mother had to rush to the toilet, as sick as a dog. Stella waited anxiously for her to come back, but the time passed and still she didn't turn up.

Eventually, careful to take the shopping-bags with her, she went to the toilet door, where she heard her mother being loudly, pathetically, sick.

'Are ye OK, Mum?' she shouted through the door, above the noise of the train.

'Ah think I'm dyin'!' her mother's muffled voice returned, and Stella was reassured by the standard exaggeration, and went back to wait.

Bess returned shortly, pale but smiling: 'I was glad tae get that up, I can tell ye!'

'But your guid trifles, Mum!' Stella protested.

'Aye well, it cannae be helped — Ah should o' kent better in ony case,' her mother sighed, nodding her head with private information kept back.

'What for? You're no' usually sick in trains . . .' Stella tried to catch her off-guard, and penetrate the mystery.

Her mother looked at Stella's serious, bright face, and said, 'Well — I suppose you'd as well be told sooner as later . . .' and lapsed into enigmatic thought.

'Told what?' Stella prodded, embarrassed, thinking that today of all days her mother was going to admit to the change of life.

'How would ye like another wee sister — or maybe a brother?' her mother asked coyly.

'A *what*?' Stella almost roared with the shock of it.

'I'm pregnant again,' her mother said, smiling smugly, having thought herself into a Hollywood frame of mind — or resolved, by one of the sleights of mind at which she was adept, not to spoil her own day.

With all the will in the world, Stella couldn't take the cue, 'But

— but — are ye *really* glad about it?' she asked tentatively, hoping to bring the truth out.

'Well, tae be frank, no, no' at first — but — what can ye dae? Ye cannae deny a wee life . . .' she said sententiously.

'But it's awfu' sair hae'in' a bairn, an' — well — have ye no' had enough?' Stella still tried to be diplomatic, and unselfish, for she certainly wasn't looking forward to the months of sickness and the weeks of false alarms, and the blow-by-blow account of the birth that she'd been through the last time.

'What's up wi' *you*? It's no' *you* hae'in' it!' her mother grew defensive.

'No. . . no — it's yoursel' I'm thinkin' about,' Stella was quick to cover this up.

'Oh, I'll manage again like I managed before . . .' Bess returned fairly cheerfully, and seemed to Stella to be all at once very young and ignorant. She went on ' — besides, it might be a *laddie* this time! Ye'd like that!'

'Right enough,' Stella immediately agreed, willing to indulge her.

'Your Dad is awfu' wantin' a laddie,' her mother went on, touchingly unsure of herself. 'He says he'll no' feel he's proved his manhood till he's gi'en me a laddie.' There was even a hint of admiration in her voice.

There were tears at the back of Stella's eyes, but she was worlds away from her mother's sentimentality, 'Oh well, in that case . . .' she murmured, not knowing what to say.

'Here's the bridge!' her mother jumped up, pulling her purse from her bag. 'Now then — a penny each,' handing one to Stella, 'and we'll both wish for a laddie!'

Her mother threw first, then Stella, with some sense of irony, threw next. Believing it would bring them luck, her mother sat back, confident, and said, 'Oh it'll be *great* tae ha'e a wee laddie!'

'Aye, — *great for the laddie*,' Stella thought miserably, feeling more like her mother's mother than her daughter.